SON OF THE

MOON

Jennifer Macaire

Published by Accent Press Ltd 2017
Octavo House
West Bute Street
Cardiff
CF10 5LJ

www.accentpress.co.uk

ISBN 9781786154651
eISBN 9781786154644

In the Aegean Sea there is still a legend that a mermaid swims, forever searching for her lost lover. If she asks a fisherman where Great Alexander is, he has but one answer to give. Otherwise, in her rage and sorrow, she will call forth a storm and drown him.

> *Mermaid: 'Where is Great Alexander?'*
> *Fisherman: 'Great Alexander lives! And still rules!'*

Chapter One

We spent the winter and spring of the lost year in the Valley of the Gods. For those who don't believe me, I invite them to go to Nysa and see for themselves.

The army had split in two: Hephaestion and Perdiccas leading the greater half of the army and Alexander taking three fighting units – nearly twenty thousand soldiers – and his precious elephants. In December we went north, leaving the sheltered valley where we had spent the last six months. The weather was grey and chill. The grass beneath our horses' hooves was dry and crackled; it sounded like a brush fire when the army moved.

We followed the Swat River, crossed it, then headed to the Nawar pass. On the way we stopped in a small village. We'd been invited by the chieftain and, since we wanted to find out as much as possible about our route, we stayed there for two days. The people were simple and friendly. They lined up and waved white kerchiefs at us. The army was so huge that it took ten hours just to cross the narrow bridge leading to the village, and one of the elephants stepped through the wooden boards, leaving a gaping hole. The villagers thought this wildly funny.

I heard that after we left, they renamed the village Iskandero. Iskander was what they called my husband – perhaps better known as Alexander the Great.

We were travelling lightly and wanted to go quickly.

1

We were to meet the rest of the army at the Indus River, but first we had to go to Nysa to find the moon's child.

The route took us through the territory of two warring tribes, the Assacenians and the Aspasians. They were already fighting against each other, and when we came into their territory, each believed that the other had enlisted us on their side. Nothing our diplomats could say could persuade them that we were simply passing through. The Assacenians attacked our column at dawn, three days after crossing the pass. They didn't take us by surprise, they'd been harassing us for days, sending scouts, spies, and shooting arrows at us from deep thickets.

Alexander was exasperated. He'd lost three men to an ambush and he was relieved to get the fighting out in the open. First we fought the Assacenians, clearing straight through them by early afternoon. In the evening we camped uneasily at the very edge of their land, wondering if the Aspasians, seeing how we'd fought their enemies, would welcome us.

If you call a brush fire lit all around us a bright 'hello', I suppose you could say we were welcomed.

'What kind of fighting is this?' griped Alexander, buckling his leather breastplate on over his short linen tunic. He adjusted his helmet and made sure his shin guards were tightly laced. 'They light fires and wait until we show ourselves in order to shoot arrows at us. By Hades, my lace is broken!' He stared at a piece of leather dangling from his hand.

The smoke stung my eyes and Chiron, never very patient, started bawling. 'I'll get you another one.' I started towards the wooden chest but he stopped me. 'No, I have to go now.' He kissed me hard and left, just another husband on his way to work in the morning.

His warhorse, Bucephalus, was ready. A groom held the reins while Alexander mounted, then handed him his shield and spear. Alexander thanked him and nudged Bucephalus with his heels. The horse needed no encouragement. His neck arched, his eyes brilliant, he cantered off.

Dawn was just breaking, but the daylight was confounded with the orange glow of the fires surrounding our encampment. The elephants, hating fire, started to bellow alarmingly. The troops lined up in even rows, the phalanx out in front, the cavalry on the flanks. The phalanx looked like a giant nightmare porcupine. It was composed of hundreds of men tightly packed together, each carrying a thirty-foot long spear. They presented a prickly, impenetrable front.

The battle that day was over by mid-morning. Alexander lost twelve men. The enemy lost half their army and sued for peace before noon.

Alexander was carried into the infirmary where I was helping Usse. His ankle had been shattered by a lance.

'Are you all right?' I asked, rushing to his side.

He stared at me, sweat pouring off his face, and his eyes two wells of pain.

'Would I come here if I was all right?' he gasped.

I sat down next to him and held his hand while Usse took off his sandal and examined the wound. When he probed, my own hand was nearly broken in Alexander's grip, and I yelped.

'Sorry,' muttered the slender Egyptian doctor, dousing the ankle with hot water mixed with different herbs. He cleansed it and put a splint around it. There wasn't much else he could do. Now we just had to pray it didn't get infected.

We stayed for three days while we organized the peace talks with both tribes. Then Alexander decided to pull out and head straight to Nysa. An ambassador for the Assacenian king told us that the child of the moon was being worshipped in Nysa.

The child of the moon was Paul, my baby, now nearly five years old. I hadn't seen him since he was ten days old.

Alexander left two divisions behind with his general Coenus while we took the rest of the army. We would all join up at the Indus River.

Ten days' marching, fifty kilometres a day. The distances were absurd, but so was Alexander's stamina. Riding Bucephalus, he drove us on. The gallant horse had already walked with his master a distance of ten thousand kilometres. I followed on my roan mare, my baby Chiron strapped to my back like an Indian papoose.

People stared, but I was used to it. They would stare no matter what I did. In a land of petite, brown-skinned, black-haired people, I was an oddity. My ancestors had been Nordic Vikings, and I had silver blonde hair and broad, high cheekbones. My eyes were blue, slanted, and chilly as an arctic glacier.

They called me the goddess Persephone, Demeter's daughter. I was often asked to bless the fields in the winter to ensure a good harvest. Nowadays, I smiled and refused; I'd done it once. Believe me, it was enough. I couldn't walk for a week.

They stared at Alexander too. Not that he was a tall blond. He was a medium-sized man with unruly, warm brown hair and parti-coloured eyes. His skin was fair, but he tanned easily and was now a smooth, reddish-brown all over. His hair had blond streaks from the sun. His cheeks flushed easily, he had high colouring. He was also beautifully made and perfectly balanced, a finely drawn man in the prime of his life.

Even I loved to look at him, and we'd been lovers since I'd met him, in 332 BC. It was now 326 BC, nearly six years had passed. He still took my breath away.

He turned his head, searching for me with his uncanny eyes. He always seemed to know when I was thinking about him. His mouth quirked up at the corners, his eyebrows drew together then relaxed. He had the most expressive face of anyone I'd ever seen. He smiled and his teeth flashed whitely. He had a slight overbite; he'd sucked his thumb for years just to spite his mother, Olympias.

Now we were going to find the baby she'd kidnapped four years ago. And I hoped that one day Olympias would suffer as terribly as I had when my baby was taken from me.

* * *

Chiron squirmed on my back and started to cry. I reined in my pony and deftly swung the papoose around in front of the saddle. The little boy was hungry again. He always seemed hungry, and he was growing fast. He was two months old, a beautiful golden child with soft brown hair that curled in tiny ringlets around his ears, and slanted hazel eyes that made him look like a little elf. He had fine bones and was a deceptively delicate looking child. He looked just like his father Plexis, better known as Hephaestion, Alexander's best friend and lover, and my lover too, obviously.

We were dirty and tired. Night was falling, and we hardly had time to set up camp. The last two days had been harrowing. Our guides had deserted us, leaving the army in a labyrinth of small valleys and twisting streams. The army, a hodgepodge amalgam of peoples and religions, reacted differently to different things.

'It's a question of getting to know everyone better,' said Alexander resignedly, after watching an entire section of archers fall on their knees in front of an albino hind one of the Egyptians had shot. The archers were Greek. They thought the hind was protected by Artemis and they were waiting for her to take revenge on the ignorant fool who'd shot her deer. Revenge from goddesses usually took the form of an earthquake or a volcano – they were expecting the worst.

The worst was our guides deserted us. They'd had enough. They'd been nice local boys, two brothers, willing to lead us to Nysa, 'a three-day march' they told us. However, they made the mistake of jumping over a large brook without first kneeling and asking permission from the water nymph, and five religious-minded Macedonians gave them a thrashing they wouldn't forget. Or forgive, apparently. We were lost.

We sent a group of men to fetch firewood, after making sure they all realized that they had to ask permission from the tree they were to cut.

'Excuse me, Desdoinia.' It was another Egyptian, speaking to the soldier in charge of firewood. 'Excuse me, I say. But how do you ask a tree anything? Where are its ears, pray tell? And how do I know if its answer is affirmative?'

I thought these were good questions and leaned over to hear the answer.

Desdoinia, a haughty-looking Persian, answered shortly. 'A tree has no ears, but the nymph living inside it does. You address the tree. She will hear you. And you speak loudly. You'll know if she's given you permission when you start cutting. If the axe slips and cuts off your leg, it means "no".'

The Egyptian looked doubtful. 'I'd rather know beforehand if she said "yes" or "no". Is there no other way to make sure? Besides,' he dug his toe in the soft ground and looked askance at Desdoinia. 'I thought green wood burned badly.'

The woodcutters left, still arguing theology, and I went to the stream to fetch some water to bathe Chiron and myself. The night was cool and would get colder. I picked up dry sticks on my way to the stream. A fire would be nice.

We camped near the stream that night after asking permission of the river god. The tent was set up when I got back. Brazza was rocking Chiron in his hammock, Axiom was busy getting dinner, and Alexander was sitting on the bed discussing with his generals which route to take. His ankle hadn't gotten infected and seemed to be healing well, but it was still in a splint, and it still pained him at night.

He leaned back on his elbows as I came in, and he smiled. The light from the blue glass lantern made his skin as pale as milk and shadowed his eyes. Craterus and Ptolemy Lagos rose when I entered. Both men were tall and gaunt, but they were as dissimilar as could be. Craterus was a pale-skinned, mournful-faced man. He had neatly trimmed dark hair. His eyes were the soft grey of a wintery sky. Ptolemy Lagos shaved his head, which was why we called him 'Baldy'. His skin was the colour of old ivory, and in the summertime he turned nearly brown. His eyes were deep and piercing, his mouth large, sensual, and curved in a smile. He was always exquisitely polite.

I was wary of polite people. Ptolemy had the same flat stare as a shark. The smile didn't fool me.

I dumped my load of firewood in the corner of the tent, put the bucket of water down, and washed my hands and face. Then I poured the water into the cauldron and started heating it for the bath. Axiom had nearly finished grilling the steaks and the smell of meat made my mouth water. Fatigue made my muscles ache. I longed to sit in a hot tub and soak, with a radio playing soft music, electric lights, and a good book in my lap. Well, in three thousand years that would be possible. Right now I'd have to settle for a quick wash in a small tub. Someone would play the lute, and I could curl up afterwards on my bed with a copy of the *Iliad*, the only story we had with us.

First I washed Chiron. He loved his bath and kicked and squealed, his legs moving in unison like an excited frog. Kick, kick, kick! When I lifted him out of the bath he yelled loudly, wailing while I dried him off in front of the fire and dressed him. He squalled until his mouth found my nipple, then he nursed greedily until he dropped off to sleep, as suddenly as only a tiny baby can.

Chiron slept, woke, and cried. He nursed again and dropped off to sleep. He had no schedule to speak of. He was a cranky, cantankerous little soul who wanted desperately to stay awake but couldn't manage to keep his eyes open after eating. I had finally figured him out. He cried easily and was prone to excess emotion. When he was still, he was very, very still; uncanny for a little fellow his age. His eyes would search and search for things to study. He got bored easily. He loved new faces. He adored pulling hair, and he sucked his fists, not his fingers. When

8

he slept, he was the most beautiful baby in the world, pure of face and peaceful. Awake, his expressions could range from gargoyle to cherub, and everything in between. He looked like Plexis, but he had Alexander's character traits. Sometimes I wondered whose child he was. I stroked Chiron's downy head, so fragile and fine. I glanced at Alexander and our eyes met. A smile moved across his face, as shy as a shadow, but his eyes were serious and deeply tender.

When Craterus and Ptolemy finished their report, we sat on the rug and ate. They told us some stories they'd heard from their soldiers. The stories were mostly about the new animals and trees they'd seen. One man swore he'd seen a red bush walking. Another man was sure he'd seen a river god who had forbidden Alexander to cross the Indus. This story took up most of the conversation, because the man in question was a priest, and we'd already had our share of trouble with a priest.

Alexander sighed and scratched his head. 'What does he want me to do?'

'Turn around and go home,' said Ptolemy, shrugging. He took a large bite of meat and mumbled, 'Ishnothingsherous.'

'What?'

Ptolemy swallowed and frowned. 'It's nothing serious. I'm so hungry I could eat an elephant.'

Alexander brightened. Elephants were his favourite subjects, after himself. 'How are they doing? Is the female any better?' Her ear had gotten infected after the last battle. An arrow had struck the mighty beast and cut her badly.

'She's fine.' Ptolemy was in charge of the elephants and the infantry around them. Craterus led the phalanx, and Alexander was head of the cavalry. We were travelling lightly; only twenty thousand of us, including slaves, priests, cooks, soldiers, scientists, doctors, grooms, scribes, pages, historians, and Chiron and me.

Forty thousand men led by Plexis and Perdiccas made up the other half of the army. Our scouts told us they had started a siege at a place called Charsadda. Apparently, the king on the far side of the Indus barred the passage to Alexander. Of the two kings in that area only Taxiles, king of Taxila, had sent diplomats and elephants to Alexander. He'd also pledged his support and gave him free passage through his lands.

The other guy hadn't been so smart. After forty days the city would surrender, be sacked, and the king killed. Plexis and Perdiccas sent news regularly, which was how we knew what was happening. Alexander loved getting mail.

After dinner, the men played chess or draughts while Alexander played the lute. He'd been well educated, and besides playing the lute he played the ceremonial oboe, the flute, and drums. He could recite Homer, Plato, and Euripides, and he knew all the constellations and stars in the sky. He could speak five languages fluently and three others well enough to make himself understood. He had studied all the ancient philosophies and the latest ones as well. Science, mathematics, history, and politics had been included in his lessons. Aristotle had been his teacher for ten years, and Alexander was still thirsty for knowledge.

I never met anyone with such a curious mind. Everything interested him. He asked questions of everyone, be they shepherd or prince, and he paid attention to their answers. I listened to him plucking the chords of the lute, his face a study in concentration. He was trying to remember a song I'd taught him. The song came from a few thousand years in the future. Normally it was played on an electric guitar, but the lute wasn't bad.

Brazza poured hot water into my tub and I sighed with pleasure as I sank into the scented water. The Persians made hundreds of different perfumes, and I had quite a few with me. Tonight I chose yellow musk-rose; the scent was divine. I put a curtain up in the corner, and my bath was behind it. It was rather a vain gesture. Everyone went around practically naked; the men marched, fought, and worked with just a short wool or linen, wrap-around skirt.

A ceremonial toga, a linen tunic to go under his armour, a pleated skirt, and a woollen cape were all the clothes Alexander possessed. I had a silk robe, a cotton shift, a linen tunic, a long linen robe, some makeshift drawstring underwear, two pairs of wool pants, a woollen jacket, and a cape.

Besides my clothes, I owned a short woman's spear given to me by Alexander's first wife – my wife-in-law? – a very fine necklace with a moonstone pendant, a gold bracelet, a horse named Lenaia in honour of an orgiastic festival, and a rocking chair, lovingly fashioned for me by Brazza.

Alexander, king of all Macedonia, Greece, Egypt, Persia, Bactria, and Sogdia, had a lamp, a table, a pen set, a golden cup, and a rug. The tent belonged to him too, of course, and he had two horses. One was the mighty Bucephalus, now almost twenty-three and turning grey around the muzzle. He had several weapons including a rather nice sword, an armoured breastplate with the head of the Gorgon Medusa enamelled on the front, and a pair of sandals. And he had a magic shield. He claimed it was Achilles' magic shield and would not go into battle without it. I wasn't reassured. His body was striped all over with scars. Sitting naked on the rug, with just a gold chain around his neck and his ankle bandaged, he looked as dangerous as one of the Siberian tigers I'd seen once before in a zoo. A scar divided his shoulder in two – from a lance that almost killed him. Another terribly gnarled scar disfigured the lower calf on his right leg; an arrow broke his fibula. His arms were striped with silver scars from sword cuts, and his ankle was in a splint; his latest wound. His nose had been broken two or three times. His forehead had a scar right down the middle; a glancing blow from a sword. His neck had a scar on the side – a rock from a catapult hit him, and he was in a coma for three days. His clavicle had a funny bump – broken during a polo match – and his thigh sported the marks of a wild boar's tusks.

Ptolemy and Craterus weren't any less marked. Ptolemy had a twisted arm from a break that healed wrongly, and Craterus had half a calf muscle missing from one leg. They didn't let those little hurts stop them, though. Ptolemy could hurl a javelin as far as anyone else, and he loved to participate in the 'goatball' games – games that left as many scars on the men as battles did.

Usse knew this. When the games began, he would start boiling his surgical instruments and heating his cauterizing irons. Stitches were unheard of in that time. They seared the wounds closed. It smelled awful and sounded worse. The patient usually screamed himself unconscious. Alexander had done so on several occasions, waking up with his voice utterly shattered.

The night was still. For once the elephants were peaceful. Taxiles had given Alexander twenty-three females and two males. The males had gone through the rutting season and had made nights miserable for everyone, except maybe the female elephants. An elephant trumpeting all night long is guaranteed to keep anyone awake.

When the generals left, Axiom helped Alexander wash, and Brazza and I cleaned and packed. We would leave early the next morning. Usse came back from the infirmary and reheated his meat on the brazier. He was excited about going to India and discovering new medical procedures. I had already told him all about germs, but he wanted something he could actually see.

For people who believed that sprites lived in trees and streams and that gods were everywhere – but not visible except on rare occasions – germs were accepted and understood. Usse wished he could actually see one, so we had grown mould, and although the spores are quite a bit bigger than germs, he got the general idea.

I wanted to try and find penicillin, and why not? I knew it was a type of mould and it had developed in close contact with human beings. It reacted to our illnesses and infections, so it was somewhere nearby, floating around. I had taken to cultivating mouldy yeast and bread, and treating the small cuts and puncture wounds gone septic. So far, I hadn't really had any success. One batch seemed to clear up a messy leg wound, but I lost the culture in a battle, and now I couldn't grow it again. The mould had been a lovely greenish blue. Usse was as fascinated as I, but he was even more interested in new plant remedies. The Indian ambassadors had brought along several doctors, and Usse spent much time with the men in deep discussion. The newest idea was burnt tiger whiskers, and Usse was both excited and apprehensive about collecting tiger whiskers.

13

We all slept in the tent. Curtains gave us privacy. Chiron slept in a hammock near me, so when he woke, which could be any time, I could see to him. Alexander slept deeply; the baby's crying didn't wake him. Everyone snored, and sometimes I dreamed that I was in a cave with bears growling or wild cats purring loudly.

Chapter Two

The dawn's light, pink and watery, filtered through a hole in the top of the tent. Axiom and Brazza were already awake, feeding bits of wood to the brazier and getting breakfast ready. Outside, everyone started to stir. I could hear the soldiers starting to take down their tents. The sound of the tent poles clicking together as they were rolled up and fastened together was like quick castanets. I heard the fluttery snorts and soft whinnies of the horses as their grooms led them to the river's edge. Then the elephants were led to water. The horses wouldn't drink after the elephants did. I didn't blame them. The elephants dug, rolled, and splashed in the mud, stirring up the water. They even gouged out the bank.

Those were the morning noises. The smell of wood burning came next as the cooks lit the fires. Then came the soft thump of thousands of bare feet as the men jogged to the mess tent and lined up to get their rations for two or three days' marching. The mess tent usually travelled at least a day ahead of us, setting up camp and getting ready to receive the rest of the army. The cavalry travelled with the cooks and there was a substantial herd of animals to be prodded along. I could hear the lowing of cows, the bleating of sheep and goats, the high cries of the children and women who accompanied the army – there were at least thirty families with children of all ages – and swearing. The soldiers always swore.

I snuggled down into the soft covers and nuzzled against Alexander's shoulder. He was awake, lying still. When I moved, his arms went around me, pulling me close. It was rare to find him in bed in the morning. Usually he got up before the dawn. However, his ankle kept him immobilized now.

I kissed his neck and nibbled his ear, making him chuckle. My hair swept over his face, a white-blonde mane. He ran his hands over my body and nudged his hips towards me. I smiled and raised my eyebrows. His mouth went soft, his eyes darkened. I didn't need to ask. I could feel his arousal. It pressed against my belly, hot, and urgent. I quivered. A kind of alchemy existed between us; a chemistry that operated on the most primitive level of sight, sound, scent, and touch. Just a look from him, a gentle touch, and my nipples would harden and tingle and a rush of heat would build between my legs; a heat that Alexander could quench with his lithe body. A play of hands, of lips, of kisses. Lovemaking that started from a look and grew steadily deeper. Legs, arms, and hair entwined. Caresses raised goose bumps all along our arms.

He took possession of me, moving surely and strongly. His face was a study in concentration, his eyes half closed. Small whimpers escaped me. I couldn't help it. My muscles turned to water and my head fell forward. He grasped my hips and pulled me harder to him, arching his back higher so that I was riding his belly like a horse. I clenched my knees around him and leaned onto his chest, my breasts brushing his ribs. I fastened my mouth on his shoulder to stifle my cries.

With a groan, he rolled over, covering my body with his, driving into me with all his weight and force. I felt as if my whole being was concentrated in one tiny pinpoint of

16

feeling that grew in my belly. It grew and grew, enveloping me, sweeping me away and carrying me on waves of pleasure. I felt Alexander spurting inside me and he cried out, once, harshly. We trembled and then lay still, our two bodies melded together.

Our bodies were still, but our hearts were pounding. I waited until my breathing quieted and the tremors stopped, then I leaned over on my elbow and looked down on my husband. His eyes were closed, he was sound asleep. His long lashes rested on his cheekbones. His mouth was slightly bruised from hard kisses, and his face was in repose for a brief time. He always fell asleep after he made love – sound asleep, as quickly as a baby with a full stomach.

I smiled tenderly, and his eyelashes fluttered as he woke up. The sleep never lasted long. His eyes, one blue, one brown stared up at me. They were clear and guileless, only a trace of impish humour marred their innocence.

'Sleep well?' I asked him, my voice purring.

'Mmm, you know it.' He smiled, and then winced. The tip of his tongue explored his bottom lip. 'Did you bite me?'

'Maybe. I don't remember.' I grinned. 'With all your cuts and bruises, what's one more?'

'One too many,' he sighed. 'I'm getting too old for this.'

'For what? Making love in the morning?'

He looked amused. 'No, for making love in the evening, the middle of the night, and then in the morning.'

'Does that mean we're not stopping for lunch?' I asked demurely.

He struggled to a sitting position. 'Look at me! I can hardly move. You're draining my strength, woman.'

'Just call me Delilah,' I said.

'Who?'

I thought for a moment. 'Samson and Delilah? It doesn't ring a bell?'

'Oh, that! But that was centuries ago. At least, let's see, seven centuries ago. Don't tell me you still talk about *him* in your time as well?' He shook his head. 'A Hebrew judge. Amazing.'

'Is that all that story is to you?'

He frowned as he ran his fingers through his hair. 'What else is there? Axiom! Is my razor ready?'

'Yes, right here. Shall I shave you now?'

'Please.' Alexander swung his legs over the side of the bed, pulling the curtains aside. His ankle made him draw his breath in with a hiss and he blanched.

'Is it worse?' I knelt on the floor and carefully examined it. It felt hot, and I frowned. 'Where's Usse?'

'He left a few minutes ago,' said Axiom, coming to the side of the bed with a bowl of hot water and a razor.

'Funny, I didn't hear him leave.' Alexander cocked an eyebrow at me. 'Did you?'

'If you're well enough to joke, it must not be serious,' I said, standing up and brushing my hands on my thighs. 'Is there any hot water left?'

'Of course.' Axiom bent over Alexander, deftly shaving his cheeks.

Chiron was still sleeping so I had five minutes to myself. I quickly washed and dressed. Then he woke, letting everyone in the camp know he was hungry.

I nursed Chiron while Axiom and Brazza took the tent down and packed. Since getting the elephants, the tent and our belongings stayed together. Our baggage was carried by a large male Indian elephant I'd named Harry Krishna, to the shocked amusement of the Indian ambassadors. He was an affectionate beast, and he liked it when I scratched his massive forehead. I enjoyed taking care of him, and I'd sometimes go with his driver down to the creek and assist in his bath. I always gave the elephant a titbit. He had a sweet tooth and especially liked almonds dipped in honey.

I had finished changing Chiron and strapping him in his backpack when my pony was led to me. I thanked the groom and mounted. Harry the elephant was almost loaded, and I could see Bucephalus being bridled. Alexander hopped out of the tent and stood, leaning against my pony as we waited for his horse.

The sun rose above the horizon. I could see it would be a bright, sunny day. A faint mist lifted off the river, and the trees around us started to rustle as the wind rose. Birds woke and their singing filled the air. I tipped my head back and breathed deeply. The air smelled fresh and clean, like the beginning of the world.

I looked down at the top of Alexander's head. His hair was neatly brushed and tied back with a leather thong. Axiom tried to tame it, but the curls that lifted off his temples and the back of his neck would tangle, and then wavy strands would escape, and at the end of the day his hair would be an unruly mane around his head, making him look like a hedonistic lion. Why wait? I reached down and ruffled his hair.

He tilted his head back at me, his eyes alight. 'This evening we will arrive in Nysa,' he said.

'How do you know? Aren't we lost?'

He snorted. 'How can we be lost? The guides are gone, we spent a day orienting ourselves, but now all is well. The route is to the north-east. Ten hours' march. If there are no great rivers we will …' His voice broke and I was shocked to see tears in his eyes.

'What is it?' I leaned down.

'I dare not hope any more. It has been too long. I have been disappointed too many times. If I do not find him here, I don't know what I'll do.' His words were simple, his voice bleak.

'We'll find him.'

'May the gods hear you,' he replied, reaching his hand out towards Bucephalus, who, with his ears pricked and his step light, trotted towards his master.

We rode steadily, stopping briefly for a rest at the height of the day when the sun made no more shadows. The air felt pleasantly cool. It was winter, but it wasn't freezing cold in the afternoon. Sometimes at night, we would get frost and the world would glitter in the starlight, especially if there was no moon. However, lately it had been mild, and I folded my woollen cape across my lap.

The sun touched the horizon. Behind us, the army spread out in a sinuous trail nearly ten kilometres long. The warmth of the afternoon left the air. I could smell smoke, somewhere someone had lit a fire. All those thoughts, like fragments of paper, flitted through my mind. We had climbed a narrow pass and arrived at the summit of a sharp, steep hill. Beyond the hill the evening mist had already obscured the valley behind it. A low, silver cloud slowly turned gold as the sun's rays touched it. The liquid notes of a songbird floated in the air, blending with the faint chirping of the first crickets and night frogs.

On either side of me, faraway snowy peaks tapped the vault of the sky. Behind me, the evening turned dark blue. The soldiers had lit torches and the orange lights flickered like a procession of fireflies. In front of me, the sun turned a deep blood red. As I topped the ridge I stopped and looked. Low clouds obscured the valley, but blue spirals of smoke told me it was inhabited.

Alexander waited for me, his horse turned sideways. The sun tinted Bucephalus's black mane and tail scarlet and gilded Alexander's head in bright gold. His face was in shadow as he looked back at me, yet I could tell he was anxious. His hands shook on his reins. I reached forward and touched him gently.

At that moment the sun's rays dipped downwards and pierced the mist. A deep green valley was shown to us in the space of a moment. My breath caught in my throat. A village nestled on the banks of a silver creek. Fields and forest were set like jewels. A lake gleamed in the distance and small cooking fires scattered like glowing topazes all around the valley.

Suddenly, a man stepped out from behind a tree. My horse shied, then quieted. Bucephalus didn't even move, he simply pricked his ears a bit and blew softly through fluttery nostrils.

'Welcome, Great Iskander, to the Valley of the Gods,' said the man, bowing low. He wore white robes and carried a long staff. I blinked. It was like meeting a character from a fantasy book. The man's pronunciation of Alexander's name was slightly different too. It sounded almost like 'Seekandher'.

'Who are you?' asked Alexander, his voice wary.

'I am the guardian of the sacred valley. Enter and be welcome. Your army may camp by the lakeside. You will find pasture and fresh water there.' He bowed again. 'You and the Lady of the Moon may come with me.'

'How amazing,' I heard myself saying.

Alexander demanded to see our child. The old man, walking in front of our horses, peered back over his shoulder and smiled. 'The child waits for you. We have kept him safe.'

'I thank you,' said Alexander stiffly. He wasn't sure, even now, that we'd finally caught up with Paul.

Neither was I. My heart thumped painfully and tears kept threatening to spill. The man seemed to sense this because he said to me, without slowing his pace, 'Worry not, daughter of Demeter. Your child awaits. You will soon behold him.'

Chiron stirred on my back, but for once, didn't cry. As he faced backwards, he had a fascinating view of the whole army coming over the narrow, high pass. In the deep blue evening their lit torches cast a warm glow upon the men and elephants. The sandy road beneath them gleamed faintly white, the trees looked dark and mysterious, and the men sang softly the song to ward off the owl spirit and to quiet the frogs.

Why they were frightened of frogs and owls I'll never understand, but the song was simple and lovely. It floated above them in the night air, like a canticle for sleep or dreams.

Chapter Three

When we arrived in the valley, a group of men waited to take Alexander and his army to the shores of the lake where a place had been readied for them. I got off my pony and stood in the gloom. My head spun. I could hardly let myself think of Paul. I gave my pony to the groom and looked uncertainly at the old man. He took my hand in his. His grip felt warm and firm. 'Fear not, my lady,' he said. 'Your son is here. I will bring you to him now. It is not fair to make you wait any longer.'

I followed him down a white sandy road between small, neat houses. People stood in the doorways bowing as I went by. The night breeze rustled the leaves of the trees, and little wind chimes made of bamboo and carved wood clicked softly in their branches. The whole forest whispered and tinkled with the sound.

The people were tall and fair and wore white robes. Their hair was dark blond or reddish brown, braided and tied back with white ribbons. They said nothing as I passed, but I could hear a murmur, like a chant, as I went by.

The last house in the village stood by itself in the midst of a large garden. Wind chimes jingled softly in the night breeze. A cuckoo called. The door opened and a woman beckoned me. I couldn't stop shaking.

Inside, lamps were lit. Yellow light danced around the walls. On the floor lay richly coloured rugs and soft cushions. A low table was set with a warm meal. Light glittered off the brass brazier and the copper bowls. However, there was nobody in the room.

'Please, don't make me wait any longer,' I whispered. 'Just let me see Paul.'

The man clapped his hands and a woman entered the room.

She led a little boy by the hand. I dropped to my knees. The boy stood and stared at me gravely. He was four and a half years old, tall, sturdy, with long, magnificent eyes in a triangular face. He had a proud nose and a wide forehead. His blond hair curled softly and lifted off the back of his neck and temples. He stood perfectly still. I hardly saw him breathe. But a pulse beat in the base of his throat. A pulse I knew so well.

I stretched my arms out to him, my vision blurring with tears. 'Come, Paul,' I said in English.

He came into my arms, laying his head gently on my shoulder. His small arms crept around my neck. I held him. I just held him. I hardly dared to breathe. It was akin to seeing a ghost.

I stood up and swung Paul into my arms, holding him on my hip. For a minute I had only one urge, to leave, to take my child and leave. Instead, I walked to the bench and sat down. I kept Paul on my lap while I unhooked Chiron's backpack and took the tiny baby in my arms. To Paul I said, 'Here's your baby brother. His name's Chiron. He's a sweet boy, and soon he'll be able to play with you.' I spoke English. I knew he wouldn't understand, but while I was pregnant I'd spoken English to Paul.

The boy twisted around and peered into my face. He seemed to be searching for something, and then satisfied, he smiled. 'Mummy,' he said, in English.

I nearly dropped Chiron.

'Do you understand me?' I gasped but he only smiled. 'Who brought him to you?' I asked the old man.

The man poured some tea and handed me the cup. 'The woman you see here. She was one of Spitamenes' servants.' He nodded towards the lady who'd brought Paul to see me. She was small with long dark hair, and stood quietly, her hands folded in front of her, her eyes downcast.

'I thank you,' I said to the woman, and she smiled shyly. 'You took good care of him, and I can see he's suffered no harm.'

'This child is marked by the moon goddess. No one can harm him,' the old man said. 'Olympias thought that Marduk would kill him, but the Babylonian god, bloodthirsty as he may be, was no match for the babe. You saw what happened.'

'The child I saved wasn't Paul! He had already left.' I cried.

'Marduk was destroyed by Paul indirectly. He didn't even need to be present. Darius took him. Then Darius was killed and Bessus took him ...'

'And Bessus was killed. And then Spitamenes ...' I looked at the child sitting on my lap and frowned. 'What does it mean?'

'It means that this child is protected by forces which have no mercy. There are forces with no souls. We call them gods. This child is protected by a god.'

'Gods have no souls?' Confusion and wild relief to have finally found Paul made my head spin.

'We will discuss theology another time.' The man's smile was amused. 'This woman was the boy's guardian and she brought him to us. She'd heard about us as a child.

The legends of our valley are numerous. She knew that he would be safe here and that he could wait for you; his mother and daughter of a goddess.'

'Thank you,' I said, still uncertain. 'Why is this valley so important?'

'It has been so for thousands of generations,' he said. 'The gods used to live here. Zeus sent his son, Dionysus, to protect him from Hera's wrath.'

I held the little boy closer. He stayed still on my lap, tipping his face up to me now and then and searching my face. His eyes were a deep blue, like twin sapphires, and they were terribly serious. 'You poor baby,' I said. 'Being taken halfway around the world, surrounded by strangers.' I kissed his forehead. 'I know how you feel, though, and I won't ever let you go again. Never.'

The man seemed amused by my words. 'The boy has been taken halfway across the world,' he said, 'but he was never in any danger. The boy is a harbinger of destruction for all those who are around him, but not for you, because you are not of our world.'

'What did you say?'

'The child cannot harm you, you are not of this world,' he repeated.

'I am not of this world?' My voice broke. 'How … how do you know all this?'

'It is written.' The man glanced towards the door. 'We have but one hour. Come.'

I stood up. The words, 'Not of this world', echoed in my head. Paul slid off my lap and ran to take refuge in the dark-haired woman's arms. Another woman came and took Chiron from me, crooning softly at him.

I followed the man into a small room lit with three torches. An ancient parchment was unrolled on a high table. It was the first time I'd seen a reading table in that time. I stepped closer. The table stood as high as my chest.

The man pointed to a passage and read aloud, *'When the two kingdoms are united beneath one man there will come a babe marked by the moon. His mother is not from this world. The babe is the moon's child and will call upon her in time of need. His father, the king, will die in his thirty-third year. His kingdom will be torn asunder. Beware, all those near the king will be swept away by the cold winds of Hades. They will disappear from the face of the earth, but their stories shall last forever.'*

I'd studied ancient texts. This one put all the rest to shame.

'How old is that?' I asked, when I'd found my voice.

'It came to us from our ancestors, travelling with them from across the mountains. We think it is three hundred centuries old.'

'Thirty thousand years? It's impossible! Writing didn't even exist then!'

'Were you around to check?' He smiled and shook his head. 'Come now, Iskander is going to arrive, and he longs to see his son.'

I let myself be led from the room. The parchment had shaken me. How could it be so precise? How had it known Alexander would die aged thirty-three? I shuddered. All his family would be killed in the murderous struggle to gain control of his empire. I knew it. Yet, how was it that everything was written down?

I knew the old man was right. If Paul entered that fray, his life wouldn't be worth much. I wouldn't be able to protect him when Alexander died. And I didn't know how to tell Alexander. How could I? It was too cruel. I could never tell him. It would destroy him. Olympias,

Alexander's mother would perish. His wives would be killed, his children murdered.

Roxanne had sent word right before we left. She had borne a son and named him Iskander. They would travel to Ecbatana in one year's time. We were going to meet there, and Alexander would see his son, a son who would die before he was ten years old.

It was dreadful knowing the future.

Alexander had gone with his army to set up camp. The night was deep before he was carried back to the village in a litter. He hobbled up the steps and stood in the doorway, uncertainty written on his face. 'Is the child here?' he asked me. He tried to keep his voice calm, but couldn't. His hands shook on the door.

'He's here. We have found our son.'

His hand tightened on the wood. 'Where?'

'There he is,' I said, moving aside and pointing to Paul sitting in the Sogdian woman's lap.

Alexander dropped to his knees in front of the child. He didn't hold out his arms. 'Paul,' he said softly. On his face was a mixture of fear and joy.

The little boy hid his face in the woman's black robe, and then timidly peeked out. His mouth trembled and dimples suddenly appeared in his cheeks. His eyes weren't frightened. He seemed to be playing a game. Alexander smiled. His eyes glittered with tears. 'Come here,' he said, and Paul ran to him.

The faces were the same, the long Byzantine eyes, the strong chins, and the bright hair. Paul put his finger in his mouth and studied Alexander gravely. His eyes were huge in his small face.

Chiron started to cry and the old woman gave him back

to me so I could nurse him. I sat near the brazier and watched Alexander and Paul. Alexander sat cross-legged in front of the table. Paul sat in his lap and seemed to have no fear of strangers. His eyes were bright and curious. He said little, but when he spoke it was clear. He spoke Greek. He had a strange accent, and I realized it was Persian. I looked down at Chiron; his mouth was open and he was snoring lightly. His fair lashes fluttered once then were still. My heart swelled. When I looked at Paul I was filled with awe. The memory of a tiny baby came back to me, but I had never known him. Was he mischievous? Was he a serious boy? Did he cry easily? I knew nothing about him. He looked sweet. I remembered a quiet baby. Mary had been sweet too. I closed my eyes. I could make no decisions tonight. I would wait. I would wait months if I had to, but in the end I would decide what would be best for Paul.

Alexander and Paul were still studying each other. There was food on the table and the old man motioned for us to serve ourselves. I thought I was hungry, but I wasn't sure I would eat. One thing my travels had taught me. Trust no one. Poison was cheap.

The old man smiled. He read my thoughts as easily as if they were written across my forehead. 'I am sorry you don't trust me yet,' he said. 'But you will. I know that, so I am not hurt. My name is Sharwah. I am descended from the first tribe that peopled this valley, as are most of the people you see. Now you have come, the valley will change. Some of your soldiers will want to stay. Anyone who wishes to settle here will be welcome.' He spread his arms. 'Tomorrow I will show you our valley and we will talk.'

'Where are Axiom and Brazza?' I looked around. I

didn't know if I could sleep without their reassuring presence.

'They have stayed behind in the tent,' said Alexander. He looked up at the man, his eyes hooded. 'If you don't mind, we would prefer to sleep there.'

'You are welcome to stay here. Beds have been prepared. But if you want to go back to your tent, watch the child carefully. He's a harbinger of destruction.' Sharwah's voice was serious.

Alexander glanced towards me, but said nothing. His arms tightened around Paul, who squirmed.

Sharwah's smile didn't waver. 'You must believe me,' he said gently. 'The child has been marked by the moon. If you don't understand, take off your necklace and hold it towards him. Then perhaps you will see.'

I didn't know how he knew I wore a necklace. It lay hidden underneath my tunic. I dipped my hand down my bodice and lifted it out. I drew it over my head and held it towards Paul, who had turned his head and was staring at me, eyes wide.

The necklace started to sing.

I dropped it on the floor and leaped backwards. It had vibrated in my hand and had given off a high-pitched whine. Even now it was humming softly. A strange glow emanated from the moonstone.

Paul stepped forward and looked down at it. His mouth curved in a wide smile. He picked up the necklace and the hum grew to a shivering, clear note. Behind me came the sound of shattering glass as a lantern broke. I whirled around and stared, mouth open, as the oil seeped out onto the floor. Luckily it hadn't been lit.

The necklace continued to sing. It seemed thrilled to be in Paul's hands. The stone glowed and cast a bluish light on the child's face. A soft moan of fear escaped me.

Alexander lifted the boy off the ground and took the necklace. He handed it back to me. How had Paul done that?

'Is it the prophecy?' he asked the old man. 'Tell me, Sharwah, is he really the son of the moon?'

'He is,' the old man replied.

'You know of the prophecy?' I asked Alexander. 'The one where, where …'

Sharwah interrupted me. 'There are more prophesies than can be counted in this world. In your world are there any left? Or have they all vanished? Or come true?'

I shook my head. 'They're just wild tales, empty puzzles, and words with no meanings.'

Alexander frowned. 'You're wrong. They are words with more than one meaning, but they are not empty. They are meant to be fulfilled, and they come to us from further in time than even *you* can imagine.' His voice was bleak. He held Paul in his arms and the child laid his head on Alexander's shoulder. 'We go now. Come, Ashley.'

'It is as you wish,' said Sharwah, bowing. 'Your litter waits outside.'

'You knew?' I blinked. 'You knew we wouldn't stay here?'

'My lady, I am old, and I am feeble …'

I gave a snort. Feeble? The old, feeble man had walked lightly down a twisting mountain trail, hopped over a rushing stream – after asking permission of the nymph – and though the distance between the pass and the village must have been five kilometres, he wasn't out of breath when he arrived.

He raised an eyebrow at me. 'I'm flattered,' he said, reading my thoughts again. 'But old and feeble as I may be, I still know the minds of men. And men who travel as much as the king need to have their familiar things around them or else their sleep is troubled. What better sanctuary than a tent?' He chuckled. 'Paul's nurse will be here tomorrow morning when you awake. Come whenever you like. The door is always open for the moon child's parents.'

We were silent on our way back to the tent. The townspeople peeped out at us when we walked by and nodded or bowed deeply. Alexander looked neither right nor left. Two strong soldiers carried him in his litter. The litter was little more than a stretcher. Alexander hated it. He refused to lie back, preferring to prop himself up and sit with his leg held awkwardly stuck out in front of him. I caught him glaring at his ankle, and then the lines on his face deepened. I fell back a step. He was proud and hadn't meant for me to see him like that.

Paul sat quietly in his lap and, halfway to the tent, the rocking motion of the litter put him to sleep. Alexander stroked his head softly. In the faint light of the stars I saw tears glitter on Alexander's face.

I carried the sleeping child into the tent and laid him on the tiny pallet Axiom had prepared. Then we all stood over him, watching as he slept. His golden hair was as bright as silk floss in the blue lamplight.

Axiom, Brazza, and Usse slept near Paul. I felt secure knowing they were there, watching over him as he slept.

Later, when the tent was still and the only sound we heard were the blasted elephants settling down for the night, I wrapped my arms around Alexander and put my mouth next to his ear. 'Tell me about the prophecy,' I ordered.

There was a sudden stillness in the tent, and I realized

that Axiom and Usse were listening.

Alexander turned to face me. 'It was a story I heard in Macedonia, but it exists in Greece, Egypt, and Persia as well. I suppose, if we ask the soldiers from Sogdia and Bactria, they will say they've heard the same thing. The story is simple. It says that the moon was once part of the mother earth, but that there was a terrible cataclysm and mother and child were separated. They were condemned to stay apart forever, never meeting each other again. Thus do the earth and the moon circle each other. Until one day, the child of the moon is born. According to the sayings, this child has the power to lure the moon back to his mother. The world will end. The gods will fall. They say the child must stay forever hidden in the sacred valley.'

'Do you believe that? It sounds so unlikely. How could staying here change anything?'

'Because this is the Valley of the Gods. Some believe that it is not really on this earth; that once we go through the pass we have entered a different world with different rules. From here the child cannot call the moon.'

I sat up. 'Usse, have you heard of this?'

A soft cough came from the far side of the tent.

'Well,' Usse spoke softly, 'I have heard tell of the prophecy, yes. They say that when the moon's child calls the moon back to earth, it will fall from the sky. It is an old legend,' he sounded doubtful. 'It is not one we usually speak of; it is more within the realm of the high priest of the moon cult.'

'And you, Axiom?' I wanted everyone's opinion.

'In my religion we have no myths about the moon's child, but that doesn't mean I haven't heard the story before. I heard say that the world will end when the child and the mother are reunited once more in the heavens. For

33

us, the moon's child is a prophet who will come and free us from our enemies. He will come with a flaming sword and he will be the king of kings.'

'Well, that counts me out,' said Alexander dryly. 'My sword never once caught on fire.'

'So, the world will end when he's reunited with his mother?' I asked.

'Well, it's vague. Supposedly there is a dragon who will swallow the sun, and then the mother will give birth in the heavens, the child will slay the dragon and evil will be vanquished for another ten thousand years.' Axiom was warming up to his story.

'Sounds wild to me,' I said, yawning.

'We'll talk about it in the morning,' said Alexander, his voice slurred with fatigue.

I fell asleep before he finished speaking.

Chapter Four

Morning in the Valley of the Gods.

A light mist floated over the flat, silver lake. The mountains in the background were shrouded in snow. The birds sang in the rushes, sweet, liquid notes to welcome the morning sun. The Egyptians began their sun chant, an ululating, sweet harmony of voices rising in the cool air. Grooms led the horses and elephants to the lake to drink. The horses walked in silence, raising their heads and snorting softly. The elephants moved like huge, grey shadows along the beach, blowing water like geysers from their trunks.

Chiron, at an age where the only thing that mattered was his stomach, woke us all up with his piercing yells.

Paul, waking up and finding himself in a strange place surrounded by strangers, started to wail. I called to him and he crawled into bed with me. I gave him a hug and he stopped crying. His eyes settled on Alexander lying next to me. He gave a little chuckle, reached over and yanked on his hair.

Alexander sat up, his handsome face rumpled with sleep. 'When the elephants stop trumpeting, Chiron starts howling. I think the Athenians are right when they say, 'The only thing more miserable than a man with children, is a man with more children'.'

'Ha, ha,' I said sourly. 'Can we apply that saying for a man with elephants, too? Harry Krishna woke me up eight times last night. Thank you, Brazza,' I said, taking Chiron from him and baring my breast. The baby grabbed a nipple and hung on for dear life. I winced.

Alexander looked at him and grinned. 'Takes after his father, doesn't he?'

I smiled. 'Which one?'

'This one.' He leaned forward and suckled the other breast, then he licked his lips and winked. 'Ambrosia must be like that; sweet, warm, and coming from a woman's breast. What more could one ask for? Chiron's absolutely right to scream for it every four hours.'

I giggled and bent my head, covering Chiron's and my nakedness with silvery hair. Alexander sat back and watched us for a while. His face reflected the contentment I felt. 'I want to talk to Sharwah some more, I don't think he told us everything,' he said.

'I agree. There's something odd about all this.' I glanced out the tent flap that Axiom had raised. Dawn was just beginning to break and the sky was streaked with salmon pink. 'It is a beautiful place. How is it that it doesn't seem to have a king or an army? Every place I've been before there have been fortifications, guards, a satrap, or a king. What is this place? Where's the temple? I looked last night when we walked through the village, but I didn't see one.'

'It is strange. And I'll tell you something else that's strange – the people don't look like any people I've ever seen.'

I frowned. 'It's like in this book I read. There was a valley with a rushing stream and a lake, where elves lived.'

'What are they?'

'They're sort of like a nymph or a sprite. Except

they're not immortal.' I tried to remember the story. 'They're magic, they make magic weapons. That's it. Maybe Sharwah is an elf.'

'You won't believe in water nymphs but you're sitting there telling me about things called nelfs that make magic weapons?' He made a droll face. 'Maybe I can ask for a magic spear that will strike down my enemies, or a flaming sword, and then I'll be the king of kings.'

'Believe me, you don't want to be the king of kings. And it's not a nelf, it's an elf.'

'That's what I said.' He leaned over and kissed Chiron on the back of his neck. 'I love that spot. It's so soft, and smells so good.' He moved his mouth over and grabbed my nipple again. 'And I love this too,' he said. Then he sighed. 'I hope my ankle will heal soon. Staying in bed in the morning is definitely tiring me out.'

'What do you mean? We're just sitting here.'

'Has Chiron finished?'

'Yes, I think so.'

'And is Paul's breakfast ready?'

I leaned over and looked. Axiom had set food on the table. 'Yes, it looks like it.'

'Good. Brazza?' he motioned to him. 'Can you take Chiron now? And Paul?' He waited until Brazza took the children then he leaned over and drew the curtain. 'This is what I mean,' he said, and his eyes were dark with desire.

Afterwards, I stretched languorously. 'I see what you mean.'

Alexander blinked and yawned. 'If I didn't know better, I would think I was becoming a sybarite.'

'But you do know better?' I teased.

'I know we're going to have to find a nurse for Paul. Brazza won't be able to look after both children,' he said fondling my breast.

'I'll see what I can do.'

'Hmm. If I don't get up now, I'll never get up. I hear footsteps.' He propped himself up on his elbow and cocked his head. 'Someone's in a hurry.'

He was right. He had ears like a bat. Craterus came in, sweeping under the tent flap, his long face mournful as usual. 'Iskander, I have news from our scouts.'

'What is it?'

'Forces are being gathered in the Swat valley northwest of here. Mostly mercenaries. They've banded together at Massaga, a fortified town.'

'Do you want to go see for yourself?' Alexander asked.

'If you think I should,' Craterus replied.

'I do,' Alexander said. 'And while you're there, see where they can attack us, where we can attack them, and all their possible routes of escape. Take fifty soldiers with you and get local guides to help.' He looked pleased. He loved planning an attack.

Craterus left, looking pleased too. He loved scouting.

I shook my head; they were like two boys with a new toy. 'Great,' I said sarcastically when Craterus had left. 'More bloodshed. Why don't you send a diplomat and see if you can talk? Maybe you can settle this with words instead of war!'

He peered at me from underneath lowered lashes. 'And will you choose the diplomat?' he asked.

'Why not?' I drew my brows together.

'And if the man's hands come back first, will you feel bad?'

'Of course!'

'Well, before I send a diplomat I prefer to see if he can be protected and what will happen if he can't be, and what

I can do if his hands come back without him. All right? I promise I won't rush in shooting arrows if I can talk first.' He tilted his head. 'How does your world conduct war?'

'It's rather complicated,' I admitted. 'Sometimes it's a civil war, in which case the outside countries stay out of it as much as possible. If another country attacks across borders, then there are allies and enemies and everyone gets involved.' I paused. 'There's no one person dragging his army around after him conquering all the territories he goes through.'

'There's not? How depressing.' He grinned. 'So all your countries are static?'

'Well, not exactly.' I scratched my head.

'And what about your weapons? You spoke to me about machines that could fly and things called "cars". Has progress also invented a better spear? Or catapult? Has it invented arrows that shoot themselves?' He said this with a mocking grin.

I had long ago decided to lie. I didn't want to give him any ideas. But most of all, I was embarrassed to come from a society that used nuclear weapons, biological warfare, and ray guns that anyone could procure and which spat death at a distance and precision that was chilling beyond Alexander's comprehension. 'No. The weapons are basically the same. Made to kill.'

'Yes, but how? I mean, there must be …' His sensitive hearing caught my half-truth.

'I want to talk about something different,' I interrupted. 'Did you notice anything else odd last night?'

'You mean, besides the weird old man, the tall, fair people, the wind chimes, the lack of a temple, and the village itself, all neat and clean? As if they had been waiting for us for days?'

39

'Well, besides that. Think!'

'No, I didn't see anything else …'

'Children! Where are the children? When we come to a village, the first ones rushing to see us are always children. We came with elephants! There should have been a crowd of kids around. Even this morning we should be able to hear children's voices.'

'It is strange,' he said. 'We'd better go. I have much to ask Sharwah.'

In daylight, the village seemed even stranger. The streets were swept and quiet. The only sound came from the hundreds of wind chimes hanging from the trees. People peeked out of doorways, but I saw no children. I started to get nervous, and I clasped Chiron tighter in my arms.

Alexander, still on his litter, was silent, but his eyes missed nothing. I could practically hear him thinking. He looked at the houses, the roads, the path through the woods, and then back up towards the high peaks and the twisting route that led to the pass. He frowned, and started searching again. I didn't know what he was looking for. Paul sat on his lap, and he seemed content there. I loved seeing them together. Their profiles were so similar.

At Sharwah's house, the door stood open. We entered, but no one was in the main room. Faintly, from the back, we heard the sound of splashing water.

Alexander hailed the old man, who answered, 'I'll be right with you. Have a seat, make yourselves welcome.'

I played with Paul. He had a wooden chariot and a little wooden horse. He also had a lump of soft clay and he was squeezing it. I showed him how to roll snakes. Chiron watched for a few seconds, got bored, cried, then fell asleep. Paul studied him carefully.

'That's a baby,' he said. 'I'm a big boy.'

'That's right.' I kissed him on the cheek and he laughed.

Sharwah came in and bowed to us. His bow was polite, but there was none of the reverence we usually got from strangers. It didn't bother me, but it did intrigue me. Alexander got straight to the point.

'Where are the children?' he asked.

Sharwah showed no surprise. 'Our children were all taken.

'Explain!' Alexander's voice was harsh.

'Our valley has been protected by the gods for thousands of years, but recently there have been great changes in the world. The pass opened not long ago. It was not always so accessible. However, a small earthquake opened the breach and our enemies came. In the old writings it says that *'Children shall suffer, men shall make strife, and gods shall live forever'*. There is a fortress on the sacred mountain which even Hercules could not capture. There lives upon that mountain a tribe of people who still sacrifice children to the living gods. They stole our children.'

'They stole your children?' I cried.

The old man held up his hand. 'We had very few. Ours is an old society and has reached its end. There were five children in the village. Aged six to thirteen. The invaders came and stole them.'

'Why?' Alexander asked.

'They are our enemies. They have been since the beginning of time.'

'And where did they go?'

'To the fortress on the top of the sacred mountain. In Aornos.'

'Is it really impregnable?' asked Alexander, leaning forward, his eyes bright.

'More than that. It has resisted everyone throughout the ages.'

'The sacred mountain? Where is it?'

'Perhaps when your ankle has healed you could go yourself and see.'

'I will capture the mountain and recover your children.' Alexander sounded sure of himself.

The old man looked dubious. 'If you do that, we will sing your praises until the end of time.'

We sat without saying anything for a while.

Paul played happily at my feet; he was a sweet little boy. He looked at me and smiled, but his eyes strayed constantly to the Sogdian woman, and I realized that for him, she was his mother.

I put my face in my hands. Sharwah's voice came to me, gently. 'I know your dilemma, my lady. I cannot help you make up your mind but I can speak. So think of this. Paul is a special child. He could grow here, surrounded by people who love him and wish him well. No one will ever hurt him. It is true that this valley is a small world, but it is unsullied and isolated. It will resist the demons of progress for longer than any other place. It will keep its innocence, its pureness. In the summertime, children can play in the lake. The stream has many fish and the forest is full of deer and wild pheasant. We are a civilized people who worship one god. Our temples are ourselves. We believe in the God-within. For us, it is a sacrilege to kill another human being, because if we do, we kill a divinity. It is not utopia. However, we were happy, until our children were taken.'

'I will get them back.' Alexander wiggled his leg

experimentally. 'In two weeks Usse said I could walk on it.'

'Rest it well until then,' I said, 'otherwise you'll make it worse.'

'I hate being wounded.'

'It's tough being a conquering hero.'

'Sarcasm doesn't become you, Ashley,' he said seriously.

That night Alexander returned to the subject of war in my world.

I lay in my husband's arms and we talked. Around us the air was filled with the gentle snores of men and Chiron. He snored too, which always made me smile. Paul didn't snore; he lay on his pallet and his small body hardly made a lump in the covers. I kept lifting the edge of the curtain to look at him.

Alexander took my hand away and drew the curtain closed. 'You were lying about the weapons – why?' he asked.

'How could you tell?'

He sighed. 'It's obvious, isn't it? You can't throw spears at flying machines. War has always moved men to do more than anything else, at least in my world.'

'You're right, of course.' I sounded sad. 'We nearly destroyed ourselves. We made weapons that killed millions of people at a time. Women, children, men, animals, the weapons made no distinction. There was no intelligence behind them. If you kill someone now, you kill him yourself. You see him die. You feel his death and it shocks you. You cannot ever be the same again. You feel responsible for their souls. I see your men after battle when the shock has worn off. The whole army sacrifices to their gods. They think of the souls they have killed. They can see the faces of their victims.'

'That's normal,' Alexander spoke softly. 'The first time you kill, you slay part of yourself. If I had known that, I never would have lifted my sword.'

'Liar.' I spoke without rancour.

'Continue. Please.'

'Our weapons dropped from one of the flying machines and destroyed whole cities ten times as great as Babylon. Everybody perished. And the poison that remained killed people for generations afterwards.'

There was a deep silence next to me. I let it sink in.

'Children not even conceived were killed, Alexander,' I said. 'The poisons warped the very matrix of the human body. Then there were the biological weapons. Weapons even more terrifying. We fought with weapons as light as air. Poison that you breathed, that floated on the wind. Whole countries were wiped out. Sickness ravaged the earth. The people who used these poisons didn't understand them themselves and caused massive death and destruction. Some were even unleashed without antidotes.' I swallowed hard. It was difficult for me to even think about the Third Great War, which had nearly annihilated the world.

'But why?' Alexander's voice sounded strained. 'Why? You said there were no more kingdoms to be conquered. No more crowns to be won. What was the reason for this?'

'I think it happened for many reasons. War doesn't usually have just one root. Like a tree, it has many. A big reason was ideological. Religion, if you can believe it, played a big part. The people of my world became too static, as you said. They separated into groups and became too rigid, refusing to acknowledge the other groups' right to exist as they pleased. Economy played a big part. The world became divided. There was obscene wealth and abject poverty. Like now, where the rich are the kings and the poor are the peasants, but on a much greater scale. The poor revolted many times, but their wars were not the bloodiest. The bloodiest wars were always those fought for ideas.'

Alexander stirred restlessly. 'I don't understand,' he said. 'I'm trying to understand why *I* fight, but it seems so much easier to explain. And to explain I must go back to my father, and perhaps, before him, and back again. The world has always fought. But not on the scale you described and not for the same reasons.'

'Tell me why you fight,' I said.

'I inherited the crown from my father, the crown of Greece and Macedonia. My father was king of Macedonia when the Greek states came to him and asked him to help them fight against the Persians who were attacking them. Before, the Greeks had always looked upon Macedonia with contempt. To them we were a bunch of sheep-herding barbarians. My father had been captured and was prisoner of war for a long time in Thebes. He grew to love everything that had to do with Greece; he loved its art, its culture, and its inventions. He wanted more than anything to unite Macedonia with Greece. He had no wish to wipe out the Greek culture. No, he wanted to become Greek himself. He helped the Greeks beat Persia, then, taking advantage of the ongoing war between Sparta and Athens, he took over all of Greece. He united the whole country, stopped the war, and gave the cities back their independence. My father became head of state but in name only. He didn't want to impose his rule. The cities were free to rule themselves. Then Darius, who had always coveted Greece, attacked. My father fought back.

'When my father got killed, he was in the midst of a war against the Persians, who had long wanted to absorb Greece into their empire. I was thrown into the battle; I had no choice but to fight. If Darius had won I would have been killed, Greece and Macedonia divided up into fiefs of Persia, and the great adventure would never have begun.'

'Oh, so to you it's a great adventure?'

'Well, yes. Not to you? I don't try and change what I've conquered. I don't kill anyone who doesn't fight. I don't tear down temples and force the people to worship anything new. They are free to choose their gods, free to continue their lives as before. They can study in Greek schools if they want. They can trade now with many different nations. I am expanding their world. From what you told me, your wars are to destroy. I fight to build. Make that my epitaph.' He grinned and his teeth gleamed in the dark.

'In my world, there was a saying: 'Fighting for peace is like fucking for virginity'.'

'That's a stupid saying,' said Alexander with the easy dismissal of a philosopher.

'Why do you say that?'

'Because it's equating four things that have nothing to do with each other. It's simple to use words to twist people's opinions. That's what my father always said about Demosthenes, the Greek lawyer. He wrote tirades against my father, the "Philippics", accusing him of being a tyrant. I ask you, if my father were a tyrant would he have left Athens a free, democratic city-state? Would he?'

'Shh, you'll wake everyone up. Of course not. Demosthenes is a loudmouth looking to sound off and trying to compensate his own lack of influence by making trouble for those he thinks need taking down a peg.'

Alexander chuckled. 'If only he could hear you.'

'Have you heard anything about the trial?'

'He got himself off, of course.' There was no rancour in his voice, only amusement. I thought that of all the reactions Demosthenes expected, that was probably the one that would sting the most. 'He's got a weak chin,' Alexander said thoughtfully. 'Perhaps that explains it.'

Then I thought of something else. 'So you were serious about creating the biggest democracy the world has ever known?'

'Of course.' He frowned. 'Didn't it turn out that way? I've given all my cities independent governments. What happens to them? What is it? Why don't you answer me?'

I shook my head. 'I can't tell you that, don't ask me, please.'

'Why is there such pain in your voice then? Did everything go wrong?'

'No, don't worry about it.' I shut my mouth. 'Goodnight.'

'Goodnight? You expect me to get any sleep now? You tell me stories about weapons that destroy cities, poisons as light as air, whole countries destroyed, and then you tell me, you say ... you say that ...' His voice broke off as he searched for the right words. 'You tell me that my ideas were never put into practice.' It was a statement, not a question, but I still said nothing. 'Ashley, speak to me. Please. Don't you see? What I'm doing isn't to destroy the world, it's for change, it's something vital. It's to build a new culture made up of all that's the best of east and west.'

'Did you ever think to ask the people if they wanted to change?' I whispered.

'What's the matter with you?' His voice was rising again. 'Who exactly do you want me to ask? Do you think the people here, in this time, have any say in the matter? Only in Athens. Only in Greece. That's what I'm trying to give to the world.'

'Power to the people?'

'Oh, very nice. Doubt and sarcasm mixed together. Thank you so much. So tell me, Ashley of the Sacred Sandals. What should I do now? Should I go liberate the children of this valley? Should I try and attack the impregnable fortress of Aornos?'

'Well, of course!' Indignation filled me.

'Of course. Go kill a bunch of people on a rock because their religion tells them to sacrifice children. Don't they have a right to worship as they please?'

'Now who's being sarcastic?'

'Stop crying. It won't work. Your attitude is childish. Are you all like that in your world? Capable of destroying each other for ideas? Building terrible weapons and not being able to control them? What else have you done to *my* world?'

'Your world?'

'Yes. My world. Paul and Chiron's world. Usse's, and Axiom's, and Brazza's – our world. In your time do people still consider it their world? Or have they become so alienated from it that they have ceased to care about it? Will they destroy it and go live on one of the many planets in space? Is that the idea?' In the dark I couldn't read his expression, but I could sense deep anger behind his words and I shivered.

'No.'

'Oh. Well, that's a relief.'

'What's a relief?' What did he mean?

'That the world is not being destroyed. Tell me, Ashley, what is your world truly like? You've told me of machines and progress. You said once that the elephants were nearly all killed. Is there any good in your world?'

'Lots of good. There are laws to protect children, so that they are not kidnapped and taken to be sacrificed.'

'No children are ever harmed in your world?'

'I didn't say that, but it's against the law to hurt a child!'

'So, your people have lost all notions of right and wrong and need laws to tell them not to harm children? Go on.'

I was flustered. 'Women can vote and work. They are considered equals in most countries.'

He pounced on that. 'Most countries? Not in all countries? In the countries where they are not considered equals, are they respected? Can they dress as they like? Obtain an abortion if they wish? Ask for a divorce?'

'No. They can't.'

'So in your time women are even more downtrodden than in my time.' His voice was wry.

'Probably.' I winced, thinking of the religious zealots who made women's lives hell in some countries.

'Certainly, you mean. Now, here and now, a woman can do all that, even a Persian woman.'

'I think I want to go to sleep.'

'I don't think you'll get much sleep.' His voice was tight.

He was right. I lay awake and wondered what on earth made me try to explain my modern mentality to a barbarian who was three thousand years my inferior and who couldn't possibly begin to comprehend the value of human rights.

Ha! Tears seeped out of the corners of my eyes. How ridiculous I must have sounded. How pompous and naïve to think that my society was any better. People were no kinder, no more intelligent, no better than they were in Alexander's time. If anything Alexander was right. We had alienated ourselves so far from nature that we had no more respect for the earth that carried us.

The Sphinx's riddle came to me then. 'What walks on four feet in the morning, two feet in the afternoon, and three feet in the evening?' The answer is 'Man'. In the morning he is a babe, crawling on his hands and knees. In the afternoon of his life he is an adult, walking on two feet, and in the evening he is old, leaning on a cane.

If I took the riddle further I could equate it with all mankind. In the morning, mankind was a child, innocent and wondering, worshipping mother earth and father sky. In the afternoon, he was an adolescent. Destructive and arrogant, nearly destroying the planet with his stupidity and lack of respect. Would mankind even make it to old age? I wondered. Three thousand years in the future mankind was still not quite grown-up. We were still not wise, and it was nearly too late.

Now it was morning. The sky turned light grey, and Axiom woke up and lit the fire. I hadn't slept, or maybe I had. Maybe the Sphinx's riddle had all been a dream.

Children in the morning. It was fitting, I thought, for the people of Alexander's time.

Chapter Five

Alexander woke up and was in a bad mood all day long. Evidently, he hadn't liked my stories about the future, and frankly, I hadn't either. But it made me appreciate this time more with its clean air, crystal clear waters in streams and lakes, and simple life.

I took Paul for a stroll in the forest. He was content to walk with me, clutching my hand and commenting about all the birds and insects he saw. I kept bending down to kiss his round cheeks. I watched him constantly, and hugged him whenever I could. I wanted to fill my senses with his presence. My heart ached and I didn't know why.

Then, Paul and I went to see an elephant and he patted it under the watchful eye of the driver. Alexander sat nearby, next to the tent. His generals had made their reports and now he sifted through the many letters he had received from Hermes, our messenger.

I saw Alexander staring at Paul. 'He's a beautiful child,' I said. 'You must have looked very much like him when you were a baby.'

'I think I was skinnier.' He grinned. 'My mother had to fight to get me to eat. And I sucked my thumb.'

'Paul is an easy child,' I agreed. 'He won't make any trouble. He's used to travel.'

'When we go, he must stay here,' said Alexander, looking up at me. He put the letters down by his side and got painfully to his feet. He limped over to me.

'What are you talking about? Of course he's coming

with us! He's my baby, I travelled halfway around the world searching for him.' My voice rose shrilly.

He looked at me sorrowfully and put his hands on my shoulders. 'He is yours no longer,' he said.

I pushed him away. 'Is that what you think?' I yelled. 'Is that what you think? He's your son! Your firstborn son! Look at him, how can you just walk away from him?'

'Do you see me walking away from him?' His voice cracked. 'Can you see what's in my heart?'

'I don't know what's in your heart. How can you abandon your own child?'

He held my arms. His hands gripped me tightly. 'You have a small memory, but don't think I do. I remember what you said to me when we were in Persepolis. You said, "When we find Paul, do not proclaim him your heir." Don't you think I wondered about that? For many nights I lay awake, just thinking about those words. Now I know what they mean. They mean that I will not be able to protect my heirs. They mean that you are afraid for his life. You are living here in this time with a sword over your head. A sword which forbids you to change anything that might affect the future. Do you think I want to put anyone I love in danger? I love my son, and so I want him to live. I will not be selfish.'

'And what about me? I can protect him! I will! I can't leave him, I won't. If I have to I will stay here with him. You can go …' I choked in anger. 'Go do whatever you have to, conquer the world, become king of kings, or whatever you want to become.' I stomped my foot on the ground.

Brazza and Axiom hid inside the tent. I could hear Chiron wailing in his hammock, and Usse poked his head outside and withdrew it just as quickly when he saw the sparks flying. Alexander and I hardly ever fought, but this battle promised to be epic. 'Paul is my child. And yours.' I added, seeing his eyes narrow. 'And if I say he comes with us, he comes.'

'And if I say he stays, he stays!'

'So say it!' I shrieked. 'But you can go without me!'

'You're going to leave me?' he asked, incredulous.

There came a shocked silence. I had forgotten how binding words were to the people of Alexander's time. 'I wasn't thinking.'

'I don't know what will become of me, but your words have wounded me in ways you will never be able to understand.' His eyes were clouded with pain.

'Alex …'

'No. Don't "Alex" me. I need to be alone to think. And I hope you will do some thinking too. You are here now, so you must accept it. Perhaps you don't believe in prophesies, but I do.' His voice was low, so low I had to strain to hear the last part of his phrase. 'And it is said that he will destroy his father to call down the moon, his mother.'

'But *I* am his mother!' I screamed, pushing him violently.

He tried to catch himself but his ankle betrayed him and he fell heavily to the ground. He sat there, not looking at me. Then he folded his arms across his knees and laid his head on them. 'And I am his father,' he said, and I saw he was crying.

My anger faded and left me ashamed. 'I'm sorry,' I said.

'Leave me alone,' he said, his voice raw.

I left him alone for a week. I packed my things and moved

into Sharwah's house with Paul. I slept in a hammock in the main room. Chiron cuddled with me. Paul slept in his own hammock near the hearth.

Ten times each day I nearly swallowed my pride and went to the tent to see Alexander. Each time my pride reared its ugly head and convinced me to wait. If he wanted to see me, he should be the one to come to the house. Why didn't he make the slightest effort to see his own son?

I wanted to be with Paul, to make up for the years I'd searched for him, for all the times I didn't know if he was alive or dead.

He was a docile child with a sunny smile and easy laughter. His travels hadn't affected him in any way I could see. He adored Maia, the Sogdian woman. It was towards her he turned when he was sleepy or sad. I knew it would take time, but in the end he would accept me as his mother.

Maia left us alone during the day, but she was always nearby. I could sense her presence. It made me cross. If Paul fell down and started to cry, she was there. When he was hungry, she brought him food. I thought it would be easier to get to know Paul if she wasn't around, but I didn't want to hurt her feelings. She obviously adored Paul. Her face lit up whenever he was with her. I frowned. It would never do; Paul had a father and a mother now. Maia would have to step aside.

When I next saw Alexander he was walking with a crutch.

He came to the house, limping, looking like a refugee from a prison camp. He was too thin. His hair was too long, and Axiom hadn't brushed it that morning, or he had, and Alexander had stuck his head in a briar bush. His face was too gaunt. His eyes had lost their sparkle. He stopped by the gate and leaned on his crutch. Sweat stood out on his brow, and he was breathing heavily. My eyes filled with tears making him look indistinct.

I blinked and the illusion shattered. It wasn't just the tears blurring my vision that made him look bad, he was ill.

I stood up, Paul's toy horse falling from my hands. 'Alex!' I cried, and ran to him. He held his arms out and I flew into them. I put my head on his shoulder. His breath was short. 'What is it?' I asked him.

'I was unwell. Usse kept me in bed nearly all week.' His voice was soft. 'I kept hoping you would come and visit me.'

I couldn't look at him. 'I'm sorry,' I said to the back of his head. 'I'm a terrible person. I thought, well, I thought you were angry with me and it made me sulk. I was acting like a spoiled brat. I'm sorry.'

'I know you are.' He sighed, his ribs moving under my hands. 'Craterus came back. He has news. We will leave in six weeks. First we go to the town, then to the mountain.'

'Will it be very dangerous?' I asked.

'So much pain in your voice.' He tilted his head. 'Did you miss me?'

I smiled through my tears. Only three more years. How could I ever tell him that? My tears fell faster, I couldn't stop them. I tried to speak but only sobs came out. I buried my face in his thin shoulder and cried.

'Well, that can mean two things,' said Alexander, tipping his head back. 'Yes, you missed me, or I need a shower and you're going to give me one right here.'

I giggled and sniffed. 'You're not supposed to make me laugh, that's Plexis's job,' I told him, wiping my wet face with the back of my hands.

'He's not here right now. I'll have to do it for him. I do need a shower. Will you wash me? I still don't feel very well.'

I helped him to the bathhouse. It meant turning around and walking back to the lake. By the time we got there I was practically carrying him. The long walk had tired his leg, and his crutch didn't help.

There was a cauldron of hot water on the fire and about twelve soldiers washing themselves. Or each other. Those Greeks! I cleared my throat and cleared a space for Alexander.

The lye soap was strong stuff made by the villagers. It stung the eyes and I didn't wash with it. The men used it though, carefully. I preferred the soft clay. It cleansed well and smelled good, thanks to the herbs Usse put in it. I smoothed it over Alexander's body, rubbing it in like a massage. Then he sat in a tub while I poured hot water over him. His hair was dirty so I washed that for him too, putting sweet oil in it then using the clay to clean it.

What I would have given for a real shampoo! I had tried everything, believe me. I tried using egg whites, egg yolks, tree bark, soured cream, fruit juice, lemon juice, vinegar, wine, ground-up chalk, you name it. Nothing really worked. I had finally come to accept that I could never get soft, shiny hair again. It was either soft and sort of oily, or shiny and dry. The best I could do was keep my scalp clean.

Alexander leaned back while I washed his hair. His face was drawn. I wished I could say something to make him feel better.

He turned and looked at me. He always seemed to know what I was thinking. His voice when he spoke was low. 'It's not your fault. It's only me. I get this way sometimes. When it strikes, I'm helpless. I feel as if the world is a dark place and the sun is cold. Usse knows how to treat this melancholy. When I'm like this, nothing seems right. Sometimes I feel that death is preferable to the confusion in my head. It is a sickness, Usse told me, and I must wait until it passes.'

'That's why you stayed away so long.'

'Mostly. That and pride. And pain. But then the darkness lifted and I saw that we were still together.'

'Together, you and I.'

'I'm sorry about Paul. We will go see Sharwah and ask if there is anything to be done. I will try and see things from your point of view. You don't believe in our prophecies, so perhaps they cannot touch you.'

I remembered the one I'd read in the back room and shuddered. 'No. I have had time to think. I cannot be selfish about a human being. Paul has the right to be happy. I think that in this valley he will have a good life.' My voice shook and tears threatened, but didn't spill.

'Oh, Ashley. I'm sorry, sorrier than I can ever say. He's a beautiful child, but I can see he is too pure for the outside world. This is truly the Valley of the Gods. He will be surrounded by love. The people here will all adore him. We've made the right decision.'

'I spent a week with our son and you haven't seen him at all. Why don't you go back to the tent to rest. I'll bring him to you.'

'I accept.' He leaned back in the tub and closed his eyes. He looked so frail. I hoped Usse had some good remedies.

That evening I took Paul to the tent to see his father. When

Maia made to follow us I told her to stay in the house and wait. The look she gave me made me feel like I'd kicked a puppy, but I didn't relent.

All the way to the tent I wondered at Alexander's words. Too pure for the outside world? I looked at Paul. He trusted everyone. He went with me as easily as he went with anyone else. He adored Maia, his nurse, but he happily left her to accompany me or one of the other villagers. He would often wander, slipping away quietly and unnoticed, only to be found watching the soldiers or in one of the houses or gardens talking to anyone he met. He was not shy and trusted everyone. His eyes were wide and guileless. He was not quite five but he spoke two languages clearly. He did seem unworldly, like a fairy child or an elf.

Chapter Six

Alexander had slept all afternoon and looked better. A cold breeze chilled the air, so the tent flap stayed closed. The light was lit, the braziers glowing, and Axiom had prepared a thick lentil soup. We ate in silence. Paul fidgeted, looking all around the tent. He's searching for Maia, I thought jealously. But no, a soft humming made him look around. It was my necklace. Ever since Paul had made it sing, I'd kept it in a small sandalwood box. Now, his very presence was making it hum.

Paul jumped up and ran to the box, crowing excitedly. He opened it and grabbed the necklace. There was a high pitched whine, a sort of joyous, mineral shriek, and the beautiful blue lamp that had followed Alexander all the way from Pella, exploded in a scintillating shower of blue sparks and flame.

I bounded across the rug, snatching Chiron out of his hammock and grabbed Paul by one arm. I pulled them both out of the tent, while Alexander, cursing heartily, rolled the rug up over the flames and smothered them.

It took ages to set the tent straight again. The lamp was gone and the rug was mortally wounded, sporting huge blackened holes. There were burned spots on Alexander's precious table. My feet were cut and bleeding. Paul clutched the singing necklace and screamed if we tried to prise it from his hands, and while he had it, its blue light cast a ghostly glow over him. Alexander's men refused to approach.

Finally, I hobbled as far as the beach, and there I pulled the necklace out of Paul's fingers and flung it into the water. I could still see it though, glowing palely in the shallows.

Back at the tent Axiom, Brazza, and Alexander tried to clear up the mess, while Alexander continued to lament over his lamp and rug. Paul crawled onto my lap, but all he wanted was Maia or the necklace.

'I want to see the necklace. I want Maia,' he said stubbornly over and over again.

Finally, I got up and limped all the way to the little house at the end of the village. It was the only way we were going to get any sleep that night. Paul trotted happily beside me. He ran to Maia, throwing himself into her arms, not even glancing at me.

Maia was too kind to give me any sort of *'I told you so'* look. I was too heartsick to care. I hopped back to the tent. Usse took care of my feet while I sat on the bed and cried.

Alexander surveyed the wreckage and sighed. 'I did hear tell the child was a harbinger of destruction.' He looked up at the tent ceiling where the empty chain swung back and forth. 'I'll miss that lamp,' he said thoughtfully.

I cried harder. 'A lamp isn't a child,' I sobbed. 'Do you have any idea how much I'll miss Paul when we leave?'

'I do, actually,' he said softly. He knelt by my side. 'But he'll be happy. Can you try, just try, to understand that he will be happy here?'

'I don't know. I've searched for so long, I've missed him so much. Only six more weeks before we leave …' My voice broke.

'I'll bring the children back, see if I don't. Then Paul will have playmates.'

'He already does. There are three families who have decided to settle here.'

'I know. And many more will stay when we finally leave.'

I sniffled. 'I threw the necklace in the lake.'

'Oh, I got it back. It was scaring the men who saw it.'

'I'm sorry about the rug and the lamp.'

'I'll get new ones. I was getting tired of that lamp anyway – too blue. I think I'll get a yellow one. I hear there are beautiful rugs in Indus. I can replace a rug and a lamp, but I could never replace you, or Paul. I've learned to live without my son. But I will never learn to live without you.' His eyes were sad.

'That's the sweetest thing you've said to me in a long time,' I told him.

'I'm sick at heart about Paul. I have tried to tell you that, but I was too proud. I was sure that you would choose to stay here with him instead of coming with me. I want you to come with me. I need you.' He said it as simply as a child, looking at me, his arms loose at his sides.

I closed my eyes. I could feel the seconds slipping by like grains of sand, the minutes like pearls on a string, sliding through my fingers. Then the hours, the days, and the months would become years, and they would fly. Three years. So little time. I would stay with Alexander. I could always come back for Paul if I wanted to. If he wanted me. Alexander did want me. He needed me. And I was a fool.

I took him in my arms. 'I'm coming with you. Never believe for one second that I would leave you.'

'I believe. Thank you.' He stroked my back, cupped my face in his hands, put his forehead against mine, and stared into my eyes. His eyes, so fey, the twin kingdoms of heaven and earth, were sad. He smiled though. 'I will take you with me to Hercules' rock. I want you to see me in action.'

'Won't there be danger?' I asked.

'Lots of danger, cold, snow, catapults, yelling, screaming, and people dying. But it will be heroic. You'll see. We'll capture a fortress no one has ever captured before, and I'll build a great statue to Nike, spirit of victory, companion of Zeus and Athena!'

'My, aren't we optimistic,' I said, raising an eyebrow. 'Just what is that stuff that Usse gives you?'

'Some sort of potion for my melancholy, why?'

'Well, I think you should give it to your whole army.'

I was just joking, but Alexander took me at my word. The results were incredible, to say the least.

Chapter Seven

We spent winter and spring in the Valley of the Gods. We got to know the quiet, fair people who lived in the tranquil valley. There were not many of them left. Isolation and a reputation for magic had kept them insular, and now with their children gone, they were even fewer than before. They farmed and fished, but ate no red meat. They had chickens for eggs. They made wine, which was, to Alexander and his men, proof that they were descendants of Dionysus. They didn't worship any gods, not even Dionysus, but they told stories and seemed to know all the old legends. Alexander's men were in awe of them and rarely strayed into the village, staying in the encampment.

The villagers, gentle, curious folk, wandered about the camp, asking questions and poking into everything. They were quite impressed with the elephants, and would line up in solemn rows to watch them being bathed in the afternoons. They would appear suddenly in the tent, looking with great interest at the furniture, the beds – they slept in hammocks – the bronze braziers – they had small stone hearths or braziers made of clay or copper – or even our clothes. They used no dyes except onion skins, and wore plain woollen robes.

They asked a million questions. They were both wise and incredibly childlike. They also had the nicest houses I'd seen in a country village. They were wood frame houses, set on stone foundations with wooden floors and walls; well insulated and sturdy. They cooked in clay pots and baked bread in ovens that would still be in use three thousand years later. They had a forge, a waterwheel to grind grain, a vast cellar where the wine was made, and a herd of shaggy goats they milked, or sheared to make their blankets and warm clothes.

Paul fitted perfectly with them. He was as silent and serious as they were. He seemed to know them all by name and they adored him. They welcomed him whenever he wandered over to visit as they worked in the gardens or milked the goats. I stayed with him as much as possible, but I always felt like an outsider looking in, whereas Paul seemed to be as much a part of the valley as the flowers or trees that grew there. He was every villager's child. He took the place of the children that had been stolen, and everyone spoiled him. He stayed as sweet and calm. The only time I saw him cry was when I'd thrown the necklace into the lake. Now I made sure he couldn't find it.

I sat on the beach and watched the sun come up. The water looked as flat and shiny as molten silver. A thin blanket of mist, no more than a few inches thick, floated just over the water. Swallows dipped below it, swooping to drink. They were navy blue, but in the morning light they looked black. An elephant trumpeted, but softly, as if he knew it was too early to wake up the camp.

A deer came down to the water's edge to drink. He walked out of the forest and peered around. I sat still so he wouldn't see me. He dipped his muzzle in the water, sipped, and then his head jerked up. His ears twitched back and forth, but he didn't run away. Instead, he dipped his head down again to drink. He had small antlers. I wondered if he was a young deer. I knew nothing about them. In my time, all the large animals had been wiped out. They were slowly being cloned and reintroduced. The earth was gradually getting cleaned up and straightened out. But we had so far to go before attaining this pristine pureness it seemed impossible.

My heart filled with the beauty of the scene. I sighed deeply, and the deer whirled around and disappeared into the forest. Chiron woke up and yawned. I had been holding him on my lap. His little face crumpled and stretched as his mouth worked. He opened his eyes, surprisingly bright and alert, and they settled on my face.

He smiled.

I blinked in surprise, and he smiled again, a real smile, not gas. He smiled, and then his mouth opened and closed a few times. He pursed his lips into a tiny rosebud and he cooed at me. The noise pleased him and he smiled again, showing his pink gums. Smiling was fun! His smile stretched from ear to ear. It was huge. He cooed and smiled, cooed and smiled, then realized he was hungry. Before he could yell I offered him my nipple. He latched on and nursed, his little hands kneading my breast like a kitten. He paused, burped, and then stared at me again. I smiled and rained kisses on his downy head.

Brazza joined me on the beach. He loved to swim in the early morning; he was impervious to cold. He walked slowly into the water and then glided silently around, his shiny bald head the only thing showing above the surface. When he finished, he dried off with a linen towel and sat next to me. He motioned for me to give him Chiron. Chiron adored Brazza. He showed him his new smile.

I went swimming. The water was icy but calm and clear as glass. I could see the gravel and weeds growing on the bottom of the lake. I could see the silver fish and the multi-coloured rocks. I dived underwater and opened my eyes. Then I floated on my back, letting just my face, my nipples, and my toes break the surface. It was like being set in silver.

The water was so clean I could drink it. On the far shore of the lake a waterfall shattered the surface, but it was a small cascade, and the noise was muted by the morning mist. I started to get cold so I swam back to the beach where Brazza and Chiron were having a smiling contest. They both won.

Brazza was a peaceful person to have around. He was a deaf-mute and a eunuch. Alexander had received him as a gift when he first went to Egypt. I'd been horrified at first, and then pitied him. However, Brazza didn't want my pity, and he certainly didn't deserve any horror. He was a cheerful person, sensitive, kind, and a wonderful cook. I adored him. We sat, leaning against each other. He held Chiron, and I made faces at my baby over Brazza's shoulder. Chiron was startled and laughed.

I wonder if all babies learn to laugh out of fright. It seems that way. Playing peek-a-boo usually starts the first laugh – seeing the mother's face popping out from behind something. The baby's relief and joy mingled with a scare. Chiron let out a burbling crow of laughter and he liked it so much he kept it up. He laughed and laughed, kicking his little legs in unison like a frog, gurgling at us.

Brazza couldn't hear him, but he could feel the vibrations the laughter made. Like music. He always knew when Alexander was singing, for example. He told us it made his teeth ache. Alexander came to the beach humming softly. Even that was enough to set teeth on edge. I saw goose bumps on Brazza's arms.

'Shh, stop singing,' I said to Alexander, not turning

66

around. 'Chiron's finally smiling at us.'

'He's smiled at me lots of times already,' Alexander boasted.

Chiron saw Alexander and his little face lit up. His mouth stretched wide and his cheeks turned pink. We hovered over him. He was our miracle that day. You would have thought that none of us had ever seen a baby smiling.

Alexander stripped and dived into the lake, splashing and swimming and kicking the water into a white, lacy froth. He looked much better. His depression lifted, he gained weight, and he was being silly again in the water.

'Ashley, oh, Ashley! Come here, I have something to show you.' A deeply mysterious voice called me, then a penis in guise of a periscope drifted by. A sputter, a laugh, and then, 'Hey, Ashley, there's an elephant under here. Look!' More clowning around. The erection was starting to get to me. I looked askance at Brazza, who hadn't heard a thing of course, totally involved in Chiron. I tapped him lightly on the shoulder and pointed to Alexander, or what we could see of him in the water.

Brazza looked at me while I motioned, then grinned. He nodded. He took Chiron into the tent for me; it was time for his nap.

I slid into the water quietly, wanting to surprise Alexander, but creeping up on him was like creeping up on a jaguar. I swam underwater, looking around, but didn't see him. Where had he gone? I came up to the surface and trod water a minute, looking this way and that through the light mist, listening. He jumped on me from behind. He dunked me underwater and swam away before I could even shout. I didn't try to catch him. He swam like a fish. I simply floated on my back, using the old *'come hither'* technique. I felt a tickle between my legs; he was underneath me blowing a stream of bubbles. I let myself sink and looked around. He was facing me underwater, his eyes full of mischief. And desire. He loved making love in the water, as did I. Our heads broke the surface and we came together. I wrapped my legs around his hips and pulled him into me. He put his face in the hollow of my shoulder and closed his eyes. He moaned softly, thrusting gently, letting the water buoy us up.

I put my mouth next to his ear and whispered while we made love. I told him all the things I loved the most about him, all the things that excited me the most. We floated for a while. Until our bodies stopped throbbing with heat and started shaking with cold. Then we pulled apart and swam back to shore. The sand was soft. We lay on it for a long time letting the sun rise and warm us. When we were dry, we went back into the tent and had breakfast.

Together, Usse and I had developed a new tonic. It was made with honey, citrus juice, raw eggs, and wheatgerm with a dose of yeast thrown in.

That was Alexander's new breakfast drink.

For lunch he had a beer with his meal. Then we all smoked a joint and relaxed. A few hours later Alexander got hungry and he'd devour a bowl of honeyed nuts. He was rapidly gaining weight.

I went to visit Paul after breakfast, leaving Chiron in Brazza's care. Alexander went to see his soldiers. There were talks about a new 'goatball' game, and Alexander wanted to make sure nobody got seriously injured.

Sharwah greeted me at the doorway. His hair was as white and fine as cobwebs. He leaned on his cane but didn't need it. He only pretended to. He looked old, but he moved about like a young man. His joints had the elasticity of youth. His eyes were a faded blue and his face a mass of wrinkles, but his voice was strong.

'Good morning!' he boomed, as I came down the path.

'Good morning. How are you?' I asked, bowing respectfully.

'Well, very well. Won't you take a walk with me? I'm going to get some honey.'

I was intrigued. I didn't often get to see Sharwah alone. I'd been dying to ask him some more questions about the prophecy.

'Where did you get that text?' I asked without preamble as we walked through the orchard.

'It has always been here. My name, Sharwah, means the one who guards the sacred parchment.'

'Sacred? But I thought you didn't worship gods?'

He chuckled. 'Why should the word "sacred" mean we believe in gods? I told you, we believe that God is within everyone. The text is sacred because it must be protected. We believe in good and evil. Paul is good, but the forces he stirs are evil.'

'Evil?'

'Real evil. It is a new concept. We have just begun to feel its presence on this earth. It has been lying dormant for centuries, but the winds of change have woken it. There will be a great battle between good and evil. That's what the parchment means when it speaks of the two kingdoms. Not east and west, not north and south, but good and evil. For nine centuries will they fight, and then there will be three centuries of light and three of darkness, alternating, until the end of time. We believe the end will come when one side or another finally triumphs.'

I did some calculating in my head. In nine hundred years it would be roughly the year 600 AD. The fighting would stop then? Then three centuries of light? Until the year 900 AD? Then three of darkness. Let's see, dark until 1100 AD. Light starting, then dark in … I frowned, losing track.

Sharwah was watching me with a smile. 'Figure it all out?' he asked.

'No,' I admitted. 'And how does Paul fit into this?'

'I have no idea.' He shrugged. 'Ah, here are the beehives. Don't make any sudden moves and you shouldn't get stung.'

I only got stung twice. Not that I really minded. I wasn't allergic to bees and I loved honey. I helped take the honeycombs out of the hives and put them in the earthenware jar Sharwah carried. The bees swarmed around us, buzzing, well, like bees, I guess. I'd never done anything like this before and thought it was great fun. I helped Sharwah put the honey away, and we walked back to his house. I sucked on my stings and on a small piece of honeycomb. I wanted to try and make a beeswax candle; mostly there were only oil lamps. I hadn't seen any candles.

Sharwah touched my arm lightly. 'Here we are, and look, Paul is waiting for us. He loves honey.'

'Don't all children?' I opened my arms and Paul ran to me. His cheeks were smooth and warm, welcoming my kisses. His blue eyes danced. I held him tightly. How could I ever leave him?

It took all my strength not to turn back. Paul sat on Sharwah's shoulders and waved, his face wreathed in smiles. His hair was a bright, curly halo. I watched him as long as I could. He never stopped smiling. Never once did his little face reflect the pain I felt. He held on to Maia's

70

hand, he perched on the old man's shoulders, and the sun glinted on his small, white teeth. He was happy staying in the beautiful valley.

I wish I felt the same. Tears blurred my vision. The little boy disappeared in a nimbus of light. The path curved, he was lost to sight.

The valley would remain inviolate, the water would stay clear, the lake would welcome the deer to drink in the early morning mist, the mountains would protect the valley, and my son would be safe here until I could come get him.

Chapter Eight

We headed north again. Alexander had decided to take the fortress of Aornos, despite the fact that it was invincible.

But before that, we had to cross a valley controlled by a village hostile to Alexander. I have no idea why they decided to resist us. It's true that Alexander didn't have his whole army with him, but he had enough. Plus we didn't want to fight. We wanted to go to the sacred mountains. But as we arrived in the valley we were attacked.

Of course, Alexander wasn't taken by surprise. Craterus had spent four weeks scouting out the area, and his spies all knew what was waiting for us. A queen ruled the village. She sent her mercenaries out to confront Alexander.

After thinking about it, when everything was finished, I came to the only obvious conclusion: the mercenaries had been getting too strong for the queen's taste, or she had no wish to pay them any more, and she used Alexander's army as a way to rid herself of them.

She would still be queen, her city would be spared, its people unhurt. However, she had to rid herself of twenty thousand hired soldiers, so she ordered them to attack us.

The fight was one-sided and bloody. After five hours the mercenaries surrendered and sued for peace. Most of them expressed the wish to join Alexander's army.

Alexander pulled back to the far side of the valley,

away from the battlefield, and set up his tent, getting ready to parley. Everything seemed to be going as normal. The fighting was over, the wounded were being carried to the infirmaries, and the diplomats and scribes were getting parchments ready and sharpening their reeds.

The talks usually started as soon as the sun touched the horizon. Alexander had bathed and was sitting behind his table. The beeswax candles I'd made were burning brightly. I was quite proud of them. We waited. The chief of the mercenaries had promised to come himself.

Meanwhile, the mercenaries camped on a small hill not far away. Their campfires flickered orange in the dusk. The sounds of women's voices and children laughing or crying floated upon the evening air, mingling with the moans and screams of the wounded and dying. The air stank with the smell of burning flesh as Usse and the doctors cauterized wounds. There had been no casualties on our side. We were in a good mood.

I lit a stick of incense and nursed Chiron on the bed behind drawn curtains. The night advanced uneasily in the valley. Alexander got up and started pacing. Something didn't seem right. The sun went down and still no one arrived. Outside the tent, the smoky air turned red with the sun's last rays, then night fell. Alexander's guards shifted uneasily, their armour clinking softly.

We looked at each other. Alexander's generals had started to arrive, ready to parley. The chief of the opposing forces should have been here already. A strange feeling prickled our skin.

Suddenly a scream rang out. Then there came a loud tumult and more yelling. Alexander cursed and ran out of the tent. I put Chiron in his hammock, went to the tent flap, and looked out. The night had dissolved into confusion and noise. Men ran back and forth, snatching up their weapons and shields. The hilltop where the mercenaries camped was strangely dark, but horrible screams and cries told me what was happening.

I stuffed my fist into my mouth and backed into the tent. Nassar, Alexander's scribe and translator, stood up, his narrow face dark with anger. 'Treason!' he cried. 'They've attacked us!'

'Hush!' I said, 'No, I don't think so. Listen, what do you hear?' My throat hurt. I wanted to scream.

He cocked his head. In the candlelight his eyes glittered. 'I hear screaming.'

'Do you hear the sound of metal striking metal? Do you hear the battle cries of men?'

'No,' he grew very still. 'I hear the screams of women and children. I hear the wind strong in the trees. I hear the cries of men, but they are not battle cries. They are begging for mercy.'

'May the gods hear them,' I whispered.

'Because Iskander's men will not,' finished Nassar.

We stood, shoulder to shoulder, until the screams were silenced.

Axiom and Brazza came back into the tent then. Their faces were ashen. 'They are all dead,' Axiom told Nassar. 'We won't need a scribe after all.'

'Where's Iskander?' I asked, but Axiom shook his head.

'He went to the village,' he said. 'He went to see the queen.'

'Was it …' I stopped and licked dry lips. 'Was it treachery? Were they going to fall on us during the night?'

Axiom looked at me, his face dark with pity. 'No, my lady. They were not. But someone went out of their way to make it seem so.'

'What happened to the children?' I asked, sinking to my knees.

'They are all dead.' Axiom spoke gently. 'And all the mercenaries are dead, but it wasn't Alexander's soldiers' doing. When we arrived it was already too late. Now they are saying that the queen sent her own soldiers to protect Iskander. He has gone to thank her.'

'To thank her?' I shrieked.

Axiom took one look at my face and caught me before I hit the ground. Nassar ran to fetch Usse who treated me for shock. Strong, sweet tea, lots of blankets. Brazza held my hand and stroked my face. I kept hearing the screams. The screams of the children rose above all the others.

I didn't sleep that night. Alexander stayed for three days in the queen's palace. I never set foot in the village. I didn't want to believe any of the stories I heard. I'd had time to think. I also thought that if I went to the palace there would be nothing to stop me from using Usse's poison on the queen.

We left that place the last week of April. I was glad to go. I had been ill the entire time we were there. I'd spent four days in bed, shivering uncontrollably, vomiting all the food I ate. It was the stomach flu. Many people caught it. Chiron nearly died from it; babies were very fragile in those days, but Usse pulled him through. Afterwards, Chiron was even crankier and I was weak, my milk thin. It took two weeks to get to the point where I felt capable of riding again.

I hated litters as much as Alexander did.

The mountains were small but sharply steep. The valleys were deep gouges or slashes in the earth. We wound up and down, straight up, and straight down. Sometimes we'd go down into a valley, find it impossible to climb out of, and have to backtrack or walk nearly the whole way around it.

While climbing out of one narrow valley, I could see the end of the army going into it. They were only a stone's throw away. We could shout to them. The march was extremely difficult, the terrain terrible, and the pace gruelling. Alexander pushed his army along as fast as they could go. Luckily, many mountain streams provided sparkling cold water to drink.

Alexander and I were on uneasy terms. We hadn't spoken in private since the massacre, and I was nursing a terrible suspicion about just exactly where he'd spent the three nights when he'd gone to *thank* the queen. I didn't dare ask him, though. I was afraid of the truth. One lesson I'd learned about that time was that men could do as they liked, whenever they liked, with whomever they liked. It had nothing to do with love or being faithful. Sometimes it was simply best to close your eyes and pretend nothing happened. Alexander would never love me less. Luckily, I didn't have to close my eyes very often.

Since we'd started marching, my spirits lifted. April snows lay deep in the bottom of the valleys. The high peaks were bathed in bright sunlight. Tall firs and fragrant laurel lined the steep paths. Sometimes we walked at the very summit of the mountains. On both sides of us were sheer drops, but it felt like walking in the clouds, like being with the gods. Ahead of us were the snowy peaks of the Hindu Kush, behind us were the valleys where smoke from the campfires spiralled up to get lost in the porcelain blue sky.

The men were in high spirits. They sang as they

marched and told stories and jokes. The idea that they were about to attack an invincible fortress didn't seem to bother them. I wondered about that, until I asked Usse why he was boiling so much water every evening. He told me he was cooking the herbs to help the soldiers feel happy. Alexander had asked Usse to give them his potion, the one he used to help when he was depressed.

I tried some; I wanted something to lift my spirits. However, it didn't have any effect on me. Perhaps it was nothing but strong tea, or maybe it only affected men. At any rate, the soldiers drank a cupful every morning and were in a good mood all day long.

The mountains were uninhabited. There was nobody to stop Alexander's inexorable march towards the fortress. He took advantage of that to send scouts nearly every day. Their mission was to draw maps. They would each take different routes, and then, back in camp, Alexander would have very detailed, nearly three-dimensional maps to guide his army. That's how he took the fortress.

We camped in a narrow valley completely hidden from view. Even our own soldiers had trouble finding it when they left it to get firewood. Alexander sent his mapmakers out and gave them instructions to draw the entire landscape surrounding the fort with all the measurements, large trees, streams, rocks, anything that he could think of. The men were gone for five days. When they came back Alexander, Craterus, and Ptolemy studied the plans. It took three days and three nights to come up with a plan, but it worked. It was crazy, but it worked.

I sat on the bed, listening. There was nothing else I could do. I suppose that if I'd been an artist I would have been happy there, painting the incredible view. However, I wasn't an artist, and I soon got bored. I wasn't an army chief, I didn't have any great ideas, and I didn't even think Alexander's idea would work. How could it? The fort was on a buttress surrounded by a wide valley. The only side we could approach was on the north side. There, a deep chasm separated us from the fortress: a chasm fifty metres wide and thirty metres deep.

I took one look and thought, 'They'll never get over that, we may as well go back now.'

Alexander bridged it. It took forty-eight hours of constant work. Whole trees were cut down, pushed into the ravine and piles of earth dumped over them. Then a makeshift platform was built onto it and pushed halfway across the chasm, and catapults set up. Alexander started lobbing stones at the fortress while his men scaled the high walls and swarmed into the fortress.

The defenders had never thought that their citadel could fall, and so they waited, like rabbits blinded in the headlights of a car, staring in horrified fascination as Alexander and his men stormed the fort.

I stayed in the tent. I could see the whole fight from my vantage point. When I was sure Alexander wasn't wounded and the battle was won, I unclenched my fists. It hadn't lasted long. From across the ravine I saw a fire being lit. Men began putting down their weapons and the doctors hurried over the bridge.

I went to the fort. The defenders had been put to death, and I don't think Alexander would have let me come had there been any danger. I walked across a rickety catwalk, the one Alexander's army had set up spanning the remaining twenty metres. It was made of rope and sticks and swayed in the wind, making me feel very much like a kite. I was glad to reach forward, grasp the rough stone parapet, and climb into the fort.

Everywhere I could see enemy soldiers lying in puddles of blood, sprawled in the graceless throes of death. I didn't look at the dead though, I searched for the children. I wanted to greet the children who would go back and play with Paul. I would tell them about him. I would ask them to tell him I loved him. I'd forgotten to say that before I left. My eyes filled with tears. A mist obscured my vision.

I turned a corner and came to a large common. There, I was surprised to see a table in the shade of a large cypress tree. At the table sat five children, their backs to me. They were sitting according to size, the tallest on my left, the smallest on my right. They took no notice of the carnage around them. They seemed to be concentrating on the food laid out before them. I thought it cruel to leave those poor children alone. There was no one around them and night was falling. They must be petrified with fear.

I rushed forward, calling to them. 'Children, children! Don't be afraid! Sharwah sent us. We'll bring you back to your families!'

Alexander caught my arm. I hadn't seen him coming. He moved so quickly. 'No, Ashley, no.' His voice was low. He was whispering.

'Let go of me,' I said. 'And congratulations by the way; I'm amazed about the fight, really. It was incredible.' I struggled to free my arm, not looking at his face. Tears wet my cheeks and I felt out of breath. 'I have to tell them about Paul!'

'Ashley.'

There was something in his voice. I stopped struggling and turned to him. His expression was desolate. Frowning uncertainly I let myself be drawn away from the tree. 'Wait, Alexander, I have to go and see the children. They must be so frightened. Why isn't anyone with them?' My voice rose. My heart knew what my brain refused to admit.

Alexander didn't answer. He gathered me into his arms. I was glad to see he was unharmed. He only had a scratch on one arm. Blood pearled along it then dripped slowly off his wrist.

'This is the first time you've touched me since you went to see that queen,' I told him in a conversational tone. 'Was it such a terrible experience?' I was surprised to hear a little gasp between my words. I was sure I felt fine. I just couldn't breathe, that's all.

He didn't answer, but a shudder ran through his body. His arms tightened around me. 'I'm sorry,' he said.

'What is it?' I asked.

'We came too late.'

I twisted my head around and stared.

The sinister stillness of the children chilled me.

The children Alexander wanted to save had been sacrificed on an altar in the centre of the fort.

Alexander didn't want me to see but I insisted. Some perverse desire to see what had happened seized me. I still don't know why I broke away and walked to the table. This time Alexander didn't stop me. He hesitated a second and then followed.

I walked slowly towards the children. The breeze lifted their hair, but otherwise they were immobile. When I got close enough to see that they were dead, I still didn't stop. It was as if the horror wasn't enough. I had to stare it in the face. I had to know.

They had been sacrificed on the stone altar and then propped up in front of a feast.

The table, the chairs, and even the food were made of straw. It was an elaborate, macabre preparation for a sacrificial fire. Burnt offerings indeed. Five faces gazed at me with unseeing eyes. Their throats had been cut, giving them wide red smiles. They had been dressed in white linen. My hands started to shake. I went to the children and I touched them on their cheeks.

'I'm sorry,' I whispered, 'so very sorry.' I knelt in front of the smallest child and took her cold hand. It was still limp. We'd almost made it in time. Fleeting warmth remained. I pressed her hand to my lips. 'Oh, sweet baby,' I breathed.

I reached up and closed her eyes. Then I closed the other children's eyes. Now they were sleeping.

Alexander didn't touch me but I heard his breathing behind me. In the back of my mind I registered the fact that he was having a bad asthma attack. That the sun had set. That the children had straw plaited into their hair, and that the smallest child was a girl. My nose started to bleed. I put my hands over my face. They were icy cold.

My vision blurred. Alexander's breathing grew worse.

We might have stood there for hours if Usse hadn't come looking for us. Chiron was hungry and was wailing, a thin cry that I heard all the way over the chasm. Usse took Alexander's shoulder and urged him towards the tent. 'Come, my lady,' he said to me. I followed. There was nothing else I wanted to see. I hadn't wanted to see this.

Chapter Nine

I was glad Onesicrite wasn't with us. The insufferable Athenian journalist would have written that Alexander killed the whole garrison to avenge the Greeks. He wouldn't have mentioned the children.

We sent their bodies back to the valley to be buried. Alexander had wooden coffins made for them, five coffins of various sizes. The smallest one had a flower carved on it.

Usse gave me a drink. It was hot, spicy wine and took some of the edge off my shock. I still couldn't believe what I'd seen. Why hadn't I stayed behind, safely in the tent? Oh no, I had to go and look. My journalist training made me want to go see what happened. But nothing would ever take the nightmares away.

Alexander caught me as I shot out of bed. He lunged across the covers and caught me around the middle. His hand clamped over my mouth, muffling my screams, and he pressed my face to his chest. His arms held me tightly until I was completely awake.

'I see them too,' he said. 'I wish you hadn't.'

I buried my face in his neck and managed to stop shaking. 'I never saw anything so horrifying.'

'I've seen worse,' he said simply.

We were whispering. The curtains were drawn. The trees leaned in the hard wind and their branches made shadows that whipped across the tent. Outside, the storm passed by slowly. Lightning flickered, thunder growled softly a moment later. Alexander held me, even after I stopped trembling. He pressed his forehead against my shoulder.

'Do you want to talk about it?' I asked him.

'I don't know.' He didn't usually sound so unsure of himself. I drew a deep breath and then guessed.

'Cxious?'

He flinched as if I'd struck him. Now it was my turn to tighten my arms. 'Plexis's brother. Yes, that's who I was thinking of.'

'You never meant to kill him. It was an accident,' I said.

'I killed someone I loved. You can't imagine how I felt afterwards. I looked down in the clay and saw that he was dead. His body was streaked with the red clay. It looked like blood.' He lifted his head and stared at me. The storm grew stronger. A flash of lightning showed Alexander's face. 'I wished that time could be stopped, that the moment could be undone, but time marched on. It was cold in the pit. I can remember standing in the wrestling pit and wondering if I could will myself to die. I wanted to stop my own heart. I closed my eyes and tried to stop it from beating. No one made a sound. Then I heard someone screaming. It was Plexis.'

'He's forgiven you,' I said. 'You must forgive yourself.'

'I'll never forgive myself. I'm a monster.' His voice broke. 'I killed Cleitus too.'

'That was unfortunate, but again, not intended,' I said.

Lightning cracked like a bullwhip in the sky, and a claw of rain scraped across the tent. Alexander pulled away and drew his knees to his chest. 'Aristotle told me that I would lose everything if I didn't learn to control my temper.'

'He's very wise,' I said cautiously. 'But he isn't you. And you're not a monster.'

'I don't know what I am any more,' he admitted.

I heard such pain in his voice. Reaching over, I drew him close to me and stroked his back. When he could breathe easier, I asked, 'Why did they kill those children?'

'It was their ceremony for the spring. They believe that only the blood of innocents makes winter lose its grip on the world. They believe in the fire god and in the god of stone. They still sacrifice to the god of spring.' He spoke in a monotone, and I shivered.

'Hush, we'll talk about it no longer. It's over now.'

We lay back down to sleep, but I slept uneasily. My dreams kept veering into nightmares. Yet every time I woke up, Alexander was there, leaning over me, soothing me with his hands and lips.

We stayed in the mountain fortress long enough to completely subdue the tribes in the area and to make sure that they would never return to the valley of Nysa to steal children for their bloody sacrifices.

Alexander wanted to leave a statue on the top of the hill. It would serve as a warning to the people of the region. He used me to put the fear of the goddess into them.

My reputation was even stronger than Alexander's. I was Hades' minion; I was Persephone, the goddess, daughter of Demeter, mother of the moon's child. Most of the time, I would have gladly given away all my titles. Like a much admired member of the royal family, I often wished I weren't so well known. However, this time I was content to dress in my finest robes and stride into a small village to put the fear of Hades into the local head honcho, who was suing for peace with Alexander.

With Usse, I put together a little show. Nothing fancy or flashy, just two small beeswax candles hidden in my palms to make it seem as if I held fire in my bare hands. The people grovelled on their knees while I held the flickering candles over my head and told them that human sacrifices were displeasing to the gods. For that reason, I said, their fortress had fallen and the defenders been slain. If they kept up the sacrifices, there was a good chance Alexander would come back and wipe them all out, simply to amuse the gods who really had nothing better to do with their time than to watch foolish mortals fighting each other.

An artist carved a likeness of me in stone. Alexander placed the statue on an outcrop of rock overlooking the Hindu Kush Mountains. It was visible for miles around. I looked back at it as we left, but the memory of the slain children made me turn away. The place was beautiful, but damned.

We joined Plexis and the other half of Alexander's army near the Indus River in May of the year 326 BC.

We made good time down the mountains. It is so much easier marching downhill.

When the brown river came into view, we shouted in unison. I rode my mare, Lenaia, and Alexander rode Bucephalus. We wore fine robes, and the soldiers around us carried tall poles fluttering with white and red flags. It was a fête.

Alexander was in a good mood and insisted on singing with his soldiers, which put a damper on *their* good mood.

Out of pity for the soldiers, bravely marching along with their hands full of flagpole and unable to clap their hands over their ears, I decided to talk to Alexander about something that had been bothering me.

'Alex,' I said. 'I've been meaning to ask you something.'

'OnWARD maRCHing BRAve Men! ON tO VICTorY We go FOrwarD!' he sang.

Well, I don't think the verb 'sing' quite describes it. Neither does shout nor growl. If cacophony were a verb it would be easier to describe what he was doing. Let's just say he was massacring a very simple marching song with only about four notes, none of which he came near.

'Alex! Be quiet! You're scaring the elephants!'

He clapped his mouth shut and the silence was literally a blessed relief. The men around us sighed deeply and started getting their normal colouring back.

'What is it?' he asked, peeved.

'Will you please tell me what exactly happened when you spent three days with the queen?'

He blushed.

I frowned. 'I see,' I said icily.

'You do?' he asked hopefully.

'I see that I can't let you out of my sight for even five minutes without you getting seduced by some sex-mad priestess or queen. What on earth am I going to do with you?' I spoke heatedly.

Alexander opened his eyes very wide. 'Me? Me? I did that? You weren't even there. Do you want to know what you can do with me?' He leered. 'Tell me some more stories about sex-mad queens and priestesses. They sound quite entertaining, but wait until we're alone. I don't want to miss a word you say.'

I narrowed my eyes. 'If I find out that you …'

'If I what?' he asked cheerfully.

I didn't answer. I was looking over his shoulder at a figure in the distance. He must have seen the look on my face because he whirled around. For a moment he didn't move. Then he dug his heels into Bucephalus's sides, and, with a wild whoop, galloped madly down the dusty road leaving me staring after him with a bemused expression.

Chiron wriggled on my back and started to whine. I dropped my reins and unhooked the backpack, pulling him around to my chest. Holding the baby in front of me, I said to him, 'There goes my husband, rushing to greet his best friend whom he hasn't seen in over three months – his best friend who just happens to be your daddy.'

I spoke in English. I didn't think anyone else would quite understand the complexities of the situation, which I'd already edited for Chiron's ears. The soldiers around me thought I said blessings. Chiron waved and gurgled happily at my breast. All he was interested in was milk. I could never understand why Chiron seemed to be the only human being who didn't mind Alexander's singing. It made most babies turn purple and scream. At first I was worried that he was deaf, but then I realized Chiron was just a little oddball. He would probably turn into one of those weird kids who love broccoli and algebra.

The sun shone, the flags flapped merrily, the soldiers sang, and the Indus River, huge, brown, and deceptively sluggish, flowed like caramel by our sides.

We were in India!

We camped on the far side of the river. The second half of Alexander's army had built a huge floating bridge. It was so sturdy even the elephants could walk over it. It took the army only a day to cross; the other half was already on the other side, and the encampment had been set up in a large, flat plain.

I stared in amazement as we arrived. After travelling for months with only about twenty thousand men, I wasn't used to the sheer size of Alexander's entire army. It took me nearly an hour to find the stables for my horse, and then I wandered around looking for the tent.

The encampment was set up with its usual precision. The stables and the bathhouses were on the eastern side, closest to the river shore. Then there were the mess tents, the infirmary, and the arsenal. Surrounding those were the smaller tents where the cooks, doctors, and scientists lived and worked. Smoke rose from nearby smithy tents, where men hammered and forged from daybreak to sunset. The smiths carved long poles for the spears, melted and cast bronze or iron spear tips, fletched arrows, sharpened arrowheads, fashioned bows, repaired armour, and fixed shields. I loved watching them work, and I would often accompany Alexander when he went to get his equipment repaired.

Children loved watching them too. The smithy tents were often surrounded by a gaggle of skinny-legged children, watching wide-eyed as the molten metal flowed into the moulds and listening to the bright clangs as the metal smiths pounded on anvils. A veritable thicket of spears leaned against their tents. The sun glinted off the bright points, an easy landmark to spot in the sprawling encampment.

Past that, in the centre of the camp, were rows and rows of small tents where the soldiers lived, usually two to a tent. They were not allowed to hang anything off their tents or put anything in the narrow alleyways separating the tents. Everything had to remain perfectly clean and the alleys clear in case they had to make a rush for it.

Each time they set up camp, the squadron leaders would make the same speech. Standing at the top of the rows they would announce, 'Soldiers of Iskander! Hail! Raise your tents up as you have been taught. Leave nothing in the alleys that may block the passage of those coming through. Store your belongings in the overhead net in your tent or under your pallet. Lean your weapons on the eastern side of your tent and put your armour on the northern side. Never leave them in the rain. Dinner will be served at sunset. Hail!'

I always liked listening to their speech. It was comforting, somehow, to hear it. It reminded me of the airline hostesses in my time. I wanted them to add, *'Thank you for joining Alexander's army and have a pleasant fight.'*

The soldiers' tents took up a great deal of space, but they were set up in such straight rows that you could see the other end of the camp in any direction. The cavalry soldiers' tents were nearest the stables.

After the soldiers' tents were the officers' tents, the generals' tents, the journalists' tents, the scribes' tents, and then the supply stores. The supplies were divided into several sections: food, cloth, articles for trade, the treasury, the scribes' supplies, the raw materials for weapons, and so on. All these were distributed around the encampment, always in the same place.

The organization of the army amazed me, and I could watch it forever and never get bored. It was an intricate dance between thousands of people. It was like a spider's web with each strand attached to a different item and everything linked together. Some strands reached all the way back to Greece, Macedonia, or Egypt, more than a year's march away. As we advanced, the strands lengthened and stretched, but instead of growing thinner and weaker, they seemed to get thicker and stronger. More and more people followed the army. There was a constant coming and going along the paths we'd taken. New routes opened. Alexander had conquered everything between the Indus and the Mediterranean Sea, and trade was the first to benefit. Mail followed. Alexander loved getting mail.

Chapter Ten

I wandered through the camp carrying Chiron in his backpack. He was a little more than five months old now, but he was a small baby. Not frail, just fine-boned. He loved to take walks. The motion put him in a good mood. I could hear him cooing. The soldiers would often come over and say 'hello' to him. They were still a bit wary of me, the goddess, but they adored Chiron. They would stand and talk to me, but behind their backs they would be making the sign for the deity they believed protected them. Not everyone, of course. There were quite a few people who greeted me without fear. The doctors were very friendly because I was sometimes Usse's reluctant assistant. And Seleucos, Alexander's general whom I had bought as a slave in Mazda and freed in Babylon, wasn't afraid. He was standing outside his tent carefully polishing the brass plaque on his armour. He looked up and saw me. A wide grin split his face, only to slip a second later.

'My lady!' he cried, his expression serious.

'What is it?' I asked. Everyone had been acting rather oddly, I realized. Crossing the river had taken me quite a while, and I hadn't seen Alexander since he'd galloped off after Plexis. Nor had I seen Plexis. Usse had gone straight to the infirmary, but Brazza and Axiom had disappeared and I couldn't find them anywhere. I frowned at Seleucos. 'Are you going to tell me what's going on?'

He licked his lips nervously. 'Nothing,' he said.

'You are a rotten liar,' I said evenly. 'Out with it.'

'Well, it's just that … uh. Well.' He frowned, searching for words. 'I can't tell you,' he finished lamely.

'I thought you were my friend.'

'I am!'

'So tell me what's going on? Why the long face?'

'My lady, Queen Roxanne is here! She's brought her babe. She came to be with Iskander. She joined the army as we were laying siege at Charsadda.'

My hand flew to my mouth.

'I wasn't supposed to tell you. I'm sorry, my lady,' said Seleucos lamely.

'Where is she staying?' I felt as if I'd just received a strong punch in the stomach. 'That little bitch. She sent word saying she'd meet us in Ecbatana.'

'She's in the royal tent.'

'The royal tent?' I choked. 'Not in Alexander's?'

'No, she has her own.'

'Well, we'll just have to sew it closed,' I muttered.

Seleucos uttered a shocked laugh.

I peered at him suspiciously. 'I'm going to give you some advice, Seleucos. Don't trust that woman. No matter what she says, no matter what she does. She has a viper in the place of her heart.'

He lost his grin and his eyes grew fearful. 'Yes, my lady, I'll remember that.'

'And stop "my ladying" me. Everyone seems to be afraid of me. I'm not a goddess. You know that.'

'I do?'

'Seleucos!'

'I do, sorry. My la … Ash … Ash … my lady.'

I heaved a sigh. 'How is Apames?'

'Very well, thank you.' He smiled happily. He was

obviously still infatuated with his wife. 'She's staying in Sogdia, but she'll join us in Ecbatana as soon as I send for her.'

I saw Alexander's tent being set up. But I hung back, now that I knew that Roxanne was lurking around somewhere. Her presence explained the new section added to the army. It was the royal court. The silly ninny had dragged along her ladies-in-waiting, the royal cooks and nannies, the royal pages, the royal entertainers, and Alexander would probably have a royal fit when he saw all that.

Then I saw something even worse. I groaned. Sitting in the shade of Roxanne's tent, busily writing, was Onesicrite, our execrable 'sex and scandal' journalist. Great. Just what I needed. I stepped back into the deep shade of a large tent and thought of different ways to get rid of everyone. A lightning bolt would come in handy right about now, I thought, scrutinizing the sky hopefully.

There was quite a bustle around Roxanne's tent. Women, pages, and slaves, all hustled back and forth between that tent, the food stores, the river, the infirmary, and the mess tent. Alexander's tent was on the far side of the new court. Not far enough away for my taste. Moreover, I would have to walk right through enemy territory to get to my tent or else take quite a long hike.

I took a long hike. I needed time to think, and I especially wanted to talk to Usse and Axiom. Roxanne was around. It was time to watch out for poison.

I found Usse in the infirmary. He was busy, but I managed to get him alone for a few minutes – long enough to tell him what he needed to know. His face grew very grave. He listened without speaking, then put his hands on my shoulders.

'Do not fear, I will take care of everything.'

Then I went in search of Axiom. He was probably in the mess hall or with the food stores getting everything settled. I didn't find him until sunset. I'd walked at least five kilometres back and forth, and I was getting as cranky and tired as Chiron.

Axiom looked worried when he saw me. I didn't search him out unless I had orders from Alexander concerning emergency meetings. Axiom was in charge of secrecy, although very few people realized it. Which was normal – it was a secret. We went to a dark corner of the storage tent to talk privately.

'What is the matter?' he asked, his dark eyes glittering in the torchlight.

'It's Roxanne. I want you to be very, very careful from now on. She has already tried to poison me once, and I'm sure she hasn't finished. I also want you to guard Alexander. Roxanne is a strange woman, and I wouldn't put it past her to drug him. Remember, she was a priestess for Anahita and she knows many potions.'

Axiom narrowed his eyes. 'She will not succeed in any of her plans. You can count on me. I will personally see to it that nothing happens to you, Iskander, or the babe,' he said firmly.

'Thank you. But you're also going to have to watch yourself, Brazza, Usse, and Plexis. Her jealousy knows no bounds.'

'It is like having a venomous serpent in our midst,' he said seriously. 'But if one knows it is there, one can watch out.'

'Take heed of her servants and who she tries to befriend,' I said. 'Try to find out who her spies are.'

'I will.' Axiom placed his hand on his heart. 'I swear.'

'I know you will,' I said. 'I trust you with my life.'

'I will not fail you.' He stood still, watching me leave, his face lined with worry.

I went back towards the tent, keeping a sharp lookout for anyone in Roxanne's cortège. I was worried. And with good reason. She was vicious, jealous, and single-minded; a rotten combination in an enemy. She also had charm and was pretty in a rather obvious way.

My mouth twisted. She was very lovely, who was I kidding? She had a perfect hourglass figure; narrow waist, wide hips, and lovely legs. Her large breasts were firm, high, and not the least bit saggy – y*et*. She had a narrow face with a high forehead and unusual colouring. Her skin was pale, her hair ebony, and her eyes were bright hazel. She had a small nose, a small mouth, a strong chin, and auburn eyebrows and eyelashes. She looked as if she had been put together with different parts of several beautiful women, but the whole picture was confusing. Her eyes were too close together, her nose too short. Her mouth folded upon itself, giving her a secretive, sly look. However, she had big tits. Frankly, it didn't matter what her face was like. She had the perfect figure. Men gave her face a quick glance and fastened their eyes on her bosom. Very few of them ever looked back up to her cynical and knowing eyes. She always wore either transparent muslin shifts or went topless, fastening a brightly coloured skirt around her waist. The skirt was usually short enough to show her legs and was often slit all the way up the front, giving glimpses of a carefully shaved sex.

She darkened her nipples with carmine, and she also did something to her sex, making it appear rather, well, I hate to say it, but she put a sort of gloss on it. I wished that she would catch something interesting, like dysentery, and have to stay in her tent for the rest of the journey. I wondered if I could arrange it. Unfortunately, Usse would never agree. She was Iskander's wife, his queen, and the mother of Iskander's son, born just after Chiron.

I would have liked to see the baby but didn't think Roxanne would let me. I wasn't going to let her within fifty feet of Chiron. I was suddenly relieved I hadn't brought Paul with me. It would have been impossible to protect a five-year-old, especially one as trusting as he was. He would have accepted any toy or sweet given to him by a stranger. I shuddered at the thought and breathed a sigh of relief.

With all that in mind, I approached Alexander's tent carefully. I wanted to make sure no one was inside. Lysimachus stood guard. I watched him for a while. He acted the same as always, but he'd been with Plexis for the past three months, and that meant that he had been with Roxanne. I decided to take a chance.

'Good evening, Lysimachus,' I said, stepping out of the shadows.

He jumped. I'd gotten good at sneaking around. I grinned.

'My lady! It's good to see you and the babe! May I see him?'

I obliged. 'Chiron, this is Lysimachus, Lysimachus, Chiron.'

'He certainly has changed,' said Lysimachus.

'He's growing. It's normal.' I smiled. 'Who's in the tent?'

'Nobody, you're the first to arrive.'

'Lysimachus, do me a favour. I'm very tired. If anyone comes to see me, tell that person I'm resting. Try not to hurt anyone's feelings, all right?'

He looked confused; I rarely gave any orders, but at that moment Chiron started to wail. Lysimachus's face cleared. 'Of course, my lady, I understand. Good evening to you.'

I ducked under the tent flap and stopped. It had all been changed.

A new rug covered the floor. Not as opulent as the old one, it was made of attractively coloured rose and violet cotton. A new glass lamp hung from the ceiling, and it swung ever so slightly, telling me that it had been recently lit. Made of pale yellow glass, delicately hand-moulded then carved, it seemed as fine as the old lamp. The light it gave was warm and made the tent look cosy. Alexander's table sat in the right hand corner, and fresh fruit filled the green jade bowl.

I poked my head out the tent and asked Lysimachus, 'Where did the fruit come from?' in a casual voice with a bright smile.

'From Queen Roxanne,' he said with an answering smile.

'How thoughtful,' I said, and withdrew my head. I looked at the fruit. Surely it wasn't poisoned, that would be far too obvious.

However, there were poisons and there were poisons. I took the fruit and put it into an old leather bag. Then I changed Chiron and put his dirty diaper on the top. I leaned out of the tent again.

'Oh, Lysimachus, I'm sorry to bother you. Will you give this old diaper bag to a slave to throw into the latrine pit? It should be buried. Chiron has suffered from an upset stomach these past few days. Tell him not to bother washing the diapers in it.'

He took the bag, frowned at its weight, smiled at me reassuringly, and called to a passing slave.

I wanted to wash the jade fruit bowl, but I'd do that tomorrow. I sighed and looked at the bed. The covers were still the same but I took them all off, searching for a thorn, a snake, or a spider. There was nothing. I shook everything out and made the bed again. I would be very careful from now on.

There were a few other differences in the tent in concession to the heat. The curtains were new. Instead of heavy tapestries they were light cotton, and the ropes holding them in place had been replaced with new ones. The tent pole had been polished, and Chiron's hammock was neatly folded away.

A thorn was in his hammock. I worked it free of the stitching and peered at it. It was a long, sharp, black thorn. Its point had been placed roughly where the baby's shoulder would be. I frowned as I held the thorn delicately between my fingers and stared thoughtfully at the little hammock. *This was war.* I put the thorn in my sandalwood box. I would ask Usse to see if it was poisoned.

I settled Chiron, and then sat down on the bed to wait. There was little hope Alexander would send Roxanne away, so I would just have to learn to live with her. I wanted to bathe, but I couldn't leave Chiron alone. Lysimachus was standing guard, yet he didn't realize how much Roxanne hated me. He had accepted gifts from her. He would let any of her entourage inside without question – he had already done so.

I sighed and lay back on the bed. I soon got bored. The minutes dragged by. Chiron slept, his little snores sounding like a bee buzzing. I stuck my legs in the air and looked at my feet. Not bad as feet went. They carried me places. I examined my hands. I had short nails, but my hands were nice with long, strong fingers from years of piano lessons. I had graceful arms from years of ballet lessons. I lifted up my tunic and stared at my body. Three pregnancies had shifted my muscles and bones. My hips were flatter and wider, and my stomach, although not flabby or round, was bigger. It was still nicely concave, but the line had changed. My breasts were large from nursing, soft, and round. They were well shaped and rather nice. Not raving beauties, but nice. When I didn't nurse they got smaller. I touched my nipples and they obediently stood up. They were small and pink, not huge and plum coloured like Roxanne's. I let my tunic fall and rolled over. I cupped my chin on my hands, wondering where everyone had gone. I needed to take a bath. I'd braided my hair tightly and pinned it up. It felt greasy. I'd brought a cake of the lye soap with me and I wanted to wash my hair with it. I'd discovered that if I mixed it with ass's milk it made an acceptable shampoo.

Because the army had a plethora of donkeys, and they all had baby donkeys, ass's milk was not hard to come by. Donkeys were very handy for the army, like little, furry, grey jeeps. They didn't eat much, worked hard, and when they died they were converted into sausage meat. Useful, attractive, and not half as stubborn as camels. Better than jeeps actually. They didn't need any roads or gasoline.

Chiron's tiny buzz-saw snore was so monotonous my eyes closed. I had just started to doze when the tent flap opened. Someone came in on noiseless feet. I smiled in my half sleep. Only one person could move so silently. There was a long moment of quiet. I opened my eyes. A man stood over Chiron's hammock. He stayed motionless, his hands clasped behind his back, bent over the hammock, an expression of intense concentration on his angular face.

'Hello, Plexis,' I said drowsily.

He came over to the bed and sat down next to me. His wavy brown hair had grown much longer and he now tied it back with a leather thong.

'Ashley,' he said. There were months of longing in his voice. His smile was sudden, and very sweet. My skin tingled. His effect on me was rapid and very physical.

I sat up and took him in my arms. 'I'm so dirty,' I moaned. 'I wish I'd seen you after my bath.'

He chuckled. 'That's all right. You're here now. I've missed you.' He held me at arm's length and looked at me. His amber eyes were clear as rainwater and his high cheekbones had a faint blush. 'You look wonderful.'

'I don't. My hair's a mess and I'm exhausted.' I wrapped my arms and legs around him and pulled him over on top of me. 'Make love to me,' I whispered, 'please?'

He nuzzled my neck. 'Soon. Right now I'm going to watch Chiron and you are going with Axiom to have a bath. He's waiting for you outside. He told me everything,' he added.

I sighed contentedly, moving my hips under his, teasing. I felt him harden and grinned. 'I'll go take a bath, but then we need to talk. And I don't know when we'll get time to do this properly,' I said softly.

'Properly? Who said anything about properly?' He was naked under his short, pleated skirt. That was his usual attire; skirt, sandals, and nothing else. Very sexy. He used his penis to nudge aside my tunic, but then he had to fumble at my drawers with his hands, suddenly urgent. 'Who invented these things?' he asked crossly, getting the knot all tangled. With a muffled curse he ripped them off, the fine muslin no match for him. He was breathing fast but then hesitated, raising an eyebrow. I grabbed his hips and pulled him into me.

He thrust hard, trembling with the effort to slow down. However, his body betrayed him, the edge of his desire too sharp to control. His breathing deepened and became hoarse. He tried to control himself, pushing up away from me.

'Don't stop,' I moaned.

'Who's stopping?' he gasped. 'After three months do you think I can stop?' He tried to slow down, but I wouldn't let him. He gave a strangled groan and let himself go, shuddering into me, his arms holding me tight.

'That wasn't fair,' he said, rolling off me. 'I wanted it to last longer.'

'Axiom's waiting outside,' I reminded him. I looked at Plexis and grinned. His hair had come loose and his face was now definitely flushed. He looked like a fallen angel. An Italian Renaissance angel after a round in the sack. Very sexy. I kissed his lips. 'Chiron is the most wonderful baby in the world,' I told him. 'Watch him carefully, and if he wakes up take him in your arms and carry him around the tent. He's curious about everything, and he loves to see new things. Don't let him touch the lamp,' I went on, straightening my tunic and taking a handful of soap with me.

The bathhouse was crowded, but as usual nobody was in the tub, a thing only sissies or women used. Real men slathered oil and sand on themselves, scraped it all off with a leather scraper, and then sluiced themselves with cold water. Some soldiers used warm water. There was always plenty heating in a huge cauldron inside the building.

There was also a pile of hot stones and herbs in the corner. Hot water was sprinkled on them to create a thick, fragrant steam. I used a big bucket to fill the tub, then I undressed and slid into the water.

Heaven couldn't be as good as this, I reflected, lying in warm water watching thirty naked men in the prime of their physical lives. They were all shapes and sizes, but all were superbly fit. Some had impressive scars or interesting tattoos. Most had beautiful bodies. A few were absolutely gorgeous. I took a deep breath and sank underwater.

The new shampoo I'd invented worked nicely. It left my hair shiny and fluffy clean. I couldn't wash my body with the lye soap, though. I had to use the kaolin clay. It was soft and didn't irritate my skin. I washed, then rinsed off, all the while admiring the men. It was my biggest bonus for being stuck here in this time. It made up for my lack of television and cinema. Well, OK, it made up for the lack of muscleman calendars. I grinned as I dressed, and then I spoke my blessing in English to the men. 'Great bodies, guys, love the tight buns, keep up the good work.'

They smiled happily. I'd said the ritual blessing. Everything was as it should be.

Axiom waited for me outside. He took his duty seriously.

Back at the tent, Alexander and Nearchus had joined Plexis. I felt suddenly very glad that I'd had time alone with Plexis before the bath. Nearchus was an uptight person. He wouldn't understand Alexander's sharing me with anyone. The fact that I had to share Alexander with several wives and lovers didn't seem to bother him a bit.

I thought he was a bore and a prig. He thought I was a dangerous spy from Hades, but he was willing to put up with me for Alexander's sake. I wondered what he thought about Roxanne. I would have to find out who my allies were and keep them firmly on my side.

He greeted me civilly, and I almost regretted thinking bad thoughts about him. Ptolemy Lagos came soon after. He had been with Alexander, so he just waved in my general direction.

I was sitting on the bed now with Brazza brushing my hair. He loved to do that. His hands were as light and dexterous as the best hairdresser's. I closed my eyes and purred.

Craterus and Coenus came in and bowed deeply to me. Antipatros gave me a genuine smile but stayed on the other side of the tent. Pharnacus followed soon after, and I felt a sharp jab of sorrow at the sight of him. He looked so very like his sister Barsine, the jolly princess I'd come to love so well. She had been Alexander's first wife and mother of his son Heracles. She had died last fall, but Pharnacus, with his fiery thatch of red hair and turquoise eyes, brought her memory vividly to life. When Alexander looked at him his face grew still, and I knew he was thinking of Barsine as well.

Perdiccas came in and greeted us. He was one of my favourite generals. He was devoted to Alexander, but he was never cold, like Nearchus. He didn't have dark, secretive eyes like Ptolemy Lagos. He wasn't as mournful looking as Craterus, or as hot-tempered as Coenus. He wasn't old, like Antipatros, or as huge and hairy as Pharnacus. He was a slight man, with straight, sandy hair and a smattering of freckles on his nose. He had light hazel eyes and an easy smile. He was also intelligent, cultivated, and one of Alexander's best tacticians. He gave me a wide smile, and, unlike most people, a kiss as well. It was a formal kiss, but he was one of the few to have no fear of me. 'My lady Ashley,' he said, 'welcome back. We missed you very much.'

The other generals made agreeing noises and I blushed.

'Why, thank you. You're too kind,' I said. 'I missed you, too. All of you. And it's nice to be back.'

The generals smiled, then frowned, harrumphed, and got back to business.

Chiron had slept soundly through everything, but at the *harrumph* he woke up and began to cry. I smiled apologetically and took him from his hammock. Then I pulled the curtain around the bed and nursed him.

'Still no schedule would Chiron follow,' I chided the little boy gently. He stopped nursing, opened his eyes, and gave me a look that clearly said, *'Will you be quiet while I'm eating?'* I grinned and kissed his downy head. He was getting rounder, the resemblance to Plexis fading. The likeness would appear again when he reached skinny childhood, but the chubby, toddler stage would hide the set of his eyes and the shape of his face. His high cheekbones were already gone; Chiron had nice, plump cheeks now. He was starting to look like anyone's chubby baby, and I was glad. The main reason was Alexander. He would need all the respect and support he could get in the difficult months ahead.

Chiron's fingers tangled in a lock of my hair as he nursed. I felt suddenly very sad. I missed Paul, even though I knew he would be safe. Chiron looked back up at me. His eyes were changing. From the slate-blue of babyhood, they were turning green. One eye looked darker than the other. I wondered if parti-coloured eyes were hereditary, and if so, who, in fact, the father was. I kissed Chiron's head again. I thought I'd really not know. I loved thinking he had parts of both men.

104

We ate dinner in the tent. The meeting still went on. Axiom brought the food. He had prepared it himself, and so I ate without any fear. I was glad, because I was hungry. Hunger pains stabbed me constantly. I was nursing, my body screamed for calories, and I wasn't getting half what I should be getting. I would have to start eating more. Now that the army was together perhaps it would be easier. The food supplies would come to the same place. Taxiles, king of Taxila, had promised to help us. We camped on his lands now. Plexis had been sending and receiving messages from him constantly. So far all the news was good.

When the generals finally left, I thought that I would be able to relax and spend a quiet evening with Alexander, Plexis, Brazza, and Axiom, but it was not to be. Lysimachus stuck his head into the tent and announced a visitor. 'Onesicrite to see you, Iskander,' he said respectfully.

I gritted my teeth as Onesicrite entered, bowed low, and spread his parchment on the table. He was oblivious to Plexis's yawns or Alexander's glassy stare.

'Will you tell me about the fortress Aornos?' he asked. 'The Athenians will be so excited to hear about it. Imagine! The very fortress Heracles himself could not bring down falls to you, his direct descendant.'

Alexander told him quickly, in very brief detail, about the attack and the outcome. Onesicrite finished his report then asked, 'And before that? Did you not visit the Valley of the Gods where Dionysus was raised? Did you partake of the wine of the gods? Did you celebrate the Bacchic revels? Was it fully as wonderful as they say?'

Alexander said that no, he had just passed through the valley, that no, he hadn't participated in any Bacchic revels, and that yes, he'd had some of the wine and it was very good. He'd even brought a good deal with him, and the next time there was a celebration, he would share it with everyone.

Onesicrite licked the nib of his reed pen and narrowed his eyes. He had been staying with Plexis's part of the army. He'd joined Roxanne's court after his lover, Callisthenes, had committed suicide. Perhaps he held Alexander responsible for Callisthenes' death, and indirectly, he was right. Alexander had imprisoned Callisthenes, and the poor man had hanged himself. But during Callisthenes' trial, Onesicrite had been horrible to him. It was as much Onesicrite's fault as anyone's that Callisthenes died. '*The guilty dog bites the hardest.*' That was a saying I'd heard often enough from Alexander.

Macedonians were great ones for sayings. Other sayings went along the lines of '*A lost goat calls the wolf*', '*Only sheared sheep can swim*', and '*A river goes farther than a puddle*'. I could understand why most of the sayings didn't make it to posterity. However, he was right about the guilty dog. I wondered who Onesicrite would bite.

He looked sideways at me, then back at Alexander. 'As you know, my king, I have been with your new queen. I have volunteered to act as her humble messenger. She greatly desires to see you this evening. As you must know, she has borne you a man-child. She would be very proud to show you your new son. What message may I bring back to her?'

His bite was much worse than his bark I decided, wincing.

Alexander gave me a reassuring smile then turned to Onesicrite and said, 'I will come see my queen and her babe when I have had my bath. I would not go to her covered in the dust and sweat of my journey. Pray tell Roxanne to expect me in one hour.'

Onesicrite smirked at me, bowed at Alexander, and backed out of the tent.

Plexis, Alexander and I looked warily at each other. The lamp flickered as the breeze blew in. Shadows danced all around us.

'I'll go take my bath now,' said Alexander rather quietly.

After he left Plexis asked me, 'What did you want to talk about?'

'Don't leave him alone with her,' I begged.

'Hush, don't say that.' He took me in his arms. 'Don't think about it. Nothing will happen to him, I promise. You're shaking!'

'Will you go with him now?' I asked. 'He needs someone with him, and I'm so tired all of a sudden.'

Plexis looked at the tent flap and sighed. I saw that and smiled. 'Go and find Alexander. And make it last longer,' I whispered. Now he did blush. I laughed.

'Are you sure?' he asked, his eyes bright.

'Of course.' I yawned and snuggled into my covers. 'Close the curtains, will you? And tell Axiom to come in the tent. I feel safer with him here.'

'There's Lysimachus,' he said.

I shook my head. 'No. Please, I only trust Axiom and Brazza.'

'All right.' He leaned over and kissed me gently. Then he left, silently as a shadow.

Chapter Eleven

I slept until Alexander came back to the tent. He reeked of strong perfume and incense, but his tense back told me volumes about the meeting between him and Roxanne.

'Do you want to talk about it?' I whispered.

He turned over and faced me. 'We're going to have to,' he said. His body was drawn tighter than a bowstring.

'Now?' I asked.

'No.' He felt me stiffen and said. 'I told her she should never have come. She took it badly. Then she wanted to make love, but I couldn't.' He sighed. 'Damn the bitch anyway. She tried it in front of Onesicrite. The Athenians are going to read about my impotence in his next newsletter.'

'I'm sorry,' I said softly.

'No you're not.' He kissed me and grinned wryly. 'And neither am I. She knows you're here, and that you have Chiron with you. She wants to see you.'

'I don't trust her,' I said.

'Neither do I,' he admitted.

I pulled him to me. 'Did you see your baby?'

'Yes. He looks like her. Dark hair, small eyes, and pale.' He was yawning as he said this, his body relaxing against mine.

I let him fall asleep, his head cradled on my arm, his hand on my breast. His breathing slowed and deepened and he slept without moving until before dawn. Towards morning he woke up, and he made love to me quietly, without speaking. We didn't need to talk, our bodies knew better than ourselves what we needed. Afterwards we just lay together. The sky turned a pale hue of rose quartz and Axiom lit the fire.

My days always started with Axiom lighting the fire. Then Alexander would get up and leave, coming back briefly to eat. I would see him again at nightfall. I buried my face in the warm, empty space he left and breathed deeply. His body had its own warmth and scent that I loved. My spirits lifted.

Chiron woke soon afterwards, and Brazza prepared breakfast. Alexander came back to the tent and ate with us. He had a faraway look in his eyes, the look of a man who has nearly reached his goal. He caught me watching him and smiled fleetingly.

'We're in India,' I told him.

'I've yet to see a singing tree, a tiger, or a wild elephant,' he said. 'By the way, I saw Roxanne. She still wants to see you.'

'Why me?' I thought for a minute. 'Very well. I'll go. But I will take Usse with me.'

Alexander sent Lysimachus with that message. I dressed carefully. Usse and I looked at each other nervously. Neither of us knew what to expect.

Roxanne hadn't changed. Birth hadn't altered her narrow hips or flat belly. If anything she looked even thinner, but her face had changed. Some women become gaunt with children. Roxanne's cheekbones were sharper, her eyes even more slanted.

She smiled and bowed, professing joy and gladness to see me again.

'I'm very flattered,' I said.

'And where is your child? I would see him without delay.' Her voice was high, but not sweet.

'I will invite you to come and see him with your own babe, so that they may play together as true brothers. My wish is that they be as close as Castor and Pollux.'

My words startled her. The crowd in the tent murmured appreciatively – and there was quite a crowd. Roxanne surrounded herself with no less than twelve slaves, three eunuchs, ten maids-in-waiting, and at least fifteen cooks and various scribes, singers, oboe players, dancers, and whatever else she felt she simply couldn't live without. Where was the baby? I looked around the tent and my eyes found the crib.

Roxanne's baby suffered from what looked like eczema combined with malnutrition and poor nerves. The tiny five-month-old boy was covered with red spots, his arms flailed when he cried out, and no one dared pick him up to soothe him.

His mother tried to act concerned, but her fingers drummed on the side of the painted wooden crib and her eyes were calculating, not worried.

'Do you nurse him still?' I asked.

'No, he has a wet-nurse,' she said. 'I never had any milk.'

'How sad,' I said quietly. 'Who is his wet-nurse?'

Roxanne smiled. 'It's an ass. Her milk is good, but the child is still poorly. Perhaps your doctor has a suggestion?'

Indeed. Things were becoming clearer. 'Find a slave with milk,' I ordered. I whirled around and took Roxanne's arm hard enough to make her wince. 'You will not interfere. Now listen to me well. I will only say this once. If you want your son to rule someday, first he must live.' I let go of her arm. She stepped back, rubbing it angrily. Her eyes were wary. Now I would see if she was dangerous when frightened, or simply when she felt on top of the situation. 'What is his name?' I asked.

'I called him Iskander, after his father.' Her voice dripped honey.

I nodded grimly. She would always back down from a head-on fight. It meant I could never turn my back on her. She was the type to attack from behind. I would be doubly careful now.

Usse and I whispered together, and then he spoke up. He bowed very low and said to Roxanne, looking down at her feet. 'You must fetch a slave woman to give him milk. He is not thriving on ass's milk. You must bathe him twice a day in water mixed with vinegar and whey milk. The water must be first boiled then cooled. You must wash his eyes with a special cloth, used only for his face.'

'But he's *my* baby!' she said. Her voice was uncertain though. She dared not protest too strongly.

'You will be happy when he has recovered completely,' I said. Then I left.

Usse and I watched the little boy carefully for a week. With regular baths, a woman's milk, and clean diapers, he soon lost his allergic rash and gained weight quickly.

He was a fey child, never crying, very quiet, and pale as the sand. He was so calm that I grew worried and asked Usse to make sure he was normal. It turned out that he was deaf. I was shocked.

I tried to remember if the child had lived. I knew Roxanne had had at least two children. One was called Alexander and had been declared heir after his father's death, but he'd died in the war between Cassander and Olympias when he was ten or eleven years old.

Usse and I decided not to tell Alexander or Roxanne

111

right away that the baby was deaf. It would be a sore blow for them. The boy was looking so much better and Roxanne seemed happy. However, we stayed no more than we had to in her tent. Neither of us ever accepted any food or drink. Although we tried not to give offense, we must have seemed extremely rude. Roxanne, egotistical maniac that she was, didn't seem to notice.

Her tent became a meeting place for those who believed in the old gods: Baal, Marduk, Ishtar, Anahita, Mot, and Ea. Two were bloodthirsty, Baal and Marduk, and one was the sex-goddess Anahita, Roxanne's cult.

She never carried her son the way I carried Chiron. Actually, I never saw her take him in her arms.

Alexander had been relieved when he saw Usse caring for Roxanne's baby. Hearing that the only thing ailing him was uncleanness made him angry. He wanted to reprimand Roxanne, but we stopped him. The best thing would be to teach her how to take care of her own child, and failing that, train one of her nurses, which is what Usse ended up doing.

However, Roxanne seemed to sense that something wasn't right with the babe and left his care to the nurse Usse had chosen. Which was probably just as well for the baby, I reflected. The poor child had been severely neglected. Now, at least he was clean and well fed, and his nurse seemed fond of him.

Roxanne's cortège marched behind the main army. It looked like a circus, I thought wryly, watching it one day as I rode. Three elephants lugged the tents. Sixteen camels carried her supplies. A large wagon full of women shrieking like a pandemonium of parrots followed. And there *were* parrots – and monkeys. The women had their pets with them. Their slaves walked alongside carrying white flags. There were priests and handmaidens in carts, and litters carried by ponies and donkeys. Roxanne rode a white mare, and I was relieved to see it wasn't the one I'd given her.

We moved slowly east. It was a week's march, and soon the only thing anyone spoke about was King Taxiles's kingdom. Would he meet us with a thousand elephants? Would his palace be more beautiful than the palaces of Greece and Persia? Did everyone wear silk? Did he have singing trees in his garden? Those were the questions everyone asked.

Chapter Twelve

We arrived early one evening. The sky was pale lavender. The mimosa trees wore yellow flowers, and the grass had grown waist-high in the fields. The dust raised by the army alerted Taxiles's scouts, and they met us just outside the city's walls.

The king and his entire army met us. They lined up with their weapons glinting gold in the setting sun.

There was a moment of confusion as Alexander and his generals wondered if we were being attacked. Before I knew what had happened, I was hustled to the back of the parade, while the cavalry rushed to the forefront and the infantry and phalanx grabbed spears. Soon Alexander's army stood wary and ready in front of Taxiles's army, and everyone stared at everyone else. There was a lot of white showing in people's eyes. The situation started to get very tense, when suddenly a lone horseman rode out from the city, waving his arms and showing clearly that he was unarmed. It was King Taxiles himself.

Alexander grabbed a translator and rode out to meet him, a flush of excitement on his cheeks. Here was the man who'd given him twenty-five elephants! They dismounted and embraced. The translator could hardly keep up as Alexander thanked him, and Taxiles apologized for the welcome.

One hundred girls ran out and started throwing flower blossoms over the road, paving our entrance with marigolds and poppies.

I urged my horse forward and joined Alexander. He and I were invited into the city. The army was shown to a huge plain not far away. Alexander and I stayed in the palace.

Taxiles proved to be absolutely enamoured of all things Greek. He wanted his kingdom to be the first to trade with Greece, and he wanted to show Alexander plans for new buildings, schools, theatres, and a gymnasium.

First, though, he wanted to settle some rather delicate matters.

The principal matter was a hefty bill he presented Alexander for all the food he'd provided for the army. Alexander paid with gold he had in the treasury.

The second matter was a bevy of unmarried daughters.

Alexander smiled bravely and said he'd find husbands for each of the girls.

'And for you, Mighty King of the West, I give you my youngest flower!' The translator spoke in a rapturous voice, exactly imitating King Taxiles's crowing manner. The king clapped his hands, and a girl came out and bowed. I choked back an exclamation. The girl was very beautiful, but only about thirteen years old. Her eyes were huge in her golden face, and her hair was so black it was nearly blue. She was naked except for flowers twined around her neck, waist, wrists, and ankles. More flowers were braided into her hair. Her lips had been painted bright red, and her eyes lined with kohl.

At a sharp word from the king, the girl knelt down, then, like a contortionist, leaned backwards to touch her head to her toes and spread her thighs wide, showing her pink sex. A slave rushed over and spread her labia open, and the translator said proudly, 'A pure virgin.'

Alexander's eyes nearly popped out of his head. So did all the other men's. The king leaned back and smiled, content with the effect. I was livid with rage. I stood up and, hiding my shaking hands behind my back, spoke in a loud voice. The translator looked at me in awe as he told King Taxiles what I was saying.

'Iskander must not be greedy. His next wife will be cursed and will kill her own parents. This girl is too young to marry. She must wait until she has reached her eighteenth year. Then she shall marry whomever she chooses. The goddess has spoken. Listen and obey.'

I had started off with a serious case of nerves and pronounced Iskander, 'Seekander'. The Indians would pronounce his name like that forever after.

King Taxiles became agitated when the translator finished. He cleared his throat and said rather hastily that the girl could wait, and that he would be content with generals or princes for his other daughters.

Alexander found many men willing to marry and stay in Taxila with the king. The city would become the biggest centre of Hellenic culture in India. Greek would be spoken there for centuries. It would become one of the greatest exchanges between east and west. Taxiles didn't know this, of course, but he seemed thrilled to meet Alexander. He wouldn't stop rubbing his hands together and beaming.

He was also very impressed with the army. He saw Alexander as the chance he'd been waiting for. To the south was his greatest enemy, the rajah Porus, whom he had been fighting against on and off for decades. Alexander had sent ambassadors to Porus asking for right of passage through his lands. The second night we stayed in Taxila, news came that the demands had been rejected, and Porus was massing his army on the banks of the river Jhelum.

Alexander grew very still when the news came. I think he was bitterly disappointed. He had been looking forward to coming to India and being received everywhere. The idea of fighting his way through India displeased him enormously. Nonetheless his military mind was already busy making plans. We left five days after we arrived.

I used those five days to go shopping. I'd been in the mountains, away from civilization for so long. I'd forgotten what it was like to go to the market, to buy food and clothes, to go to the theatre, or eat at a restaurant.

I insisted Alexander accompany me and do all those things, except the restaurant. There weren't really any restaurants in those times, just food stands in the market place. We strolled through the city. The people acclaimed us, and everyone tossed flowers at us; flowers and coloured rice. I loved it. I felt like a bride the entire time.

Alexander covered me in beautiful, bright silks and cottons, and we ate curried lamb and peacocks. Alexander loved Indian food and Taxiles adored Greek art. Alexander's men put on sports exhibitions in the plains, and the people of the city swarmed out to see them every evening.

Lanterns made of coloured silk, and ribbons of bright cotton decorated everything. All the hues were bright and vibrant. *Gold! Red! Pink! Violet!* they screamed. The Greeks were entranced. It was a mutual love affair between the pure, classical Greek style and the colourful, elaborate Indian manner. It was sparkling white marble meeting bright fuchsia silk. It was like cold vanilla ice-cream and hot fudge sauce. It was calm restraint meeting wild abandon. Everyone exclaimed at everything. There

117

wasn't a single thing that the Indians didn't adore about the Greeks, and the Greeks thought that everything in Taxila was fabulous.

For five days, there was one big party going on. We walked through the streets on carpets of flowers, ate to the songs and instruments of India, and made love in a huge bed in an airy room overlooking a garden filled with the deep, mysterious, intoxicating fragrances of India.

The moon rose and hung fat and satisfied in the sky. The stars twinkled and shone. Alexander wrapped yellow silk covers around us and kissed me from my toes to my nose, saying all the dirty words he'd already picked up from the Indians.

He had an amazing ear for languages.

Besides all the obvious bodily functions, he'd picked up orders such as: 'Give me', 'I want', 'Don't touch', and 'Hot!' – that was for the curry – 'Please' and 'Thank you', 'How much?', and 'Beautiful'. Five days in India and he was already ordering the servants around, much to their hilarity, when he told them 'want the window to eat hot curry now'. He was trying to tell them to open the window because we were hot. To tell the servant to change Chiron's diaper he said, 'Go away please baby shit.'

The servants loved him. They were always walking in on us. They were never embarrassed by anything we were doing. I was embarrassed. King Taxiles showed Alexander some erotic drawings and miniatures from a thick folder. Alexander turned bright red and looked over at me. I raised my eyebrows and asked to see, but Alexander told me to forget it. He was blushing.

The winding streets of the city fascinated the Greeks. It was old and romantic, with flowers growing everywhere, and bright cloth hanging from windows as women dried their washing.

We bought a new rug for the tent. We already had one, but in Taxila I fell in love with the bright colours of India. I wanted a beautiful rug to take the place of the exquisite one Paul had destroyed.

I found one made of silk. It had deep red, turquoise, yellow, gold, and all the colours of the sunset and sunrise woven into a huge, intricate pattern. It cost a fortune but I traded some jewellery Alexander had given me.

I had the rug taken to the tent as a surprise. I also bought some toys for Chiron: a rattle made of a gaily painted gourd, a ball made of soft suede, and yards and yards of soft, airy cotton to dress him.

I bought the exact same things for Roxanne's baby, all the while knowing the poor child would probably never receive them. Our mistrust was mutual.

For Plexis, I bought an erotic painting. For each of Alexander's generals, I bought a light cotton robe. Cotton was not well known in Greece, the only cotton that came that far was often rough and poor quality. The Egyptians had yet to start cultivating it. This cotton was a big hit, especially in the wonderful colours the Indians dyed it, bright scarlet, deep jade, buttery yellow and hot, peppery orange.

The whole army had changed its 'look' by the time we moved off towards the kingdom of Porus. We were bright and gay. Instead of white, everyone now wore vivid splashes of colour. I decked my mare with necklaces of marigolds, wore a fuchsia robe, wrapped Chiron in royal blue, and tied sunny yellow ribbons in my hair.

King Taxiles rode with us. He was coming to fight his enemy with five thousand of his own soldiers. He and the generals came into our tent every night, sat on the marvellous silk rug, and plotted and planned until the wee hours.

'Porus,' said Taxiles, 'is a cunning leader, an excellent tactician, and has an invincible army. He has nearly fifteen hundred war chariots pulled by fast horses. He has five hundred elephants, and cavalry fifteen thousand strong. He has thirty thousand infantrymen, and thirty thousand archers. His men are known for their bravery and skill. It will be a very close battle.'

Alexander listened to everything Taxiles and Meroes, another Indian rajah who had joined him, had to tell him. As before, he had detailed maps drawn up. They showed the river, the land on either side, and the sort of soil and vegetation. He was searching for things like deep sand, slick mud, or soft, crumbling dirt. He wanted to know everything. All day he would talk to the Indians, and during the night he drew up plans.

We marched across the plains towards rolling hills. We were heading more or less south, through Taxiles's lands. Behind us, Coenus had gone to fetch all the boats Alexander had used to cross the Indus, and he was busily dismantling them and hurrying them towards our meeting place on the banks of the Jhelum River – in Alexander's time it was called the Hydaspes.

We marched quickly. Alexander wanted to see exactly where he was going to have to fight, and he would need time to observe the enemy. He was all nerves during the march, barely sleeping, eating only when we begged him, and then hardly tasting anything. He would chew a few mouthfuls then spring to his feet again and start pacing.

By day he rode or walked. He didn't ride Bucephalus. The stallion was resting in the herd of army horses. He used his new stallion, the one Plexis had picked out for him. He liked this horse well enough, but between Bucephalus and Alexander there existed a deep affection. The old warhorse would act like a colt whenever his master approached. He would trot over to Alexander, lay his great head on his shoulder, and nibble at his hair.

Bucephalus was a stocky horse. He wasn't a lean, pure thoroughbred-type. Those horses wouldn't exist for another two thousand years. The horses of Alexander's time were more like ponies. Some had Arab traits. Most had big heads, strong legs, round rumps, and high withers. Bucephalus had a wide, deep chest and a huge head. His eyes were canny. His coat was a warm bay, with a black mane and tail. A white mark on his forehead, shaped like a bull, gave him his name. When he was ridden, his neck arched and his eyes blazed like a tiger's. He would flare his black, velvet nostrils, showing their blood-red interior, and he would whinny piercingly.

The warhorses screamed when they charged, and it made a heart-stopping, blood-curdling sound. Bucephalus, with his thick neck and heavy head, made a sound that was more like a lion's roar.

Alexander counted on his cavalry to win most of his battles, and this battle was to be no different.

We crossed undulating hills and low mountains before coming to the top of the Nandana Pass. From here, the whole of the river plain was visible. The sun glinting off the narrow ribbon of water, made it look like a flame. There were flat plains leading to the water's edge as far as the eye could see in either direction. And directly in front of us, across the river, Porus's army camped, determined not to let Alexander pass.

We set up camp, and Alexander gave orders as to the

121

placement of everything. We were supposed to make it look as if we had decided to settle there all summer.

The river had effectively started its annual flood, and very soon would be impossible to cross. The snows from the Himalayas were melting, and the icy waters would swell the river to four times its normal size. Already the river was no longer a sluggish caramel-coloured flow, but swirled and eddied with the force of new waters coming from the mighty mountain streams. It frothed white in some places, small waves curling and breaking over floating branches and underwater boulders. The banks on our side sloped gently downwards. The water lapped at them invitingly. In contrast, on the opposite shore, steep banks leapt ten feet into the air, and they offered a crumbly and unsure footing. The horses could swim across, but could they clamber out? Perhaps, but surely not with the weight of Porus's army facing them down.

And the weight of his army was the elephants. Horses are frightened of elephants. All Porus had to do was line his elephants up along the bank and Alexander was stymied.

Alexander sent scouts up and down the river to search for passageways.

For nearly three weeks, we played an elaborate game with Porus.

First, Alexander made it seem as if we were settling down for the summer. He made sure Porus saw the enormous shipments of grain arriving for the army's sustenance. Then he started the feints.

Like the boy who cried wolf, he lined his army up in attacking formation and pretended to attack two or three times a day. The men would scream their battle cries, the horses would gallop madly back and forth, and the catapults and javelins would be deployed.

Porus rushed to the defence each time. His elephants lumbered over, the artillery fanned out, the archers knelt, readying themselves.

Alexander watched all this with great interest. Each time, Alexander subtly changed his method of attack. Each time, Porus saw the change and adjusted his defence accordingly.

Alexander was euphoric. The harder the problem the more he loved it. This was a great puzzle, and he'd already figured out all the pieces. At night he would toss and turn, getting up four or five times to pace and mutter. During the day he galloped back and forth, a huge grin on his face. He was manic, excited, exhilarated. He would often leap off his horse after a false attack and rush into the tent, grab me, and throw me onto the bed to ravish me. Everyone would scatter, and I would find myself in the arms of my husband, joyous and incandescent.

I watched him with an indulgent smile. I was his greatest admirer. What else could I be? What else could I do? I loved him, my heart sang when he was near me, when I saw him I was just as euphoric because his elation was contagious. Everyone in the camp believed in him. Everyone bathed in his glow. The grand adventure had swept them up and was carrying them along as easily as twigs in the flooded river.

Then word came that Coenus was approaching with the boats, and the plan moved to stage two. The false alerts doubled. Porus had not a minute's respite. He was unable to watch the whole river at once, or choose one place as the most likely to defend. He was obliged to split up his army, giving the chariots to his son, and deploying his infantry and cavalry in two or three places.

Meanwhile, Alexander disguised one of his generals in his own clothes, put him on Bucephalus, and bade him to continue the false alarms. He himself had to organize his real attack. One that Porus hadn't even begun to suspect because of its sheer audacity.

Twenty-five miles away was a high cliff, where the hills of the Great Salt Ridge came right down to the water's edge and formed a strong promontory. Behind it, a deep valley cut into the mountain's flank, easily big enough to hide half of Alexander's army. Now came the tricky part.

Under cover of night, over several nights, parts of the army crept away. They hid in the valley and their places were taken up by the civilians following the army. Everyone was involved in the deception. Women dressed as soldiers and held shields. Doctors and scientists rode horses and carried bows. Everyone spread out, tents were left behind, and dummies were stuffed and placed in strategic positions. To the watching army on the other side of the river, it was impossible to tell that fully twenty thousand men and horses had gradually disappeared.

And Alexander's look-alike continued to ride up and down, shouting, waving, and giving the call to attack.

Porus finally stopped answering the false attacks and stood back warily. Watching. Now was Alexander's chance. He seized it during a severe thunderstorm in the dead of night.

Chapter Thirteen

I stayed in the tent with Axiom, Brazza, and Chiron, pacing up and down while the rain battered the roof, and the wind and thunder deafened us. The lamp swung back and forth. Shadows reared and subsided, our eyes were deep, black pools of worry. Chiron cried angrily and slept fitfully.

Craterus had been left behind with his cavalry, the phalanx, and the Indian army with Taxiles and Meroes. His orders were simply to stand. Not to attempt any crossing until he was sure there was no way he could be pushed back by Porus's army. If he saw that Alexander's army needed help, and he could make it across, he was to deploy the boat-bridge. If Alexander's army started to win, he was to cross right away, swimming the horses and crossing the men on the bridge in order to give chase to the retreating army. If he saw Alexander losing, he was to take me, Roxanne, and the rest of the civilians and retreat to Taxila. Then we were to return to our respective countries, except for me. I would be accompanied by Craterus to the Valley of Nysa.

I didn't see Alexander's part of the fight, but I know exactly what happened. Between his words, the storm, and the sounds of the battle there was woven a tale out of the night. The story of the Battle of Porus.

Arrian starts his story this way:

"It was a dark and stormy night ..."

A bolt of lightning crashed into the valley, hitting a tall tree, electrocuting three of the cavalry horses tied beneath it. There was a brief moment of panic, but it quickly subsided as the men concentrated their efforts on setting up the floating bridge across the raging river.

The storm slashed downwards with such strength that the men could hardly see a hand's breadth in front of them. Torches were put out instantly in the deluge and, anyway, Alexander had ordered complete darkness. Only the flaming tree offered a flickering red light. The smoke showed the driving rain. The river lit by flashes of lightning churned heavy and wild as a living thing.

The boats were recalcitrant, bucking and twisting. However, the men had lots of practice and soon the bridge was completed. The infantry walked across, with the cavalry swimming their horses in the lee of the bridge. It offered shelter, at least from logs or branches sweeping down upon them. Two hours later most of the men had made it to the shore, but Alexander, who had been among the first to cross on his valiant Bucephalus, discovered that they had been misled, and instead of arriving on the opposite shore, they had hit an island. Forty feet of swiftly flowing river stood between them and the opposite shore. Alexander went first. It was too late to bring over the bridge, they would have to wade or swim. He hoped that it wasn't too deep.

Bucephalus plunged in, snorting and shaking his great head. Soon the water was up to his belly, swirling around his legs. Only the blue lightning flashes lit the darkness, and the thunder made all shouting impossible. Bucephalus hit deep water and for a second his head was submerged, then he surged upwards, blowing water out of his nostrils like a whale. He struggled against the current, swimming with just his nose in the air, snorting furiously. Right away though, he found a footing and hauled himself out of the water. Limbs trembling, sides heaving, he stood still for a moment, recovering his wind. Then he threw his head up and whinnied. His voice climbed over the storm and the thunder. The other horses answered. The men leaped forward.

Alexander had to hurry. The night would not hide them indefinitely. He gathered the cavalry around him. Plexis had five hundred cavalry under his command as well as the Royal Guard, Perdiccas and Demetrius each had five hundred cavalry, Coenus had his battalion and the phalanx, and there were archers and infantry.

Alexander put the Royal Guard and Plexis with the hipparchies to his right. To his left, he put Perdiccas. In front of everyone he deployed his mounted archers. Behind were the infantry, with Coenus and his battalion, the phalanx was in the middle, and the archers were on the wings. Then he set off as fast as the army could go towards Porus.

It was a six-hour chase through the blackest night. The horses had better night vision than the men, but two men were killed outright when their mounts stepped in deep holes, pitching them over their heads. Another horse screamed and died not long after, perhaps bitten by a snake. By some miracle none of Alexander's men were bitten in the rush through the fields and river-plains.

Six hours of running, then walking to get one's breath back, then running again. The horses trotted steadily. Alexander didn't want to get too far ahead of his foot soldiers. Only when he felt they were close to where Porus would certainly meet them, did he urge Bucephalus into a headlong gallop, the rest of the cavalry racing along after him. The ground shook with their charge. He was planning on buying time for his infantry to rest, but it meant sparing neither his horse nor himself.

Porus's scouts saw Alexander's army and ran to tell their leader. Even knowing he had been duped, Porus didn't panic or think of giving up the fight. To give himself time to deploy his elephants and cavalry, he sent his son with a thousand chariots and two hipparchies of cavalry to slow Alexander's charge.

The rainstorm acted in Alexander's favour now, bogging down the chariots and slowing their charge. Unable to swing around in time to face the sweeping charge of Alexander's cavalry, the chariots were cut down and the men, including Porus's son, slaughtered.

It was still night, though a grey line was showing under the heavy belly of the clouds. Dawn was coming. The attack had begun in earnest.

Porus was caught between Alexander's troops on his side of the river and Craterus's troops on the far side, still in position to cross at any moment. However, Porus decided to engage Alexander fully, thinking – rightly, I'm sure – that if he managed to kill the young king, the rest of the army would be lost. Therefore, he called his troops, blowing mournfully on a huge horn.

The elephants made an impenetrable forest, while Porus's archers, shooting from behind, kept Alexander's army at bay. But Alexander had time to develop a strategy against this, and he set off at full gallop with his cavalry. Porus's cavalry, lined up behind the elephant line, followed them, running parallel to all Alexander's movements. While they dashed back and forth, the elephants swung uneasily from side to side. The infantry, arriving now, stealthily took their places behind Alexander. They had marched all night, twenty-five miles in a thunderstorm, and they were tired. Alexander gave them time to rest using his cavalry as a diversion – and then not as a diversion. As soon as Porus decided it had been a distraction and made the decision to attack, Alexander suddenly split his cavalry in two, sending Coenus and Perdiccas to the left, taking Plexis and Demetrius to the right, flanking Porus's army. Seleucos stayed with the phalanx and with his cavalry. The result was that the Indians were obliged to quickly split up in two groups, one facing Alexander's cavalry, the other meeting Perdiccas. In the middle, all was confusion.

The phalanx charged and the archers rushed in, aiming at the elephants and their drivers. The beasts, wounded and driverless, started to bellow and charge, stampeding thoughtlessly over Porus's army. Alexander's men, being in the open, were able to retreat and dodge, but Porus's army was caught in a trap of its own making. They were caught between the elephants and the bulk of the rest of their army, with Alexander's cavalry on either side.

The shrill trumpeting of the wounded elephants brought me rushing to the river's edge. I could see the top part of the battle: the elephants towered over everything else. I was too low to see anything other than the elephants. Cursing, I ran to the wooden tower Craterus had built to view the scene. He and two other generals were in it, surveying the battle. I couldn't tell by their faces what was happening. If they were surprised to see me, they said nothing. Silently they made room for me between them.

At first all I saw was confusion. The elephants were badly wounded. Blood poured off their heads and bodies, and they had retreated into an instinctive huddle, facing their enemy. They raised their trunks and trumpeted mournfully. Shaking their massive heads, flapping their ears, they slowly backed away from the prickly thicket of spears Alexander's phalanx presented.

Arrian describes them as looking like boats being rowed backwards as they retreated. I will always have that image of the great, sad beasts shaking their heads back and forth in an almost stately fashion, as their mournful cries mingled with the screams of the wounded and dying.

When the elephants started moving backwards, Craterus began shouting, and the bridge that had been hidden behind bales of hay and stacks of wood was rolled out and pushed over the river. Soon Craterus's cavalry and foot soldiers were rushing towards the opposite shore to finish the battle.

The sun was very high now. The storm had left the air sultry and heavy. It felt like being inside a sauna. There was no shade on the battlefield. The brassy heat shimmered as the men struggled and fought. Now I could see Alexander's cavalry. He was in the fiercest fighting. Plexis fought on his right side, Perdiccas on his left. The horses were covered with white lather. It was nearly impossible to distinguish anyone. Everyone was striped with blood.

As I watched, there came a tight knot of Indians towards Alexander. I held my breath. They rode armoured horses and used them to clear a path through the archers. When they reached Alexander's group they dropped their heavy shields and drew sharp swords. The sunlight flashed on the metal as they raised their arms to attack.

Alexander managed to deflect the blows with his round shield, letting go of Bucephalus's reins and twisting his body around to face his attackers. His sword jabbed out from beneath the shield, keeping the men at bay. Perdiccas took a nasty blow on the leg but his horse reared, saving him. When he came down, Perdiccas had recovered enough to riposte, fighting to clear some space. Plexis was on the right, and he took the brunt of the attack. Light of build and flexible, he could dodge and turn, avoiding blows while dealing out his own. Using his legs to control his horse, he brought his horsemanship into play. But the ground was wet with rain and blood and the hours of marching and fighting were taking their toll. His horse was young, not experienced like Bucephalus. When a sword cut his chest he veered and Plexis met an attacker head on. He didn't have time to duck; the blow caught him on the temple and he fell.

My legs suddenly gave out. Through a blur of tears I could see Alexander had lunged forward, using the superior weight and strength of Bucephalus to smother his opponents. With a fresh wave of cavalry rushing to join him, Alexander soon gained fifty yards of ground and cleared through the enemy. I couldn't see Plexis anywhere. His horse was rider-less, but then, so were many horses. I took huge, deep breaths to try to calm myself. My nose, never any good in an emergency, bled profusely. I stood, gripping the wood so tightly my fingers whitened. I saw Alexander, he had cleared a space around him. He and Perdiccas were fighting back to back. Around them stood Alexander's men, the infantry and the archers, holding their positions.

As soon as Craterus reached the opposite shore, mass confusion scattered Porus's ranks, who were now set upon from all sides. Shouting, cursing, and screaming hysterically, they tried to find an escape route, but they were caught in a vice. Porus, on his elephant, called out to his men, swinging his arms, telling them to attack, and attack again. But the battle was lost. It had been lost from the moment Alexander divided his troops and outflanked the elephants. Suddenly there was silence.

The men were exhausted. I could hear their breath coming in great sobs, and the high whistle of the horses' breathing sounded like steam engines. The metallic clash of weapons stopped. The elephants stopped trumpeting. The men stopped screaming.

Craterus held his men in check now. They were fresh, quivering, shining in the sun, ready to move in and slaughter Porus's army at a word from Alexander. The silence was tense.

A voice rang out. It was Alexander's. Hoarse, broken, but absolutely triumphant.

'Do you concede?' he called.

Porus spoke no Greek, but Alexander's tone of voice said everything. He raised his arms. 'No!' he shouted.

There was a minute's shocked silence as his men digested this bit of news, then they seemed to draw their collective breath and plunged back into the fray.

It became a massacre. At a motion from Alexander, Craterus let loose his men and they swept in from the river, fresh, strong, yelling, and screeching. Their weapons were not yet dulled with blood and they flashed in the hard sun. They arrived at a full gallop and the shock of the collision was deafening. Their horses had the weight and the impetus of a freight train, and they ploughed twenty feet into the mass of foot soldiers. There were men flying through the air. The sound was dreadful, like an avalanche. The soldiers started to scream again.

I cried out in anguish at the sight and covered my face

with my hands but didn't dare look away. Alexander was out there, his sword lifting and falling, his face a terrible mask of fury and exhaustion. Porus's army turned and fled. As soon as a space opened for them they scattered. Only Porus still fought on standing on his howdah. His elephant was covered with thick leather armour and his drivers had huge shields.

Then an arrow struck Porus's shoulder and I saw him fall to his knees. Surely he must give up now? Taxiles thought the same thing as I, for he rode his horse towards his enemy and called up to him to surrender, but Porus, in a fit of rage, nearly ran over him with his elephant. Only Taxiles's horse's agility saved him.

Then Meroes, the other Indian rajah rode over and spoke urgently to him.

There was another lull in the battle. Craterus's men were like hunting dogs that have been called back. They turned reluctantly. Everyone else stood in place. Most were swaying, white-faced and drained from the battle. Shock was setting in and soon they would collapse.

Porus bade his elephant to kneel and he dismounted. I gasped. He was nearly seven feet tall, with a stern, beautifully sculpted face. He wore a blue and orange silk robe.

He took his armour off, no easy feat with an arrow still planted in his shoulder. Then he let it drop onto the blood-soaked ground.

Alexander rode up on Bucephalus. The great horse walked stiffly. His sides heaved like bellows and he was covered in white foam and sweat. He had galloped nearly fifty miles in one night. He'd swum a river and had been in a battle that had lasted a full eight hours.

Alexander dismounted, letting the reins drop to the

ground. He walked over to Porus, and, as was his custom, knelt at the rajah's feet.

Porus stood motionless, looking over Alexander's head. Then he took a deep breath and looked down at the young king.

I couldn't see his face, he was too far away. But the set of his shoulders spoke of a grief that could never be assuaged. I didn't know then that he'd lost his eldest son in the battle.

Alexander got back to his feet and said something to Porus, who replied shortly. There were no translators around, but I could imagine Alexander saying in his fledgling Hindi, 'Hot curry day, tired to death, what want you?'

What he really said was, 'How shall I treat you?'

Porus replied, 'Like a king.'

Alexander smiled gravely. 'Ask what you wish, I will grant it to you.'

Porus answered, 'I have already asked for what I wish.'

'You will always be a king for me. Your kingdom is your own. And I will add to it all the lands that I have conquered on the far side of the river, so that never again will you have to face an enemy across these shores.'

Porus bowed low. He became one of Alexander's most fervent followers from that moment on. He motioned to his men to start counting the dead and took Alexander by the arm. They walked towards his elephant. Porus wanted to go to his palace to break the news to his wives and the rest of his family.

The dead amounted to about twenty thousand on Porus's side, including his son, and nearly a thousand on Alexander's side, including Bucephalus. For although the mighty warhorse had carried his master safely through the battle with never a foot placed wrong or a stumble, his great heart gave out as soon as the battle was over.

It was almost as if the horse had waited to make sure that Alexander was no longer on his back and no longer had any need of his services. He had stood still while Alexander spoke to Porus, and had watched, his ears pricked forward, as his master took the tall Indian's arm to help him over the slippery ground towards the waiting elephant. Then he'd turned his head – his heavy, great head, with his wise eyes and white mark shaped like a bull – towards the mountains. And, with one last look towards the west, towards the land where he was born, he sank slowly to the ground, rolled over, and died.

A cry went up from the watching soldiers, and Alexander spun around. His hand fell from the rajah's arm and he froze. Even from where I was, I could see his face contorting. Then he rushed towards his horse, throwing himself across Bucephalus's neck.

I scrambled down the scaffolding and dashed across the floating bridge, grabbing for handholds as the river tossed it about. I had to run across a muddy, blood-soaked battlefield. I leaped over bodies of men and horses, sliding and stumbling, my breath whistling in my tight throat. I knew I had to get to Alexander. He was so unrestrained. His joy and grief knew no bounds. This loss would devastate him.

I scrambled over the last twenty metres, calling Alexander's name. He sat cradling his horse's head in his lap, saying over and over, 'Buci, Buci, Buci …'

He looked up as I arrived. 'Ashley,' he said hoarsely. Then, 'Your nose is bleeding.'

'Don't worry about me.' I squatted down next to him. 'You were wonderful,' I said. 'Incredible. I watched the whole battle from the tower. Now I know why men will study this battle, sing songs about it, and write stories about it for thousands of years. It was amazing.'

'Do they really?' He smiled, but tears ran down his cheeks. 'Was it so great?' His voice was raw and broken.

'More than great,' I assured him. I looked down at his hands, wrapped in Bucephalus's mane. One of them was bleeding and swollen. 'If you want, I'll make you a bracelet with some of his hair.'

'I'd like that,' he said simply, and watched as I carefully plucked ten hairs from the horse's long mane. 'He was my horse,' he said softly.

'He was more than that!' I said. 'Why, if everyone had a horse like Bucephalus, they would be the luckiest of men.'

'As was I.'

'As you still are,' I said firmly, taking his face in my hands and kissing his mouth.

We sat for a moment, Alexander's hands twisting and twining in his horse's mane. Then he bent over and put his cheek on the great animal's neck. 'I'll miss you, old fellow,' he whispered. 'You and I, we travelled far together.' He got to his feet and took my arm, helping me up. 'Thank you for coming to me,' he said simply.

'What did you say to Porus?' I asked.

'I tried to say he'd be treated like a king. I think he understood me.'

I smiled. 'I'm sure he did. Let's go back to the tent now. You need to rest.' His legs were trembling violently, the shock of the battle was taking its toll. I flagged down a litter and made him get on it.

'I have to see my men,' he said. He was still crying.

'Let Perdiccas take over, he'll get everyone settled.

You have to learn to give over the reins. You'll kill yourself if you go on like this.' My voice was shaking. I was afraid he would ask for Plexis.

'Get Nearchus, tell him to …' His voice broke.

'Please, just lie down.' I motioned for the men to start walking back to the camp.

'I have to go with Porus,' he protested, but I held his shoulder.

'No. Let them prepare the funerals. They have so many dead.' My face twisted. 'You can't see from here, but Craterus slaughtered nearly all Porus's infantry.'

'What a waste,' he sighed.

My hand tightened on his arm. 'War is nothing but waste,' I said tiredly. 'But that never seems to stop it, does it?'

Chapter Fourteen

Alexander fell asleep on the litter. His face was so colourless I was frightened, but Usse told me he was unharmed except for a broken bone in his left hand.

They found Plexis on the battlefield. He wasn't dead, as I'd feared, but he was unconscious. He'd taken a blow to the head, his arm was broken, and Usse had to cauterize a nasty wound on his side. He lay for three days in a light coma.

Alexander was up and about the next morning, but I was strict. He wasn't leaving the tent without Usse's permission and he had to eat something. Roxanne sent messages every half hour, demanding to see Alexander. I sent back a message telling her to leave him alone for at least a week. That didn't please her, but she was powerless to do anything but complain.

Usse pronounced Alexander fit, so that afternoon we attended the funeral of Porus's son. The dead were cremated. The soldiers' remains were sent to their families. Porus's son was burned along with his young wife on a special pyre in the palace's courtyard.

I had heard about *suttee* from vague tales, but in my time, it was a custom that had died out so long ago that it had been forgotten. At first, I didn't notice the slender woman following the funeral cortège. She wore scarlet robes. Her unbound hair fell to her heels, which was what first caught my eye, and she looked lovely and terribly young, maybe fifteen or sixteen.

I was standing with the Greek dignitaries. Alexander was with Porus. His wives were in a separate section by themselves – he had twelve – and his other children were gathered around the pyre. Porus's son had been wrapped in white cotton, and flowers were strewn all over his body. His face was not covered, and I saw that the young man, who must have been only twenty, was as handsome as his father.

They laid his body on the tall pyre, and that's when the girl hitched up her skirts in one hand and clambered onto the wood. She settled herself cross-legged by her husband's head and took it on her lap. I frowned. Something didn't seem right. *The dry wood will burn so quickly, she'd better kiss him farewell and hurry away*, I thought. But no, the torch was carried nearer and nearer and she still didn't move.

I saw Alexander tilt his head, as if trying to understand, and then his face froze.

I knew his expressions so well. Horror, pity, and understanding fled across his face. Then his features hardened into a marble mask that let no feelings through.

Puzzled, I turned back to the funeral where the first flames started licking the wood. All around me the Greeks shifted their feet, muttering uneasily, but Alexander frowned at us. From across the fire we caught his stern gaze and we became silent and motionless.

Plexis was still in the tent, floating in a world between wakefulness and sleep. I wished I could be there. Reality was too sharp. Nothing blurred the edges of the flames or the screams.

The girl's hair burned first and she started to shriek as the pain hit her. There was simply no way to be prepared for such a thing. It must have been horrible. She stood up and tried to run, but her feet fell through the burning wood and her dress caught fire. She raised her hands to the sky, and her features seemed to melt like hot wax. I tried to scream, but my throat was too tight. She fell in slow motion, a flaming candle in a shower of sparks. It seemed to me that she screamed for an eternity.

My mouth was open, my limbs trembling. I backed into Nearchus, standing just behind me. He gripped my shoulders. I think that if he hadn't been there, I would have just kept backing up, backing up, until I got to the tent. My breath came in sharp gasps and my nose bled, blood dripping off my chin. I tried to staunch it, but my hands shook so much I couldn't control them. I stood, my hands waving frantically in front of my bloody face, until Alexander managed to leave his place and come to me.

He spoke sharply, but I couldn't understand him. I just gaped at him. I could hear him, but the sounds coming from his mouth made no sense. Then he slapped me.

It jolted me out of my shock. 'Please Ashley, get hold of yourself. The Indians believe that the couple will go directly to Paradise. Look, see the smoke? Their souls are rising towards the sky.'

He tried to turn my head back to the pyre but I wouldn't look. I screwed my eyes shut and whispered, 'Stop, just stop it!'

'Hush. I cannot.'

'It's barbaric,' I said brokenly. I tried to push him away, but my arms were about as strong as marshmallows at that point. I still shivered with shock. Even the sight of the battle hadn't shaken me so badly. Alexander clasped me until I could breathe. When he was sure I was better, he sent me back to the tent with Nearchus and Perdiccas. He stayed for all the ceremonies. He honoured the dead.

He mourned every soldier as if they were all his men.

I lay in my bed and sobbed, not even noticing when Plexis, groggy and unsure where he was, crawled into bed next to me and asked if the battle was over.

Chapter Fifteen

We spent two weeks with Porus. Alexander was busy with Nearchus, who had come into his own at last getting his navy ready. Alexander was planning to sail down the Indus.

First, Alexander had something to do. He designed a shrine for his horse Bucephalus and founded a city in the stallion's honour. The shrine was built on the flank of a steep hill overlooking the river where they had crossed at night. It was a small temple made of white marble; just a simple altar. A carving of Bucephalus was made in the stone. I'll always wonder who ended up with that treasure. I never saw it in a museum. It was a life-size fresco of a horse carved into a block of marble with no rider, or harness – just free. For nearly a week, Alexander cried bitterly every time he thought of his horse. Then he dried his tears, cut his hair short as a sign of mourning, and got to know his new horse, named Dolphin.

Near the banks of the river where we camped, he founded another city, calling it Nikaea – after Nike, goddess of victory. Bucephala, the city of the 'famous horse', became a small trading town, and the legend of Bucephalus became an Indian legend. The story was about a goddess who rode Bucephalus to earth and stayed to marry a king. I had always liked that legend. Now I knew where it came from.

It was now monsoon season: muggy, hot, torrid, rainy, humid ... I'm trying to find all the adjectives to describe what the next three months were like. We sweltered. The air felt as thick as water and the heat was oppressive. We wilted at nine in the morning, and when the sun went down there was still an hour of suffocating heat before the – relative – cool of evening set in.

All our leather goods got mouldy. The Greeks and Macedonians, coming from dry countries with nice climates, were astounded. The barbarians, huge, red-haired, and furry as bears, begged to go back to their mountain homes before they melted away.

Alexander took pity on his troops of mountain men, and he did send quite a few of them back. Pharnabazus couldn't stand the heat, but he was determined to remain by his brother-in-law's side.

We stayed in our camp two more weeks, then we moved inland, trying to find some shade. Porus had taken his family to the mountains where he usually spent the summer months. He left the palace for us if we pleased, but Alexander was shy about staying somewhere without his host. I could understand that. We wandered about the city, but we stayed at the camp with the soldiers. And Roxanne.

She was beginning to get on my nerves. She would simply not accept her role of fourth wife. Well, I suppose it sounds ridiculous, but I didn't like the girl. She was too sly, too cunning, and too much in love with Alexander's power to leave him alone. And most of all she wanted to do away with the competition, which is the real reason I didn't like her.

The competition being Chiron and me, of course. She still hadn't caught on to Plexis. Plexis who shared our tent

– although, believe me, it was so hot that nobody slept together. We stayed as far apart as possible. We lifted up the tent walls and slept with the night breeze cooling our bodies.

One night, someone slipped in the tent and tried to kill Chiron. He had been poorly, cranky with the heat and whining, so I had put him at the foot of my bed. He wasn't in his little hammock. We woke up when Axiom screamed. He had never screamed before. The sound catapulted Alexander out of bed, and he stood naked in the middle of the tent, his eyes wild, asking, 'What is it? What is it?'

Chiron started to wail, and I had to grab him before he rolled off the bed.

Axiom stared at Chiron. Then he stared into the hammock Chiron usually slept in. His eyes rolled up in his head and he dropped to the floor.

In Chiron's hammock was a small cobra.

I felt faint when I saw that. Alexander lifted the slithery reptile out of the hammock with the point of his sword then he tossed it in the air and sliced its head off with a quick slash.

Plexis, who could sleep through anything, sat up and blinked. He yawned, looked at the headless snake next to his pallet, and lay back down. Then he shot upright. 'What in Hades is that?' he yelled, scrambling to his feet.

'A cobra.' I clutched Chiron tighter. 'The tail doesn't sting, it's the fangs that have the poison.'

'I know that!' said Plexis. His broken arm was still in a sling and he moved it gingerly.

Axiom was sitting on the floor rubbing his face. 'When I woke up, I glanced in Chiron's hammock, as I do every morning. I saw a huge snail. I was shocked. I thought, 'what happened to Chiron?' and I poked the snail. It reared up and hissed at me. I swear, for a moment I thought that Chiron had been turned into a snake. I hate snakes,' he said in a shaking voice.

'I don't hate them, but it's best to watch out. These snakes are more deadly than the vipers you have in Greece. Their poison is a neurotoxin, I believe,' I went on, oblivious to the fact I was holding Chiron so tightly he was crying, and I was gibbering. 'When they bite, you have to rush to the hospital and get an anti-venom shot. They make those with horse's blood you know, it's really quite interesting …'

Alexander sat next to me and pried Chiron out of my grasp. He handed the screaming boy to Brazza, then he took me in his arms. 'Ashley, be quiet. It's all right. Chiron's fine and the snake is dead. Porus told me about such beasts. We will be careful. I have a surprise for you. Do you know what it is?'

I turned to face him, I still felt strangely cold despite the heat. 'What is it?'

'We're going to go towards the great sacred river in the east. It may be cooler there. I've heard tales of trees so large a whole army can shelter under one, and there are sages who will speak of the mysteries of the world. I've decided to leave half the army here and take the other half west. In three months, we will meet and sail down the Indus.'

'That sounds nice,' I said cautiously.

'I thought you would like the idea.'

'Well, I have an even better idea. Let's go home now.' I was staring at the serpent, my face stiff.

He looked at me in shock. 'You don't want to come with me?'

I glanced up at him. The tone of his voice made me flinch. 'I'm sorry. Of course I do. But can you promise me something?'

'It depends,' he said warily.

'Install Roxanne and her court in Porus's palace until we return. I think she's responsible for the snake in Chiron's bed.'

He started to say something, but thought the better of it. 'Fine,' he said shortly and left the tent. The sun was starting to rise. It was going to be a busy day.

We travelled through the summer's heat towards the heart of India. The men would have liked the voyage a great deal more if the weather had been clement, but the sky was a hot brass bowl cupped over our heads, and when the sun didn't shine it rained; waterfalls of water fell upon us. We all took off our clothes and went naked. That was the first thing that lifted our spirits. When the sun shone, we draped the light, brightly coloured Indian cottons over our heads, and I devised parasols for everyone.

It made the army look positively friendly. A bunch of naked men carrying red and pink parasols.

Feet were the next problem. Damp, sore, infected feet. We had to wear sandals all the time. The leather rotted quickly, so the sandal maker was the busiest man in the army during the march.

Snakes were not much trouble. The vibration the army made as it walked warned the serpents that we were coming, and they cleared the area. But the scouts were bitten often, and we lost nearly ten men to cobra bites. The horses were hot, but they didn't suffer from snake bites. However, any cut that wasn't immediately disinfected became a dangerous wound. Usse and his doctors made antiseptic every evening when we camped and supplied the whole army with salves and creams.

The ground was so wet that we slept in hammocks. It was nice, except when it rained. At first our hammocks filled up like bathtubs. Then we traded our cloth hammocks for the open-weave kind. We all slept better after that.

We managed to stay more or less healthy, but there were cases of malaria that the doctors treated with fever nuts and a drink made from ginger, cinnamon and grapefruit.

The land was rich and we didn't suffer from hunger, but food spoiled so quickly that we had to be very careful. We lost a few soldiers to food poisoning.

We crossed four rivers, endless plains, skirted the mountains, and arrived in front of the mighty Beas River after four weeks' march.

Chapter Sixteen

We were exhausted. The heat and the humidity were unrelenting. Mosquitoes buzzed everywhere, and I was as cranky as Chiron. He was seven months old. He sat up by himself, and I'd invented a sort of saddle with a little roof over it so he could ride and still be in the shade. However, I'd nearly run out of mosquito cream and Usse couldn't find any more citronella. The mosquitoes drove us crazy. They were dreadful.

We sat on the banks of the Beas River and we stared at the churning, muddy expanse of water with the flat plains stretching after it. Flat as far as the eye could see. It wasn't even a particularly pretty place, and we all decided, 'This is it. We're not moving another inch.'

All of us except Alexander, of course.

It was like being with a huge, hyperactive, unnaturally healthy five-year-old. He was full of energy. The heat, the mosquitoes, the dysentery – none of this got to him.

He darted into a huge clump of reeds and speared a three metre cobra, pulling it out by the tail. He decided it wasn't quite dead when it suddenly twisted around and tried to strike at him. He danced backwards with a pleased laugh and teased the monster before dispatching it with a careless chop, hardly even looking at it.

We all looked at him. I could hear the other men's thoughts. They went along these lines: *'It's all fine for him. His father was a god, his ancestors were immortal.'*

'Look at that fool, nothing can kill him. If the snake bit him the snake would probably be the one to suffer the most.'
'Look at us, covered with mosquito welts, bleeding from the arse, our feet a mass of soggy blisters, and our hair growing mould. Even the lice in our hair have mould on them. And look at that guy! Can't he sit down and relax?'
'What's he doing now?' 'Shit! Is there another snake in that bush?!'

The men around me all jumped backwards as the female cobra shot out of the tall grass. Alexander had somehow found the nest. There was a moment's mass hysteria as everyone panicked and tried to climb into everyone else's arms. Including the horses. Then Alexander, crowing loudly, leaned over and grabbed the snake. Cracking it like a bullwhip he snapped the head right off, making it sail ten metres in the air to land with a 'plop' in the river.

'There are eggs here too!' he cried happily.

We looked at each other. It was time for someone to say something, but nobody knew quite what, or how. Most of the men looked at me, hopefully, but I just smiled wryly. No way. I had to live with the guy. I wasn't going to be the one to announce the mutiny.

It was Coenus who stood up and accepted the burden. I reached over and squeezed his hand affectionately. He looked down at me and his mouth quirked. He cleared his throat.

Alexander wiped his hands on his thighs and turned to us, smiling. The smile slid across his face like oil though, he knew us too well.

'What is it?' he asked, frowning.

'My king,' began Coenus, then stopped. He drew a deep breath and started again. 'Iskander. I speak on the behalf of the army, on behalf of the soldiers, and on behalf of your lady wif …' He stopped when I jabbed his leg.

'Not me,' I whispered.

'On behalf of the rank and file,' he continued, rubbing his leg. 'We have succeeded beyond our wildest dreams. You have recaptured the crown of Persia, which is yours by right, and we have reached the very heart of Indus. Now it is time to return, my king. We would go back and see our families. We are tired, our bodies and spirits are broken and wounded. We cannot go on. Please, sire, the sign of a great leader is knowing when his men want to stop.'

There was silence after his speech. Some men were weeping, though. They saw in Alexander's face his desolation and bitter disappointment, and they felt his heartbreak as strongly as their own fatigue.

'I'm sorry,' whispered Coenus.

Alexander looked down at his feet. Two bright patches appeared in his cheeks. He blinked hard, biting his lips. The face of a thwarted child. However, he raised his head and faced them. The child tried to take over, but the king held on. 'Very well,' he said. 'I agree. We will return.' He stopped and drew a deep breath. 'But I will go on.'

There was a shocked murmur, and he held up both hands. 'No, listen to me. I will go on to the sacred river. It is a ten-day march from here. While I am gone I want you to construct twelve altars to the twelve great gods of Olympus. Make them of grass and green wood, and when I return in twenty-four days' time we will burn them and sacrifice to the gods.'

There was a furious cheering from the soldiers. Now everyone was weeping. The adventure was over, we were going home.

Coenus, Plexis, and I accompanied Alexander to the river Ganges. Riding with us, were Usse, twenty cavalry, thirty Indian guides, two translators, and Chiron, of course.

The trip was actually easier. After crossing the Beas River the land sloped gently upwards. We were heading towards the mightiest river in India and the fabled city of Patna, a city that rivalled even Babylon, the biggest city the ancient Greeks could imagine.

The weather seemed to favour us, sending light rain but no deluges, and clouds kept the heat bearable.

We marched as quickly as our horses would take us, and in ten days we came within sight of the holiest of rivers, the sacred Ganges.

Our Indian guides and translators prostrated themselves when they saw it. They remained kneeling for an hour, moaning and chanting while we stared, quite awed by their fervour. Then we trotted down the rocky road leading to the river bank, where we were met by the great rajah of India himself, the Rajah of the Ganges.

He had heard of Alexander's coming and knew we were unarmed. Therefore he met us simply, with only one thousand of his three thousand elephants and only fifty thousand of his hundred thousand cavalry.

And only thirty of his one hundred wives. Next to him, Porus was a monk.

Alexander's spirits lifted. We spent three days being fêted in a magnificent palace on the banks of the sacred river. Every night there was a feast. There was music and dancing all day and all night, and the king asked Alexander to accept humble presents such as fifty horses, a new tent, a white elephant, and at least a ton of silks and cottons for his wives.

Alexander stared in fascination at the bevy of beautiful women surrounding the king. 'I have but one real wife,' he said, 'my lady Ashley. Although I do have two other wives I married for politics. Did you do the same?' he asked.

The rajah laughed, a rich sound that came out of his thick torso. He was a very large man, his skin was shiny brown, his black hair hidden beneath a light blue silk turban. 'No, I married my wives because they were the flowers of my kingdom, the most beautiful women in the world. If you wish I will offer you an Indian woman to take as a wife.'

Alexander looked at me hopefully. I mouthed 'No!' silently but very definitely.

'I'm sorry, but I must decline,' he said with a trace of mischief in his eyes. 'I think your women are far too beautiful for me. If I took one back my whole army would insist on getting Indian wives as well.'

'I understand completely,' said the rajah.

'Of course, if you had fifty thousand such flowers you wanted to give away, well, then I really couldn't refuse.'

The translator wiped away the sweat from his brow as he said this, but the rajah had cottoned on to Alexander's humour and smiled broadly. 'I will give the order directly! Tomorrow fifty thousand beautiful women will be at the gates of the city, waiting to accompany you.'

Alexander scratched his head. 'Well, I couldn't possibly make such delicate flowers march. You'll have to throw in fifty thousand elephants.'

'Elephants?' the rajah's eyebrows lifted. 'Why not horses?'

'If there's anything I know about beautiful women, your Highness, it's that they never travel without at least a ton of clothing, jewellery, make-up, maids, and sometimes their own mothers.'

'True, so true.' The rajah sighed. 'I have to withdraw my offer then, with great regret.'

'*Your* biggest regret is not getting the elephants,' I muttered to Alexander.

He winked at me.

'Are you happy?' he asked, as we lay in each other's arms. The palace was cool. Our room overlooked the river Ganges, and I was entranced by the scene unfolding before me every morning.

Ochre steps led down to the river's edge. As the sun rose it touched the stone, turning it to molten gold. A trumpet would blow in the temple next to the river, and sixty or seventy trumpets would answer from the depths of the city. Flocks of white birds would flap into the air seemingly cast aloft on the notes of the music.

The people of the city awoke and went to the stairs to make their ablutions in the flowing water. Hip deep, they stood in the river and washed their bodies and hair. The children sat on the steps as their mothers poured the water over their heads, scrubbing them clean. The women washed their long, black hair then braided it tightly to dry in waves. Afterwards, everyone bowed towards the river before throwing a bouquet of flowers or handful of rice into the waters.

The city was built along the river banks. The buildings were painted bright colours; cotton and silk awnings glowed. Small boats plied the water. There were fishermen, traders, and even ferryboats to take people back and forth. The little boats had yellow or red triangular sails. The boats were painted bright colours, and the fishermen threw nets into the water to catch silver fish.

Special stairs had been built for elephants. The great beasts would lumber down them, swim across the river, then climb out on the other side. The elephants were decorated as richly as the women. Jewellery hung from their foreheads, they were painted bright colours, and they had gold rings on their tusks. Even their ears were pierced and hung with jewellery or garlands. Their drivers were proud men, who often had their sons on their laps as they rode the great beasts. Many of the drivers had carefully trimmed moustaches and goatees. They wore tight jackets made of bright silks, and their sons wore identical costumes.

Flowers grew everywhere. They climbed on vines into the palace itself and bloomed under spreading trees in the markets and in the streets. They clambered onto roofs, down terraces, spilled into the windows and were trained over doorways in an opulent, fragrant profusion of blossoms. Everywhere was colour and perfume. The marketplace reeked of curry and saffron, cardamom and cinnamon. Metres and metres of marigolds strung in bright orange ropes decorated everything. There were birds in cages singing sweetly.

Alexander and I sat in the marketplace on the wall of a marble fountain and watched in wide-eyed wonder as a caravan came to deposit its goods in front of us. The caravan came from the mountains of Kashmir. We examined the fine wool – as soft as cobwebs and warm as embers. Alexander offered me a delicately woven shawl of the precious stuff. Then he bought me two sapphires, as blue as my eyes. He had them set in earrings for me. The trader showed us strings of amber, amethyst, jade, and even some rubies.

Alexander decided to bring back a ruby for Roxanne,

and he had it set in a bracelet for her. Then he bought some of the cashmere cloth for Stateira, the wife he'd left in Babylon. He'd send it back by post. It would reach her in roughly a year and a half. Surface mail. Special delivery.

As in most cities, a man standing on a raised platform shouted out the daily news. He would chant the going prices for staple goods first then move on to the more interesting news and gossip. Most newscasts followed the same pattern. Our translator obligingly translated the morning news, adopting the nasal, singsong voice of the 'news-caller'.

'Grains stable, cotton prices the same as yesterday's, no change for goat milk either. Silver is up two points, gold up four. Good clay jars are fetching nine rupees in the market. Butter and oil have gone down, five points each. Hair ribbons are on sale over by the fountain, and there's a special on parrots. Let's see, a caravan from Kashmir has just arrived. Hurry before all the goods are gone. Tonight there's to be a show at the open air theatre, the story of the Vishnu avatar.'

'The what?' I interrupted.

Alexander frowned at me. 'Avatar, it means a divinity taking a human form.'

The man calling the news looked down at me to make sure I wouldn't interrupt again, and then he cleared his throat. 'Our illustrious visitor Sikander, the western king, has consented to stay another night. Anyone seeking opportunity in the west should contact his generals. There was a flood three weeks ago near Benares, the price of silk is expected to rise as high as the waters.' He finished, took a deep breath, and then started all over again.

Alexander tossed him a coin and we strolled away.

155

'Anyone seeking opportunity in the west?' I asked, raising an eyebrow.

'As my father always said to me,' he answered seriously 'go west, young man.'

'So you went east?'

'I was a contrary kid. When I get back we'll go to Africa, and then I'll go west. I've heard tell of a country called Gaul where they use cheese as weapons.'

We travelled back to the army waiting by the river Beas. They had taken Alexander's altar suggestion very seriously, building huge towers of wood and grass, but they'd set them on blocks of square-cut stone. Each one was carved with the name of a god. On the one dedicated to Demeter I found my portrait, carved into the stone, staring back at me. Very spooky.

'Do you think your mother will appreciate that?' the artist asked me nervously.

'I think so,' I answered cautiously. I wasn't sure, actually, what my mother would think. If she ever did see the likeness it would be three thousand years in the future. Besides, she probably wouldn't recognize me even if she did see it. She hardly looked at me except to say 'Ashley, stop slouching. Stop sulking. Honestly, no one will ever want to marry you.'

Her only goal in life had been to marry me off to someone and be free to turn her attention back to her orchids. I was never allowed into her greenhouse, so I have no idea if her flowers were beautiful. She was afraid I'd lose my head completely and tear them to shreds, I suppose. The idea had, on occasion, occurred to me.

I *had* been married. She'd arranged it, and I'd gone along, being only sixteen, inexperienced, and docile. My husband had been a sadistic bastard, only interested in my money and my looks, showing me off during endless dinner parties as his trophy wife, and taking advantage of my submissiveness to beat me senseless nearly every night. He was careful not to bruise my face. After six months, I found the courage to crawl out of the window and escape. It was the bravest thing I'd ever done. After following orders for sixteen years, I'd done something on my own. And then I'd decided to go to Tempus University and major in time-travelling journalism.

I stared at the face carved in the stone and tried not to notice the look the artist had put in the eyes. A cold, implacable stare gazed back at me. As unfeeling as an Ice Queen, the name I'd been afflicted with in college. I'd liked college. The feeling wasn't mutual. From the boys I snubbed, to the girls I was afraid to talk to, to the teachers who were jealous of my money, to the dean who hated my title – everyone waited with bated breath for me to fail or show some weakness.

My only weakness was my stupid nose. If I refused to let my feelings show my nose had no such qualms. As I stared at the portrait, blood ran down my chin and dripped to the ground.

The artist was so pleased he cried. The ancient Greeks thought my nosebleeds were a blessing from the gods.

Chapter Seventeen

The altars were ready. Alexander had prepared a great speech, but when the time came he was so moved that all he could say was, 'It's been wonderful.'

Well, not exactly, but that was the spirit. Then he torched the altars, and we roasted a few cows and had a huge barbecue on the banks of the river. The full moon was bright yellow. I was sitting on a woven grass mat next to Plexis; he was uncharacteristically silent.

'What's the matter?' I asked him. 'Does your arm hurt?' It had healed quickly, but I knew it still ached sometimes.

He held Chiron on his lap. He handed the baby a bone to gnaw on and stared at him moodily. 'No, my arm is fine. I was thinking of what the oracle said.'

'Which one?'

'The one that said I would see the sacred river and the twelve altars, then die.'

'Oh, that one.' I was silent a moment, thinking. 'If it makes you feel any better, you look perfectly healthy,' I said cheerfully.

He stared at me, tears in his eyes. 'Don't you care?' he asked.

I kicked myself mentally. He was quite serious about this oracle thing. 'Of course I do!' I moved closer to him and put my arm around his shoulders. When I touched him I felt a shiver of delight. It had been so long since I'd made love to him, and his body reacted to mine like a magnet. His eyes became all pupil.

'Ashley,' he whispered.

I closed my eyes. I felt myself blushing. There was a throbbing between my legs and my chest felt tight.

I didn't hesitate. Life was short. I was well placed to know that. I took Chiron, put him in Usse's lap, and then took Plexis's hand. We left the circle of firelight, nervously, I admit, thinking of snakes. But the army had set up a real camp while we'd been gone, so I led Plexis to our tent.

The night was sultry, the air like hot silk on our bodies. I spread a cotton sheet on the grass next to the tent and pulled Plexis down beside me. He was trembling, urgent, and I let him take me a first time, quickly. Then, when his breathing had slowed, I made him take me again, and this time we really made love. This time we shared our bodies and our desires, slowly, heartbreakingly, tenderly.

I wrapped my legs around his hips and held him to me, feeling his orgasm calling mine, and I answered. I let myself go – let myself be swept along. Our bodies slid and glided together. Sweat gleamed in the starlight. His skin was dark, mine light. I arched against him and let my body drink its fill. Then we lay still, and I waited until my tremors stopped. I sighed deeply. Goose bumps rose on my arms. Plexis leaned over me and his lips brushed my nipples.

The yearning came back as sharply and poignantly as before. I moaned and opened my legs. His hands cupped my face as he soothed me. 'Shh, shhh,' he whispered.

Someone else knelt between my legs. Alexander. His eyes in the moonlight were fey. I met him halfway, and this time I didn't hold back. We grappled like wrestlers, gasping and twisting, striving to immobilize each other. He was stronger than I, but I was supple and had never been wounded in battle. I knew all his weaknesses, every torn muscle, and each broken bone. His body was still magnificent, but it had its foibles, and I had the hunger of a she-lion. Under the swollen moon, I felt as if there were fire beneath my skin, as if my blood were electricity.

He came, crying hoarsely in my ear. I felt his body jerking into mine, and I suddenly let all my muscles go loose, letting the storm take me as it would, giving myself to the yellow moon, to the hot air, to the monsoon clouds darkening the horizon.

Alexander lifted me and carried me into the tent. He laid me on the bed and we slept deeply until dawn. The heat didn't wake me for once. I slept the boneless sleep of fulfillment, a smile on my lips. Chiron woke me. I stood, stretched languorously, then looked at Alexander who cocked a satirical eyebrow at me.

'Sleep well?' he asked.

'Mmm, yes.' I grinned, then grimaced. 'Ow, did you bite my lip?'

He leered, 'And a lot of other things.'

Plexis rose and took Chiron from his hammock, holding him at arm's length. 'Is this smelly thing yours?' he asked me.

'I'm afraid so,' I took the baby. 'I'm off to the river to bathe. Who wants to come?'

Alexander came with me to the river. Dawn was breaking. The sky was shell-coloured, pale pink and coral along the horizon, darkening gradually to the west. There were still stars faintly visible where the heart of India lay, still sleeping.

Alexander and I waded into the river, and I stripped

Chiron. He was a water baby, splashing and gurgling happily when I lowered him into the cool water. The sun's rays found us and gilded our bodies. Alexander was rose and gold, his hair a bright crown. He stood next to me, the water swirling around his hips.

Chiron was hungry, and I held him to my breast and nursed him as I stood waist deep in the water, feeling the tug of my baby's mouth on my nipple, the tingle of warm milk, and the flow of the water moving around my legs. I tipped my head back, my face to the sun, my eyes closed. Birds sang. Wind rustled the tall grass. If paradise existed, I thought, it must be like this.

As Alexander and I watched, a tiger came to the edge of the river to drink. His coat blazed in the dawn. He was not more than fifty feet away from us, but I was unafraid. It was because of Alexander.

The tiger lifted its heavy head and saw us. Alexander, king of men, and the tiger, king of beasts, stared at each other. The tiger didn't blink. Alexander stood in front of me, his arms crossed on his chest, unmoving. They gazed at each other for a very long time. They almost seemed to be communicating, and perhaps they were. Was Alexander showing him the power he had, telling him silently about the men who followed him and the kingdoms he'd conquered? Was the tiger saying, *'Yes, but I am free, and you will always be a king in chains'*?

Whatever it was, they both seemed to feel it deeply. The tiger finally lowered his head, turned around, and disappeared into the tall grass as silently as he'd come. Alexander turned to me, tears running down his cheeks.

We sat on a high bank with a spectacular view of the rising sun and the river in front of us. Alexander was melancholy.

'What is it?' I asked. 'Please tell me.'

Moodily, he plucked a blade of grass. 'The earth is round? You said it was round. Can we go straight on until we get back home?'

'No, we can't. There's a big ocean that cuts the world in half. But, Alexander, listen to me. The distance we've walked is equal to halfway around the earth. If that ocean weren't there we could have kept on walking. I promise. I'm sorry.'

'So, now we turn around and head home, and when we get there, it will be as if I've walked all the way around the earth?' His voice was dreamy again. His sorrow lifted.

'That's right.'

'So in a way, I've succeeded.'

'You've succeeded in so many other, important ways,' I whispered.

'This was important to me,' he said.

He would never know how much he'd accomplished. I couldn't let him die without knowing what he'd done. 'And the kingdom? Bringing east together with the west? Opening new trade routes? Founding beautiful new cities? Bringing Hellenistic culture to the very gates of China? That's not important? All those people you've shifted, moved, and inspired – they will never be the same. The world will never be the same, all because of you. What you've done is change the world,' I said. 'Do you know how amazing that is? Only incredible people with fantastic dreams can do that.'

'I'm incredible?' His voice held a note of interest in it now. He loved flattery.

'Incredible, amazing, fantastic, Alexander the Great. And I love you.' I took his face in my hands and drew him towards me. 'And you kiss better than anyone I've ever known.'

Now he was really smiling. 'I think I'd like that on my epitaph; "He was incredible, and an amazing kisser."'

'Look at Chiron,' I said. The little boy had stopped nursing and was sitting peacefully, his open mouth still on my nipple, his eyes dreamy.

'A wise man,' Alexander approved. Then he tipped his head to the sky. 'Please, Zeus, let this one live. I long to grow old with my children beside me.' He smiled self-consciously. 'I made a wish. Did you hear? Hush, I see by your face you want to speak, but say nothing, just put your head on my chest, and let me hold both of you. Behind us there is sorrow, before us is pain. But right now, here on the banks of the river, there is nothing but peace.'

Chapter Eighteen

In late September we arrived back in Porus's kingdom. He had returned from his mountain retreat. For the next two months there were endless dinner parties given by Alexander, Porus, and even Taxiles, in vain attempts to outdo each other. There were sports, games, festivals, and the Greeks sacrificed willy-nilly, as October, the month with the most religious ceremonies, got under way. We used up so many cows that the herds dwindled alarmingly.

It was about this time that an Indian holy man joined our camp.

I say 'about this time', because nobody was quite sure when he'd arrived. Some said he'd followed us from the Ganges, others said he was from a place near Taxila, and that he'd been around for a while, observing us. Whatever it was, one day I woke up, and there was another person sleeping in our tent.

It took me a few days to get used to him.

His name was Kalanos, and he was sweet, holy, very spiritual, and unworldly. That still didn't mean I liked it when he poked his head through the curtains one night as Alexander and I made love.

He said he wanted to see how the king made his children.

I opened and shut my mouth like a fish. Alexander tilted his head to the side, and Plexis, who was – thank goodness – over in his own pallet, whooped with laughter.

Alexander, who hadn't moved from his position between my legs, stared at the wide, innocent eyes of Kalanos and said, 'I do it the same way as any other man.'

'Well, that's a relief,' said Kalanos, and closed the curtains.

Plexis chuckled all night long, ruining my sleep.

Kalanos was full of wise sayings and maxims, which endeared him to the Greeks. They were always looking for a cliché. I hoped that he would get to meet Aristotle. Alexander spent hours with Kalanos discussing philosophy and science. Kalanos was interested in the scientific theories that Aristotle had started to talk about, like: 'The earth is round,' and, 'The planets and the sun all revolve around the earth, they are not static in the heavens'.

For the people of that time, the earth was the centre of the universe. Well, why not? I wasn't about to correct them. I loved to sit in on these talk sessions. Kalanos, with his garbled Greek, and Alexander, who hashed his Hindi, adored philosophical discussions. They were also good listeners, which is a rare thing in a talkative person.

I was a listener. I would sit in front of Alexander, his arms around me, and my face to the firelight, listening as the men spoke of the wondrous things they'd seen in India: banyan trees with their spreading branches, suttee, the men who never cut their hair or fingernails, – this really intrigued everyone – strange animals, elephants, – still a big thrill – the white elephant that Alexander had brought back from the Ganges, snakes, and the sacred river.

Everything was described in great detail. Kalanos would explain what he could, and the scribes and botanists would carefully transcribe everything.

There was a whole tent dedicated to these journals.

Everything that happened, that was said, that was seen, got written down. Scientists, doctors, botanists, and journalists followed the army and collected information. Alexander insisted on having everything written in triplicate and kept in three different tents. He was right to do so, because the only light at the time came from oil lamps, and parchment has a tendency to burn quickly.

Moreover, Alexander was already amassing material for his precious new library in Alexandria. He wanted Babylon to be the seat of his new government, but he wanted Alexandria to become a beacon of learning and knowledge throughout the world.

To the Indians, he gave detailed instructions to reach his cities, so that they could trade and share their learning.

We had only been back a few weeks when Coenus, Alexander's general and good friend, fell ill. He had malaria and dysentery. Usse nursed him. At first we thought he'd be all right; almost everyone came down with fever and chills, the symptoms of malaria. The fever nuts that we took every day, boiled as tea, helped.

Coenus, however, grew worse, and we moved him into our tent. Alexander slept by his side, holding his hand, wiping his brow with cool water, and begging him to get well. Usse watched him day and night, giving him doses of willow bark tea. We all prayed, and several goats and cows were sacrificed by various priests. In spite of all that, he died suddenly at dawn. His heart simply gave out. He wasn't young any more and, like most of us, was worn down.

It was a terrible blow to Alexander. He had not lost any of his generals in his battles, and his childhood friend had died from sickness and fatigue. He felt guilty. He kept saying, 'If only I'd turned back before! But for the sake of a few days, I've lost my friend.'

Onesicrite, our execrable 'sex-and-scandal' journalist got hold of this titbit and changed it, hinting that Coenus had been poisoned.

Plexis sought him out and broke his nose. I don't know how Plexis saw Onesicrite's journal; he wouldn't even show it to Alexander. But Plexis had spies everywhere. He was one of those people who could blend in. He could hang out with any crowd and be 'one of the guys'. Everyone liked Plexis, and Plexis got along with everyone, except Onesicrite. The broken nose was the second time Plexis had attacked the insufferable journalist.

Usse smiled as he bandaged Plexis's knuckles. He didn't care for Onesicrite either.

Alexander built a huge tomb for Coenus, and we sacrificed more cows. There was a week of mourning.

It was well into November when Roxanne's son took ill. It was soon after Coenus's funeral, and Alexander didn't pay much heed. It must be said that the little boy was sickly. A poor diet when he was small, neglect, and the hot, humid climate all combined to make the baby ill. Usse went to see him regularly, so we weren't worried. We were worried, though, when we were woken up one morning by banshee wails.

Roxanne came to our tent – something she'd never done – screeching and tearing at her hair. 'Your son is dead!' she screamed at Alexander. He got out of bed and threw a robe over his shoulders. She followed him, sobbing, as he rushed to her tent.

I ran behind them, calling to Usse to come quickly.

When I saw the baby, I gave a cry of horror. He had

died of asphyxiation. His little face was blue, his tongue stuck straight out. I clapped my hands to my mouth, my nose started bleeding.

Usse came in and stopped when he saw the babe. His face darkened and he looked from Roxanne to her maids, standing in a row and wailing.

'Where is the babe's nurse?' he asked.

Roxanne pointed to a corner of the tent, and I leaned over to look. A woman's feet were visible, sticking out from underneath a muslin sheet.

'What happened?' asked Alexander. His breathing was strained. I saw Usse frown as he looked at him.

'She let the babe die,' said Roxanne. For someone who had just been wailing and crying, she sounded remarkably cool.

'She's dead?' My voice rose to a squeak.

'Well of course! The stupid bitch killed my baby!' Roxanne stamped her foot. I turned green. I felt physically sick. In a moment I would vomit. I staggered out of the tent and threw up on one of the maid's monkeys chained to the tent post. He didn't seem to mind. Plainly, the poor creature hadn't eaten in days.

I gagged and rushed to my tent. Behind me, I could hear Roxanne's cries. 'Don't leave me!' she shouted.

Plexis saw me coming, but I just grabbed my bathing things and rushed out again. He would have followed me, but there was nobody else in the tent, and I didn't want to leave Chiron alone.

'Watch the baby!' I cried, and fled to the bathhouse.

I took a hot bath, had a good cry, brushed my teeth, washed my hair, and tried to scrub away the memory of that poor little boy, so obviously smothered in his crib.

Chapter Nineteen

Alexander told me, after the baby had been buried and the religious rites performed, that he would never touch Roxanne again.

We were lying in each other's arms. The sweat on our bodies had dried. I was feeling languorous after a nice round in the sack. I opened one eye to see if he spoke seriously or if it were just a reaction after our lovemaking.

'Too tired?' I joked.

'No, I mean it. I will never touch her again.'

'Don't say that,' I begged. 'The history books say you had a son by Roxanne, one that lived.' I nearly said lived longer, but I bit off the word.

'I don't care.' His voice was flat. I'd rarely seen him so angry. 'She said the child was cursed. She said he was deaf.'

'That's not a curse!' I said.

'No, but it was a good enough excuse for her.'

'Did she kill her own child?' I asked, shuddering.

'Usse thinks so, but he says the babe wouldn't have lived long anyway. He was too frail.'

'And whose fault was that?' I snarled.

'She's a witch,' said Alexander. 'And I will not go near her again. I'm dividing us into three parts. Plexis will take the cavalry and the elephants and stay on the eastern side of the river, Craterus will take the western side, and Nearchus will navigate in the middle on his boats. I will go with Plexis. You will stay with Nearchus, and Roxanne will be with Craterus. There will be less danger on the river,' he said, hushing my protests. 'Porus says that the tribes living to the south are barbaric and most are hostile to my crossing their territories. We may have to fight and I don't want to have to worry about you and Chiron.'

I smiled through my tears, kissing him. 'And I can't worry about you?'

'Why should you? You know when I'm going to die.' He said it simply but it was like a knife in my chest. I couldn't breathe for a moment.

'I will never tell you that,' I said. 'Even if you are on your deathbed I will lie and say you're going to get better. It's unnatural to know the hour of one's death. And who knows, after two thousand years, there's a good chance that the history books are wrong.' I tried to speak as lightly as he did, but the pain was nearly unbearable. Luckily it was dark, and my face was in shadow.

He kissed me. 'Oh, Ashley, don't be sad. The time we've had together has been the most magnificent time in my life. Even if I die tomorrow, I will die happy.'

'Ha,' I snorted, 'you say that now. But if I told you that you were going to die tomorrow, believe me, you would not be happy.'

'You don't know me very well, do you?' he asked softly. He wrapped his arms around me and rolled over on top of me. 'I'm Uranus and you're Gaia, we're the sky and the earth.' He moved slightly, just enough for me to feel his intent. With a smile I spread my legs and welcomed him. 'Now I can die happy,' he said with a groan.

'I wish you would just die quiet.' It was Plexis. He lifted his head and stared at us. 'Can't a person get any sleep around here?' He peered closer. 'Didn't you just get

170

through doing that?' he asked.

Alexander kept moving. 'If you don't be quiet I'm going to ask *you* to go sleep with Roxanne. That way …' – he broke off and moaned, then continued, '… that way I don't have to bother.'

I gave a shocked laugh. 'I will admit the idea seems like a good one. Except, not Plexis,' I gasped, arching my back.

'Shhh,' he said.

I wrapped my arms around Alexander. Urgency grew in my belly. Plexis sighed deeply and drew the curtains closed, but we didn't notice. All I could feel was Alexander moving steadily within me; all I could hear was my own harsh breathing. The air around us started to tremble. Bright colours danced in my head as I felt my hips rise to meet Alexander's hard thrusts. There was an instant where everything froze and then, like a house of cards tumbling down, our bodies shattered together. We held each other to keep from being swept away. It would always be like this. We would always need to reassure each other with words, caresses, and with our bodies. Together we were invincible.

Afterwards Alexander ran his hands down my body, calming my tremors.

'So cool and fine,' he whispered. 'I feel as if I've quenched my thirst at an enchanted fountain.'

'That's a sweet thing to say,' I said, smiling in the darkness.

'You make me feel sweet.' He took my chin in his hands and kissed me deeply. His mouth was soft, mine was bruised. My head felt too heavy for my neck. I fell asleep before he finished kissing me.

The forces split into three parts; the navy sailing on the river, and the two others following along on either side. They would try to stay within sight, although because of the terrain, it might not always be possible.

From the deck of Nearchus's boat, I could see Alexander's column on my left, and on my right, Craterus's half of the army. I could see Alexander's half better because he had the elephants with him. Their heads were visible above the tall grass and reeds.

Alexander wanted to go thirty kilometres a day. That meant the scouts had to work hard. They had to make sure that the encampment would be defensible and that there were no hostile tribes massing against us.

At first, the trip was like a huge holiday river cruise. The tribes near Porus had learned of his defeat and of Alexander's mighty army, so they came to greet us with gifts and promises of allegiance. Alexander was in high spirits, his men were euphoric, and we were heading home.

Nearchus had more than fifteen hundred boats under his command. The Phoenician and Egyptians had fashioned them from reeds and wood, and some of them were rigged like the boats that navigated the Nile and Indus three thousand years in the future. The sails were linen or cotton, and most were dyed bright colours.

The boats had oars and rowers, and I had fun teaching them to sing the famous, 'Row, row, row your boat gently down the stream'. The men sang phonetically, in English. They were positive they were singing the god's blessings in a sacred language, and I'll admit to a few theological qualms when I saw the fervour with which the men applied themselves to the song.

To make up for it, I taught them to sing it as a round,

and the river echoed with the music all morning. We were glad Alexander was too far away to be heard, but I think he sang once, because the elephants started to stampede.

Some boats transported grain and there were boats for the livestock; the army's food supplies now travelled mainly by water. I slept on the boat. Alexander wouldn't let Chiron and me go ashore. He was too nervous about enemies. He knew the danger would come from the east, and he was right. Two weeks after we set out, we were attacked during the night.

The army was always ready for an assault, so everyone knew exactly what to do. I would stay in the boat, huddled with Brazza and Axiom, until the battle ended. If anything happened to Alexander, Nearchus was to set me ashore where Craterus had orders to take me and Chiron directly to Nysa.

The battle was brief, just a skirmish. The enemy had been testing the army. The next morning Alexander called a meeting, and he decided to strike back. He reasoned that if he did nothing, he'd be harassed all the way down the river. Plus he was mad. One of the elephants had been killed.

The cavalry and the infantry were gone all day. Nearchus paced on the deck. I was too nervous to pace. The weather was getting cool, the river had shrunk and the banks were high on either side of us. Nearchus didn't like to be hemmed in, and he always tried to find the largest part of the river so that he could manoeuvre. Downstream was the boat-bridge, which was set up every time we stopped. That way, the whole army could cross from one side of the river to the other in a matter of hours.

The siege towers were erected as well; there were four, two on each side of the river being used for observation. A small catapult was on top of each tower for breaking into cities with high walls. Very useful. Everyone should have at least one. I decided to climb a tower to see what was going on, but Nearchus, who was at best a stuffy person, said 'no', I had to stay on board. Alexander had told him to watch me, and he wasn't going to let me out of his sight. I smiled sweetly and told him I was going to lie on the deck and sunbathe.

He didn't say anything. He was not a talkative fellow, except when he started talking about boats, and then you couldn't get him to shut up. I propped my chin on my hands and watched him as he moved around the boat. I was waiting for my chance to escape. I'd decided to go climb a lookout tower.

The day dragged by. Chiron woke from his nap, and I sat him in his bouncy sling-seat in the shade and played pat-a-cake with him. He was easily bored, but pat-a-cake games would keep him entertained for hours if I changed the songs and the rhythms often enough, and if I made enough funny faces at him. He adored funny faces. He would imitate me perfectly, like a little clown. He was starting to crawl. He had started like most babies, getting up on his hands and knees and rocking back and forth until he got the courage to move his hands. Now he would crawl all over the deck if I let him.

I kept him tied to the mast. He could crawl five feet in any direction, but he couldn't leave the shade of the awning. I also had the toys Plexis made for him. Alexander wasn't particularly deft, but Plexis could carve birds and alligators from pieces of wood, and he made them articulated, so that the alligator would seem to walk and wag its tail, and the bird hopped and flapped wings with real feathers in them.

Chiron pulled the feathers out, but they were made to

pop out. I would just poke them back in the holes. Chiron watched me and then tried to do it himself, his little face screwed up in concentration. Other toys included nesting baskets, balls, beads on string, a puppet, a rattle, and a doll made of cloth. The doll had no face, no hair, no arms nor legs, but Chiron clutched it tightly every night when he went to sleep, and if he misplaced it he would wail. Kalanos had made it for him.

The old man was also on the boat with me. He squatted in the shade next to Chiron and spoke to him seriously in Hindi. I asked him what he was saying, and the holy man said he was telling Chiron all about his own childhood, and that Chiron understood perfectly and would remember everything he said when he was old enough to talk.

I was doubtful. It didn't seem to me that he understood anything, but he did love to watch Kalanos's beard as he talked. It waggled back and forth, and Chiron seemed quite hypnotized.

When evening came, I found a moment to escape, leaping lightly from boat to boat until I got to the bridge, then I walked across to the shore and climbed up a tower.

The sentry made room for me by his side, and I gazed out over the plains. There was no sign of the battle. The village was further inland. I soon got bored and turned towards Craterus's side of the river.

Roxanne's court looked like a three-ring circus. The tents were gaudy with bright colours, flags flapped gaily in the breeze. Dogs, parrots, and monkeys were tied to every available post. The women dressed in the robes Alexander had brought back for them from Patna, so they were brilliant in orange, scarlet, and saffron yellow. Roxanne had been sulking since we left Taxiles's kingdom. The death of her baby might have something to do with her mood, but I doubted it. I was sure she was angry because Alexander had told her, in no uncertain terms, that the marriage was over. He'd asked her to return to her own people, but she'd refused. She still thought she could win him over.

I could see her walking around her tent. She was leading a white dog by a string, trying to teach it to follow her. I thought she might have better luck if she would stop turning around to kick it each time it pulled backwards.

Her face was frozen in its usual thin scowl. She had recently adopted the Persian-style dress, but she slit the long skirt up to the thigh and tied it with a wide sash at the waist. She hadn't yet taken to covering her breasts. She must have sensed my thoughts or felt my gaze, because she raised her head and spotted me. She had an uncanny stare. Her eyes were very pale, like green glass. She saw me in the tower and frowned. Perhaps she thought I was spying on her. I gave her a friendly wave. She turned to glance behind her, she thought I was waving to someone else. I let my hand fall and my face grew still. She stiffened when she realized I'd been waving at her. For a minute she didn't move. Then she straightened her shoulders and stared at me. She didn't make a gesture. Her look was a mute challenge filled with hatred – she'd seen my pity.

I climbed down the tower, my heart strangely heavy. I shouldn't have worried about her. She had been receiving mail from our mutual mother-in-law. Olympias wrote to her nearly every month. Alexander knew, of course. Perhaps he even read the letters. I don't know for sure. The two women had a busy correspondence: two witches giving each other advice on oracles and potions, and what to do to get rid of a rival.

176

Chapter Twenty

Alexander came back late that evening after subduing the enemy. The army rested for four days as we took care of the wounded, buried the dead, and made the appropriate sacrifices to the various divinities the soldiers worshipped.

Between the six or seven main pantheon of gods that the Egyptians, the Greeks, the Phoenicians, the Bactrians, the Sogdians, the Barbarians, and the Indians adored, we had quite a list to choose from. The priests were, on the whole, a nice group. They were willing to honour everyone else's beliefs just as long as their gods were honoured too. The gods were easy to please. They seemed to like being sung to, having things burned in their honour, and having altars built with their names carved all over them.

During the Greek ceremonies, I had a role to play as Demeter's daughter. The busiest time of year for me was midwinter, when I was supposed to bless the fields and ready them for the sowing. The funeral ceremonies were also for Hades – and for Hermes. Hermes, the gods' messenger, was in charge of leading the new souls towards the kingdom of the dead where Hades ruled.

Brave warriors were supposed to go to a beautiful field where they would spend eternity. I, Queen of the Dead, spent my time – supposedly – in a barren garden, treeless except for one, a pomegranate tree. Everything in the garden was frozen and glittery with precious jewels instead of flowers. That explained my white hair and frosty blue eyes. I had long ago stopped trying to convince people I was human. They didn't want to hear it. Making a job out of it made me feel better about impersonating a goddess. Part of my job was overseeing religious ceremonies. I put a lot of effort into memorising my lines and not giggling at critical moments. I also learned everything I could about my alter ego.

Persephone was Demeter's daughter, a young girl who loved walking in the fields and picking wild flowers. One day, while her mother was napping, she wandered away, and Hades, god of the dead, saw her and fell madly in love. He got into his chariot pulled by six black horses and burst out of the ground, snatching the unfortunate girl by the waist. He turned around and plunged underground and the earth closed behind him. No one saw but a swineherd, who was shocked to see all his pigs disappear down a deep crevice.

Demeter woke up and called for her daughter, but she was nowhere to be found. Frantic with worry, Demeter rushed about, looking everywhere. She asked the sun, but the clouds had covered him that day. She asked the wind, but he had been elsewhere. All the other gods joined the search, but nobody could find Persephone. She had vanished from the face of the earth. Nobody thought for one second to look underground in the cold, barren kingdom of Hades.

Then the swineherd told Demeter what he'd seen, and she immediately guessed what had happened. Furious, she stormed to Olympus and told Zeus that if he didn't fetch Persephone she would let the earth starve – as goddess of the harvest she could. When Zeus asked, Hades refused to free his new queen. Demeter mourned her daughter.

Winter came, the earth turned barren, the plants didn't grow, and Demeter crossed her arms and waited.

Hades finally relented and set Persephone free, but as she ran joyfully up towards the surface of the earth, a dry laugh stopped her. It was Hades' gardener. In his hand was a half-eaten pomegranate. Persephone had nibbled the seeds one day as she wandered sadly through the darkness. According to the rules of the gods, she had to stay with Hades, since she had tasted the food of the dead.

Zeus decided otherwise. She had only eaten six seeds, so she would spend six months a year with Hades. Ever since, winter comes, and the earth lies fallow for six months. After, she rejoins her mother, and Demeter's joy brings spring to the world.

My part in the funeral ceremony was brief. I begged my husband, Hades, to listen to me. The men we were sending him had been mighty warriors who deserved to live forever in the sunny meadow reserved for heroes.

Then I drank some wine and waved my arms gracefully, spoke a few words in English, and everyone was happy. Hades, they reasoned, was still in love with me and would listen to my pleas. The fact that Alexander had kidnapped me meant he would be punished once he was dead, but everyone knew Hades couldn't do anything to the living.

I drank the wine and bowed deeply. It was a hot day and the ceremonial wine was cool and fresh. I was about to drink more, when the wooden platform I stood on slewed sideways, spilling me, the wine, and the ten priests who were standing with me, onto the ground.

It wasn't a big fall, I landed on soft dirt, which saved me from any bruises. The platform had fallen because of soldiers leaning against it. Alexander rushed over shouting and moving everyone, making sure no one had been hurt. Everyone was laughing and shouting at the Egyptian engineer who had built the platform. The poor fellow knelt and banged his head on the ground until Alexander told him to stop.

He got to me last. I was already on my feet, and I was laughing at the silly monkey who'd latched onto the wineskin and was drinking from it, exactly like a little man.

Alexander sighed in annoyance and snatched the wineskin from the monkey. He held it upside down and two drops fell out. It was empty. The monkey looked up at us and hiccupped. Then he got to his feet and staggered around, his tail jerking up and down as he tried to find his balance. He sat down suddenly, a comic expression on his little face, then he keeled over. Dead drunk. We all burst out laughing.

Alexander nudged the monkey with his foot. The animal didn't budge. He didn't even blink his eyes. Odd. His eyes were wide open.

I stopped giggling as cold realization washed over me. Not dead drunk. Just dead. My knees gave away and I sat heavily on the ground.

Alexander looked at the monkey and then back at me. All the colour drained from his face. His pupils grew huge. He whirled around and grabbed a soldier. 'Get Usse. Tell him to come to my tent. Hurry, man!' The soldier left running. Alexander picked me up and ran to the tent.

When he put me down, I was amazed to see that my legs wouldn't hold me. An icy trickle ran through me veins. I shivered despite the heat. I had been poisoned. That was the only thought that was coherent to me. Poison.

I was going to die.

Poisons in those days were powerful, deadly weapons. When you were poisoned you died unless you were treated immediately by someone who knew what to do. Even then you usually perished, writhing in great agony.

Usse knew what to do, and it wasn't pleasant. He made me drink a horrible mixture, and I vomited for what seemed like hours.

Time went weird, seeming to stretch into infinity. Sounds were long, drawn-out moans. I couldn't understand what people were saying. My stomach heaved and heaved. Usse held my head and Alexander paced back and forth, imploring the gods, or whatever, to spare me. Plexis came running. He grabbed Alexander and shook him. Alexander was as white as chalk. I was green. When nothing was left in my stomach, Usse ground up some charcoal, mixed it with honey, and poured it down my throat. That came right back up, but he kept making more and giving it to me. I couldn't move my arms, my hands were frozen. I started to shake. There was a lull while Usse searched through his medicine chest for something. I lay on the ground. Nothing seemed to matter any more. There was a hideous pain in my stomach, and I thought I'd feel much better after I was dead. Anything was better than this. My head was splitting, and I saw white spots each time I opened my eyes.

Usse came back and prised my mouth open. I thought I had tasted the worst, but no, *this* was the worst. I struggled and choked, but he had a funnel. Then he sat and held me, with his arms wrapped tightly around my head and chest, keeping me sitting upright. His hands were wiry and strong. One was cupped around my jaw, keeping it shut. The other stroked my throat, as if I were a cat, and I felt the pain start to ebb.

When I could move my hands and legs, he let go. I managed to stay in a sitting position for a few seconds before slumping to the ground. Usse picked me up and carried me to my bed.

I felt as if I'd gone fifteen rounds with a bulldozer. My muscles screamed, and my stomach told me, in no uncertain terms what it thought about the whole proceeding.

I couldn't talk for three days. My throat was raw. Not that I wanted to talk. I wanted to sleep. I woke up briefly to crawl to the chamber pot or to drink water. Otherwise I slept. Axiom and Brazza took care of Chiron, and Usse watched over me like a dark angel, his narrow face tight with worry.

Alexander tried to find out who had put poison in the wineskin, but of course, it was impossible. The wineskin was the one I always used for the ceremonies. It was kept in our tent, but it had been taken to the supply tent to be filled. There it had lain unguarded for half a day. Anyone could have taken it.

However, a few days later, one of Roxanne's ladies-in-waiting disappeared. A fisherman found her body downriver and brought it back to camp. I didn't think anything about it, until one evening, when Alexander was gone, Roxanne arrived in my tent unannounced. 'I have come to tell you what my oracle said,' she proclaimed. I was in the tent with Chiron. Axiom had gone to get dinner and Brazza was at the baths. Lysimachus was nowhere to be seen, so I was alone with the mad princess. I'd long ago decided she was crazy.

'My oracle said that my lady-in-waiting, Orianne, put poison in your wine and Demeter, your mother, struck her down as she went to bathe in the river.' Her voice was toneless, as if she were telling me it looked like rain.

'Was this the girl the fisherman found? How do you know it was my mother's doing?' I asked.

'She called a great crocodile to seize Orianne and drag her into the water to drown.' Roxanne shrugged. 'I have heard that the crocodile god is one of your protectors,' she added seriously.

I knew where she had heard that. Our mutual mother-in-law, the divine Olympias – may she rot in Hades. 'I'm sorry that your lady-in-waiting died,' I told her. I wasn't sure what else she wanted me to say. Her pale eyes darted over my face, then around the tent. 'Can I get you anything?' I asked her.

'I'd like a drink,' she said. She sat on the rug and stared at me. Her face was without any expression. I would have thought she was pretty, but she frightened me.

'Certainly.' I poured a cup of watered wine and gave it to her. She sipped it politely then set it down on the table. She looked around.

'It's very peaceful in your tent. Does Iskander hate noise so much?'

'No, he doesn't hate noise but he likes quiet. So do I.' I didn't know whether I should stand or sit. Finally I sat, but not too close to her.

'Where did you grow up? In which country? Was your father a great king? Or is it true what they say, that you are the goddess Persephone?' She leaned towards me as she spoke. Some people, I noticed, have no sense of personal space. Roxanne was one of them. She always wanted to get too close to me, which made me jumpy.

'I grew up in a country far from Persia, nearer to Macedonia. My father was a powerful man and very old

183

when I was born. My name is Ashley, not Persephone, and I am mortal and not very exciting, I'm afraid.'

She smiled. 'My father said you were *quite* exciting.'

My teeth drew blood from my lip. Her father had raped me in the temple of Anahita. I lowered my eyes, afraid she would see the murderous thoughts running through my head. 'Don't you miss your family?' I managed to ask in a voice that sounded almost normal.

'My family? No. I miss my palace and the temple. I'd been a priestess there since I turned thirteen. I am looking forward to going to Babylon. Iskander said it will be the seat of his new government. Are you happy to go there too?' She took a lock of her long hair in her mouth and sucked on it.

'I've been there before,' I said shortly.

'Oh, how lucky you are! I forgot how much you've travelled. So tell me, how was the sacred valley of Nysa? I heard many things about it from the soldiers who accompanied you. They told me of a child. The Child of the Moon. Is it true he is Iskander's child?'

I looked at Roxanne. Her expression was bland, but I didn't trust her. She received letters from Olympias. Instead I said, 'I never told you how sorry I was that your son died. I hope you will forgive me.'

Her expression didn't change. 'How sweet. Thank you. I am sorry too. He was my firstborn. But I will have more.'

'I'm sure of that,' I said.

'The oracle told me I would have another son very soon. I will call him Alexander. Now, why don't you answer my question? Is it true you have a son in Nysa?'

I frowned. 'Why do you want to know?'

'Because Olympias writes to me that she longs to see her grandchildren, and she wonders if you will bring the

Son of the Moon to Babylon.' She took the lock of hair out of her mouth and gnawed on a cuticle.

'No. He must stay in the sacred valley.'

'How curious. My oracle made no mention of that. Well, it was lovely speaking to you.' She got to her feet with a strange, jerky motion and bowed to me. Then she backed out of the tent, bowing constantly. When she was gone, I heaved a sigh. I was shaking. I had no idea what she was up to, but for the first time I was grateful that Paul wasn't with me.

Chapter Twenty-One

We sailed down the river, the army following along on the banks. Alexander was nervous. The tribes around us were hostile, hardly a day went by that one or two scouts didn't get shot at or killed by an arrow.

Arrows were my nightmare. I hated them. Because of some silly misunderstanding, all the arrow wounds were sent to me. The soldiers thought I worked miracles. I had simply taken off a soldier's armour one day. He had thought he was wounded, but the arrow was stuck in the leather. It fell onto the floor; the man didn't have a scratch.

Two days after Alexander's fight in a place called Tulambi, someone galloped over to the riverside and yelled my name. I poked my head out of the galley, and saw a man on his horse holding another man across his lap. I could see the arrow sticking out of his chest. I clambered into a dinghy to be rowed ashore. Meanwhile, I sent word to Usse to come and help me. I had no special powers concerning arrows.

The man riding the horse was Plexis, the arrow was stuck in one of his soldiers. The man, a scout, had somehow managed to make it back to the main army before collapsing.

Usse and I put him on a table and looked at each other. Usse hated arrows as much as I did. This one looked dreadful. It was stuck in the man's breast, to the right of his sternum, just underneath his clavicle. Usse prepared a poultice, and then, muttering a prayer, he used a copper separator to open the wound and yanked the arrow out. The man screamed and fainted.

I had been trying to grow penicillin. All my moulds were kept in glass jars. In the heat of India, I had managed to get some spectacular examples. Now Usse raised his eyebrows at me and pointed to a lovely blue-green mould. We decided to try it. The man's wound was deep. The arrow had somehow missed major arteries and Usse hoped the lung had been spared. We packed some mould into the poultice and bandaged everything tightly. A wound like that, in the heat and humidity, would certainly fester. If it did, the man would die within three or four days.

We moved him onto the boat with us. We fixed up a hammock and slung it in the shade. He was still alive the next morning but terribly weak and could hardly drink the broth Axiom made for him.

That evening, Alexander made the decision to attack a large, fortified town to the south where the scout had been ambushed. For Alexander, an arrow was as good as a declaration of war. Early the next morning, he and his troops set off at a gallop across the plains.

Nearchus would sail down river and meet the army that evening. Alexander was blithely confident. The city was fortified, but not large. There didn't seem to be much of an army defending it, so he thought he'd go, put the fear of 'Sikander' into them, and continue his route unhindered. What he feared the most was an attack from behind, so he preferred to make sure the enemy was vanquished before moving on.

I watched the army moving off. Then we sailed down river and camped at a bend. I decided to go ashore and left Chiron with Brazza and Kalanos. Axiom was getting supplies, and Nearchus had gone to do whatever admirals have to do when nearly two thousand boats all arrive somewhere at once.

I was nervous. The weather that day seemed odd. There was no wind, and the sun burned in the sky. The air felt heavy with electricity. Some people can feel storms coming – I was one of them. My head hurt and my eyes stung. Prickles ran up and down my arms, and there was an ache between my shoulder blades. The storm would hit that night. I went to find Nearchus to tell him. Luckily, he listened to me.

Everyone believed me. They figured goddesses knew things. Nearchus told me to go tell Craterus, and I did, bouncing across the boat-bridge, cheerful despite the strange heat and despite Alexander's absence. He'd be back soon, full of the energy that the battles gave him, hectic and nervous. Then he'd talk all night until the shock wore off. We'd make love, and he'd fall asleep. I walked along the river bank looking for Craterus, thinking about Alexander, and worrying about the coming storm.

Craterus listened to my prophecy about the 'tempest' – that's what he called it. I just told him he might want to get ready for a big rain. During the monsoon season we thought we'd seen everything, although I hadn't gotten a feeling this strong before. The hair stood up on my arms.

That afternoon, as we were setting up camp, a lone horseman came galloping towards us. He was going flat out and his horse was covered with white lather. He had obviously come from the battle. He shouted for me. Great. Another arrow wound.

It was Seleucos. I frowned when I saw him. He didn't bother to dismount. 'Come quickly,' he said urgently. 'It's Iskander.'

Those four words chilled me. In a sudden panic, I ran to the stables and called to the groom to bridle Lenaia, then I went to get Usse. He took one look at my face, at my nose that had begun to bleed, and grabbed his medical bag. Before we left, I also took the jar with the blue mould. The wounded soldier on our boat hadn't developed a fever yet. He was looking better.

We rode back upriver as fast as we could. Nearchus would come with a boat to fetch Alexander. When Seleucos had told Nearchus to bring a boat I'd nearly fainted. Only a very severe wound could keep him from riding. Twice I nearly fell off my horse. My head was spinning. I felt like throwing up, but I didn't stop.

Seleucos had been with Alexander. As we rode he shouted the story to us. They had arrived at the town in the morning. The town's defenders had refused to parley and had shot arrows at the ambassadors. Alexander had then cordoned off the town and prepared the siege towers. They catapulted the walls and he propped ladders up against them. The defenders couldn't stop the assault, and Alexander, seeing how smoothly everything was going, was one of the first up the ladder. Luckily, Seleucos and Perdiccas had been with him.

As they reached the top of the ladder, the siege tower suddenly lurched forward, unbalanced by the catapult which had not been properly tied down. The huge engine crashed into the ladder, leaving Alexander, Seleucos, and Perdiccas balanced on the top of the wall. They were stuck. They couldn't leap back down, it was a fifty-foot drop into an empty moat lined with flagstones. Standing on the top of the wall was out of the question, they were vulnerable from all sides. But behind the wall, and not too far away, was a huge tree. If they could make it to that shelter, they could wait until the main army broke down the wall or the gate. They didn't hesitate. They leapt off the wall taking the defenders by surprise. They rushed to the tree, putting it at their backs.

The next twenty minutes were like being in Hades's realm, Seleucos told us, his voice strained as he relived the horror of it. They stayed behind their shields, Alexander and Perdiccas standing, and Seleucos crouching. Alexander took his sword in his left hand and fought on the left side, Perdiccas took the right, and they slashed at the men all around them. For twenty minutes they kept five hundred men at bay. It was hopeless. Their arms burned with fatigue, the sweat blinded them, but Alexander wouldn't give up. Shouting at them that help was on its way, he lunged from behind the shield to hack at an Indian, and at that instant an arrow hit his chest. He fell to his knees and tried to yank the arrow out. The pain made him scream. He grasped a low hanging branch and tried to pull himself upright. Blood spurted out of the wound, cutting off his respiration. Grey with shock, he pitched forward. Seleucos managed to keep him covered with his shield. Seleucos and Perdiccas could see the pool of blood forming at their feet but could do nothing but continue to defend their fallen leader.

Just when all seemed lost, the wall came crashing down, and Alexander's army swarmed into the city, routing the Indians.

The soldiers lifted Alexander to his feet, but he was unconscious and they had to carry him on a litter to a temporary campsite. Seleucos had leapt on his horse as soon as he got out of the city and had ridden to fetch Usse and me. Nobody else dared touch Alexander. This probably saved his life.

When we got to the place where the camp had been set up, my heart nearly stopped. There was a crowd around the tent, milling aimlessly, and everyone was wailing and keening. The storm I'd felt all day was building in the north, huge dark clouds roiled on the horizon, and the air burned my throat.

I threw myself off my horse, fell in the dust then scrabbled to my feet. 'Where is he?' I cried, my voice breaking.

Usse was calmer than I. He'd heard Seleucos's recital, and he'd already formed an idea of what the wound was like. First he washed his hands and made me do the same. Usse was now a firm believer in germs, and he took great pains to foil the 'micro-monsters' as he called them.

Alexander lay on a table. He was conscious, but looked awful. He panted, and I could see the pulse in his throat. It was like a sparrow's heartbeat. Each time he took a breath, it was with a little groan. An arrow was planted deeply in his chest. Even I could see that this was serious.

There existed a story, a rumour that Alexander had, in fact, died in India, and that the man who came back at the head of his army was a stand-in. It was a wild story, but the people in a certain region in India claimed Alexander was buried near their town in an ancient temple.

As I remembered that, there came a loud rumble of thunder. Usse glanced uneasily at the sky and gave curt orders to the soldiers standing behind him to secure the tent against the storm.

Alexander opened his eyes and gazed at me. His breathing made a *'huh, huh, huh'* noise. It was painful to hear.

I took his hand and kissed it. 'I'm right here,' I said softly.

Standing around him were Perdiccas, Plexis, and Ptolemy Lagos. They had tears on their cheeks; their faces were tragic.

Alexander's eyes were dark with pain. The pupils hid the iris, and I wasn't sure he'd even heard me. Then faintly his hand squeezed mine. Even this small effort made sweat pop out on his brow. He trembled.

Usse stood still, assessing the wound, touching Alexander's neck, his wrists, and his head lightly. Then he looked at me and said, 'We have no choice. We must pull the arrow straight out.'

Alexander closed his eyes. I felt the blood leave my face. The arrow was deeply embedded. It had certainly hit something vital.

We got to work. First we had to cut off his armour. We stripped him and laid a muslin sheet over his lower body. The arrow had pinned his armour to his chest, so all we could do was cut around it – without moving the arrow. Usse was very firm about that. Then we carefully lifted the armour off, sliding it from under his back.

Immediately, Usse sluiced Alexander's body with water mixed with an antiseptic and cleaned the skin around the wound. Afterwards, he prepared a poultice with herbs and the mould. He had to pull the arrow out, and he had to be quick – if air got into the chest cavity, the lung would collapse, and Alexander would die within minutes. Usse positioned the spreaders and clamps. Everything had to be done at the same time.

We looked at each other. Alexander sensed it was time. He tightened his grip on my hand. I bent down and kissed him on the lips. I whispered into his ear, 'You don't die in India.' A faint smile flickered across his lips.

Usse's assistant actioned the spreader, and Usse yanked

the arrow out of Alexander's chest.

There was a fountain of blood and air bubbles as well. The lung had been punctured. Usse flung the arrow behind him and slapped the poultice with the mould on the wound, pressing as hard as he could. Then he stretched a piece of fine leather bandage across Alexander's chest. The bandage had been made from a membrane peeled from the hide of an ox and boiled until it was soft. It covered Alexander's chest, sealing off the wound so that no air could get in. Wide bands of linen held it in place. After, Usse spread melted wax over everything.

I didn't take my eyes from Alexander's throat where his pulse beat erratically. Then the heartbeat disappeared. His body grew strangely limp. His eyes opened, but they were devoid of life. I recoiled instinctively from the horror of death. Then I sank to my knees and looked up at the sky just visible through the top of the tent.

'Please,' I whispered. 'Let him live. I need him. I love him. He still has two more years to live – just two more years. Let me have them, please.' The sky gave no sign of having heard me. The black clouds gathered and churned. I glanced at my husband, tears obscuring my vision. Suddenly there was a tremor in his body and his pulse beat again. It was still faint, but it meant the shock of having the arrow pulled out had passed.

Shock, as much as the arrow, nearly killed Alexander. We stood at his side, holding the bandages in place for nearly an hour. Finally, his cheeks turned pink again and the blue faded from his lips. He was still unconscious though. We carefully wrapped another bandage around him. When it was in place and Usse was sure no air could get in, he stepped back with a huge sigh.

'I have done what I can. Now his life is in the hands of

the gods.'

I looked down at my husband. His eyes were open. He tried to say something, but the effort was too much for him. A rictus of pain crossed his face, and he passed out again.

For three days he hovered between life and death. His will to live was stronger than death, though. His body burned with fever, but perhaps the heat killed the germs or the mould did work. Whatever the reason, his wound, although nearly mortal, didn't become infected.

Nearchus had brought the boat back upriver, with Chiron, Brazza, and Axiom aboard. I didn't sleep there. I was too frightened for Alexander. I stayed next to him, leaving him only long enough to nurse Chiron.

Chapter Twenty-Two

After three days, we carried him to the boat and sailed down the river. Even the slight rocking movement of the boat caused his wound to ache, and his breathing was harsh groans by the time we arrived at the camp.

His soldiers had lined up on the banks of the river. They stayed silent as Nearchus manoeuvred the boat towards the dock. As we glided up, I could hear a high-pitched wailing. My skin prickled. It was Roxanne. She rushed along the river's edge, keeping pace with the boat. She had smeared her face with ashes. I realized that she believed Alexander was dead.

I said to Plexis, 'Keep her away. You're the only one who can stop her. The silly bitch will throw herself across his body. If he is jarred it will kill him.'

He glanced at Alexander and leapt onto the shore, intercepting Roxanne.

'No,' he said, loud enough for everyone to hear. 'You mustn't touch him. He's not dead, just grievously injured. Go back to your tent, pray to your gods, and make sacrifices. That is all we can do for now.'

The army sacrificed to the gods, they chanted and prayed. And they talked about the huge storm that had raged but hadn't shed a single drop of water on the tent where Alexander lay wounded.

The storm had been an electrical heat storm. Huge

black clouds had cast flickering blue and green lightning back and forth in the sky. Then gigantic reddish lightning bolts fell to the ground. The air around us crackled and sparked. Our hair stood on end and the metal tips on the spears glowed. St. Elmo's fire ran up and down the tent poles, and the men hid their eyes and wailed in fear.

Usse had seen the fire before, so he wasn't frightened. But hardly anyone else knew what it was. I knew, of course, but I'd never actually seen it and was startled. I didn't fall to my knees and scream though. I was beyond that. I had believed Alexander would die.

For three days and nights I didn't sleep. None of us did. We watched as Alexander struggled to live. We prayed, we cried, then we stopped crying and stood numbly, while Usse kept the fires burning in the brazier and boiled water.

Usse felt useful as long as he was fighting germs. He made tonics for Alexander to drink, and every time he woke up Usse spooned hot broth into his mouth, though most of the time he couldn't swallow it. His body seemed to waste away. His ribs and his cheekbones pressed against his hot skin. He moaned in his sleep, sometimes delirious, sometimes lucid. When he was lucid he thought he was dying.

We stayed for a week in the encampment. Every day the soldiers lined up outside the tent and asked to see Alexander. They were grief-stricken. Roxanne and Onesicrite claimed he was dead.

I refused to let Roxanne visit Alexander. I wouldn't even let her cross the river. I was insane with worry, exhaustion, and grief. However, the soldiers grew fearful. They insisted on seeing their leader. Craterus, Ptolemy Lagos, Plexis, Leonnatus, and Perdiccas were allowed to see Alexander. They tried to tell their soldiers that he was slowly recuperating, but that his wound was still life-threatening and he couldn't be moved. The men disbelieved them. They muttered fearfully that Alexander had died, and that we were hiding the truth.

Finally, Alexander heard the men's cries. He was propped up in bed, drinking hot broth, but still not eating anything. His breathing caused him pain. His colour was still bad, and any effort made his lips turn grey. He decided to mount his warhorse and ride along the edge of the river to show himself to his men.

I nearly had hysterics, but Usse calmed me. He understood Alexander. Perhaps he was the only man who ever truly did.

He had the horse drugged so that there was no way that he would make the slightest jarring movement when the men started to cheer. Because cheer they did. When they saw Alexander sitting on his horse, they wore out their voices screaming.

Plexis and Perdiccas walked on either side of Alexander, surreptitiously holding onto his legs. Seleucos held the horse's bridle and Usse walked behind, watching Alexander with his dark, piercing eyes, his narrow face solemn, but, at the same time, proud.

After an hour, Alexander started to slump in the saddle and was taken quickly back to his bed. The wound had started bleeding again. Blood was visible under the bandage, but Usse wouldn't remove it until he was sure the lung was sealed off.

I was sure it was going to get infected. I thought the mould would never work, that the arrow had gone too deep, and that Alexander would die. Yet somehow he pulled through those first days and first weeks.

The soldier Plexis had brought to us was in the infirmary recuperating. He was doing well. Usse took off his bandage and we marvelled at the healthy, pink skin around the wound. Usse pressed it carefully; there was no sign of heat or redness. It hadn't gotten infected. We stared at each other, hope in our eyes. What if that mould was the right one? We hardly dared say it out loud.

At last Usse decided to unwrap Alexander's bandages. We lay him carefully on a table and Usse prepared a new poultice with the mould. He peeled the bandage from Alexander's chest and cautiously washed the wound. It was a deep, angry-looking thing that disappeared between two ribs and plunged straight into his chest. However, it wasn't full of pus, as Usse had feared. It was not pretty, but it seemed to be healing slowly. Usse put a new poultice on it, and from then on changed it every day. He still put a piece of thin leather and wax over it though. We sailed down the river until we came to a place where two rivers joined, and here we rested for nearly four months while Alexander recuperated.

The countryside was pretty, with gentle hills, and the weather stayed clement. Alexander founded another city, calling it the City of the Confluence, or sometimes, the City of Tears.

We were not sad here but I cried often. To have almost lost Alexander only made me dread the future more.

That year, I celebrated Christmas with the people in my tent. I had little presents for everyone, sang Christmas carols, and lit some beeswax candles. I'd decorated the tent in red and green, the traditional colours of Christmas. It was actually a month after Christmas, but Alexander was finally well enough to move around, and I needed to

198

celebrate. I wanted to give the people I loved a gift, but I didn't know exactly what. I knew that stories were greatly appreciated in this time. What really would have knocked them out would have been a holographic DVD player with a fantastic film. Failing that, I decided to tell the story of King Arthur.

I was not a particularly good storyteller. I knew I wasn't very good, so I didn't try to embellish. I simply used my memory, which was sharp and clear, to recite the story as I'd read it.

When I was finished, there was a deep silence. I had been speaking for what seemed like hours. The fire had gone out in the brazier and the only light came from the moon. Chiron snored softly in Brazza's arms, and Axiom sat cross-legged on the rug, his chin in his hands.

Alexander, to whom the story had been dedicated, was motionless. He had not asked a single question, unlike Plexis who hadn't stopped interrupting.

I'd answered all his questions: 'What was the idea of chivalry?'; 'What was a joust?'; 'Why didn't Merlin tell Arthur that Morgan was his sister?'; 'Couldn't Arthur and Lancelot just share Guinevere?' Plexis wanted to understand everything. He was upset when he heard that King Arthur was killed in battle and his sword lost in the lake. He'd been fascinated when I came to the part about the sword in the stone and the singing light coming down over young Arthur.

'Can you tell me that part again?' he asked, when I'd finished the tale. 'What was the singing light?'

Alexander stirred and said clearly, 'I saw a light like that.'

We gaped at him. He smiled. 'When I was lying on the table and Usse said he was going to pull the arrow out, I knew I was dying. My life's blood would leave me and I would die. Then Ashley leaned over me and said, 'You don't die in India.''

This statement caused quite a stir in the audience. Usse glanced sharply at me and Plexis drew his breath in with a hiss.

Axiom clapped his hands. 'Go on,' he said.

'I remember clearly when you said that,' Alexander said, speaking to me. 'I smiled. You kissed me. I thought the last thing I would feel was the touch of your lips, and I was almost happy.'

He reached and took my hand. 'And then there came a pain like never I had felt before. The arrow tore out of my chest and hurt so much I passed out. Everything went black, and I remember feeling only relief. The pain had gone. I was dead. There came a white light. Cleaner, brighter, more beautiful than any light I've ever seen. It was pure light, untainted by any colours at all. That light made me realize that the sun's illumination is just a poor imitation of real light. Even the word "light" has nothing to do with what I saw. It was soft and I could feel it touch me. It flowed like water around me and seemed to fill my veins. I found myself floating in the air. I know you won't believe me, but I could see all of you. You were bending over me, holding something on my chest, and I was suddenly shocked to see my own body.

'I looked at myself. I could sense the part of me that was floating, and it was made of the light. It was pure, and I was filled with wonder. My body lying on the table was covered with blood and was soiled. It was made of clay. I had a feeling of revulsion for my own body, but was incapable of detaching my gaze from it. Perhaps it was because I wasn't dead. I could perceive a faint pulse beating in that body of clay, and that pulse was like a chain that kept me from floating away. I found myself wishing the pulse would stop, because I could sense the pain that waited for me in that ruined body. I say "ruined" because I could see each scar, each broken bone, and each hurt I'd ever suffered as if they were freshly made. My whole body was nothing but a battlefield. Then you looked up, Ashley. You looked up and stared right at me. I saw your lips move. You said, "Please. Let him live. I need him. I love him. Give me just the time that's left, please.".'

I stared at him. He was still smiling. My lips were cold. I felt faint. I did remember, but I hadn't said that, exactly.

'And then the light disappeared and the blackness came to claim me. The blackness and the pain. I didn't want to return to the body I'd seen. After being part of that light, my body was cold and mundane. I hated it. But I returned. Because you asked me to,' he said, looking straight at me. 'I thought I would hate you when the pain washed over me. Feeling my body around me again was like drowning in mud.

'But I had to return. Because the only thing that remotely feels or looks like that amazing light I saw is love. It's as simple as that. Was that what King Arthur had to learn before he died?'

My own smile twisted my mouth awry, and my face was wet with tears. 'I don't know. I hope that's part of what the story's trying to teach us. I'll have to tell you the story of Jesus some day. He was another man who wanted to show us that love could save the world.'

'Well, maybe it did,' said Alexander thoughtfully. 'Maybe, in a way, it did.'

Chapter Twenty-Three

Alexander slept without any sleeping draught that night. The pain that had plagued him for weeks was ebbing. He was still weak, but he was getting better. Each day saw him stronger. And, like most active people, he started to chafe and fret at being cooped up in bed.

'I want to see the new city,' he said.

'No, you have to rest.' I was firm. We were facing each other over the chessboard. Alexander was winning, but it didn't seem to matter.

'I am tired of sitting in bed,' he said and tossed the chessboard to the floor.

'Oh, stop being such a baby.' I picked up the pieces all the while conscious of his glare. I brushed my hands on my robe and crossed my arms. 'All right. Out with it.'

'With what?' He looked wary now.

'Something is bothering you. I know what it is, but I won't say anything until you do.'

'If you know what it is, then you know why I'm upset!' he cried. He stopped shouting and ran his hands through his hair. 'And you know I can't tell you about it. You already told me you'd never talk to me about my future.'

'That's right.'

'But now you have to. Don't you see? I saw you. I heard what you said. I hear it every day, every hour, all the time. *Two more years*. That's what you said.' His voice broke. 'Two more years. Why, Ashley, why did you have to say that?'

I sat next to him. I had a sudden, very sharp pain in my belly. I touched his hand, but he pulled it away from me. I realized that he hadn't touched me once since he'd woken up. I closed my eyes. I couldn't bear seeing the desolation in his gaze.

'Tell me,' he said. 'What should I do? Should I name an heir? Who will rule when I'm gone?' A muscle jumped in his jaw.

I shook my head mutely.

'Answer me, by Zeus!' His hand shot out and he hit me, knocking me off the bed. For a wounded guy, he still had a mean jab.

I sat on the floor, stunned. He'd never lost his temper with me before. I put my hand to my face. My nose was bleeding, but that wasn't his fault. He'd hit my shoulder. I didn't dare speak. I thought I'd probably vomit.

'I'm sorry.' He crawled off the bed.

'Get back in bed, Usse will kill you.'

'No. I don't die for another twenty-four months.' His voice was strangely calm.

'Do you think I'm happy about that?'

He shrugged. 'Maybe now you are.'

'How can you say that?' I cried.

'I don't know. I had a shock. First, I thought I'd die when the arrow struck me, then I was sure it was all over when Usse pulled it out. Now, I know I'll recover. It doesn't make me feel any better. In some perverse way, I almost feel like killing myself right now, just to spit in Atropos's eye.'

'The Fate who cuts the thread of life,' I recited hollowly, remembering Callisthenes's lessons.

'I see you paid attention to your tutor,' he said dryly.

'Well, now it's your chance to remember what yours said. What would Aristotle say if he knew you had decided to give up?'

'Give up?' he said. 'Who's giving up?'

'You are. But I have a new tactic for you.'

'A tactic?' His mouth quirked. 'How interesting.'

'Pay attention, you might learn something.'

'You're not the only one with a good memory,' said Alexander.

'But I'm the only one who can save you.' I drew a deep breath. 'This is what we're going to do. You're going to pretend you never heard me say what you think I said. And I will do everything in my power, when the time comes, to save your life.'

'You'll have changed time,' he warned. 'You'll be destroyed by your Time Gods.'

'But you will die. Or rather, you'll give the impression you died. Do you think you can do that? Will your pride and ego let you walk away from your empire in the prime of your life?'

'My pride and ego? Do you think all I care about is myself?'

'No. That's exactly the opposite of what I meant.' I took a deep breath. 'Let me start over again. I want to give you a chance to cheat fate, but I want you to understand what it means. You must walk away from everything, and I am afraid to ask you to do that. You've worked so hard to do something so extraordinary. It's not fair.'

He looked at me through narrowed eyes. 'If I understand you correctly, my death is something that could be avoided.'

'I'm not sure,' I said. 'Nobody knows exactly what you died of.'

'That does complicate things. What about the date?'

'The date is known, yes.' I hesitated.

'Go on.'

'I don't want to hurt you any more,' I said. 'Don't look at me like that. I'm so sorry. You shouldn't have heard. It's as if the gods have been playing puppet games with us.'

'I want to know something,' he said. 'What happens to my empire when I die? Who do I name as a successor?'

'Nobody,' I whispered.

'Nobody?' He gave a startled jerk then cried out in pain as his wound hurt him. He gasped for a moment then drew a shaky breath. 'Fine. So my generals fight it out between themselves.'

It was a statement, not a question. I frowned. 'What happens after your death must not concern you. If you want me to save you, you have to disappear from the timeline. You must spend the rest of your life invisible.'

'Or else we are destroyed?' he laughed hollowly.

'That's right. Or else we will both be destroyed. You, our children, and me.'

'What exactly do you suggest I do?' he asked, wincing.

'You said you wanted to go all around the world,' I said quietly. 'Would you travel with me? Would you like to go to Africa and see the wild elephants? To the great north to see the reindeer pulling the sleighs through the eternal snow? We can go to China and see the dragon festivals. We can go north, south, east, and west. Wherever you wish, we can go. Only this time, instead of fighting and conquering, you can simply go to see and wonder. And I will go with you.'

'You alone would still love me if I were not king,' he said softly. 'I always said that, didn't I?'

'Me, and Plexis, and Usse, and Axiom, and Brazza.' I smiled through my tears. 'And Chiron and Paul. Before we go, could we first go to the sacred valley and get Paul? I would take him with us.'

'I didn't say I would go,' he said slowly.

I blinked, sending more tears down my cheeks.

'Please say yes,' I whispered.

'Why?'

'Because I can't live without you, and knowing when you will die is killing me as surely as it hurts you. I dread each day that ends. Every time the sun sets a part of me dies. Every month that passes is a door closing behind me. Each minute is like sand falling through a sieve.'

'To me as well,' he said. 'Come here, Ashley.' He opened his arms to me. 'Help me back in the bed. I'm still weak as a worm.'

'Weak as a worm?' I smiled. 'A Macedonian saying, no doubt?'

'Yes, why? What do your people say?'

'Weak as a kitten.'

'Well, I don't know why you laugh. A kitten is stronger than a worm any day.' He sounded cross, but he smiled suddenly. 'I will think about it. And I will think about what you're saying. But first I have to know three things.'

'Ask, I'll try and answer,' I said cautiously.

'First, does my kingdom collapse entirely?'

'No. It splits into three major parts. Egypt, all of Persia and Greece, and then Macedonia, which keeps its independence.'

'All right. I won't ask who rules the pieces, I will find out soon enough. So, what happens to my son Heracles?'

I shook my head. 'Nobody knows. I think his family, seeing the conflicts and the power of the generals, decided to keep him far from the throne. His death is not recorded.'

'Neither is his life, though,' said Alexander sadly.

'I'm sorry,' I said inanely.

'Third question.' He drew a deep breath. 'Why did you decide to tell me the truth? You could have denied ever saying what you did. You could have told me I was delirious, that it was just a result of the pain or the wound. Why did you admit it? Why?'

'Can't you guess?'

'I think so, but I want to hear it from you.'

'Because I'm tired of being a puppet for the gods,' I said. I held his gaze. 'It is my turn to spit in Atropos's eye. And I'm going to do it with the most famous person on earth.'

There was a long silence. Alexander's breathing was remarkably clear.

'You have thought about this for a long time.'

Another statement.

I barely smiled. 'Since we left the Sacred Valley.'

'Did you know I could hear you?'

Our eyes were locked together. I felt savage ice in my veins. I was doing something that could bring the gates of time crashing down. 'I hoped you could hear me. I thought you were dying. I had to bring you back. I told you that I would lie to you even if you were on your deathbed. I had to say something that you would believe. I had to tell the truth. I'm sorry; sorry for your dreams and sorry for your empire. But I'm not sorry for you, Alex. You will always be Alexander, no matter if you're king of the world or simply someone living in a tent. Like the tiger. No matter what anyone calls him, he's still a tiger.'

'The tiger?' he said, with a smile. His eyes were full of tears. They hesitated on the edge of his lashes, then spilled down his cheeks. He brushed them away. 'Perhaps I *will* come with you,' he said. 'If I do, we will both laugh at the Fates as they tangle their threads and scream in frustration.'

'I hope that's what will happen,' I said. 'There's always the chance I won't be able to save you.'

'Let me think about this. It's all very strange.' His voice had almost found its old timbre.

'While you're thinking, can I get you something to eat? I'm worried about you. You're much too thin.'

His mouth twitched. His eyes, the blue and the brown, were perfectly candid. 'I know what I'd like to have.'

'Oh? And what's that?

'Chiron's dinner.' His voice was bland.

I gave a shocked laugh. 'You can't be serious?'

'Why not? I have no appetite and don't feel like eating anything. The only thing I want is your milk. Will you, please?' He was serious.

I sighed, took off my tunic and crawled onto the bed next to Alexander. 'I'm going to wean him soon,' I warned him.

'Not until I get better,' he said as he burrowed his face in my breast.

He fell asleep just like a baby, his mouth still on my breast, his long lashes lying on his cheeks, a faint smile tugging the corners of his mouth. I kissed him tenderly. I had almost told the truth. Nobody knew exactly what he died of, but nearly everyone said it was malaria. It had killed Coenus. If Alexander fell ill, chances were he'd die, no matter what I did.

Chapter Twenty-Four

Further down river was the kingdom of King Musicanus. Alexander was too weak to fight any battles, but his army was strong. Plexis and Perdiccas led the cavalry. King Musicanus fought several half-hearted skirmishes with us, but they were more like jousts with no losses on either side. He sent ambassadors and diplomats to Alexander, and we sent our men. Soon we received an invitation to his court.

Alexander was bored. He couldn't ride, he'd read the few books we had a hundred times, TV wasn't invented so he couldn't watch the sports channel, and I had my hands full with Chiron. I couldn't tell him stories or cater to him all day.

'Let nature take its course,' Usse said each day when Alexander grew impatient.

So Alexander was glad to visit the king, and we sent word saying we would meet him in his court in three days, giving Alexander time to plan for treason.

Nassar, our scribe and translator, was very sceptical. 'I don't like the idea of your going to his palace,' he told me. 'I've heard things on the river.'

'What things?' I asked, 'I mean, besides the songs the soldiers sing as they row, the cries of the vendors paddling around us, the clamour of the people lined up on the river banks, and the complaints of Onesicrite?'

'Onesicrite is bored because Alexander won't talk to

him for more than five minutes at a time,' said Nassar with a grin.

'Well, he should go back to Roxanne's court, he'll feel right at home with the chattering monkeys, the screeching parrots, and the shrieking women.'

'He thinks he's needed to record Alexander's journal.'

I sighed. 'I wish he would fall overboard. Why don't I like that fellow? He's never actually done anything bad to me.'

Nassar pursed his lips. 'Maybe because he's always complaining, he's insufferable, asks a thousand questions, and never listens for a single answer?'

'So, what did you hear on the river?' I asked.

Nassar frowned. 'It's vague, but people say that King Musicanus is in dire danger from his own Brahmins. They are the warrior caste, and they wish to fight Iskander in order to die valiantly. They believe that King Musicanus is taking away their glory by making peace with Iskander. It's getting tense in the area.'

'Perhaps you should tell Iskander,' I said. 'Shall we go find him?'

'Onesicrite went below. He must be with your husband.'

'Honestly,' I said. 'We *would* be stuck with him now. Why did Bulos have to break his hand?'

I was referring to Aristobulus, Alexander's personal historian, who had followed the army since the beginning. He wrote a neat, concise military journal and didn't plague us with silly questions. Or complain. We called him 'Bulos' because the Greeks loved nicknames, and hardly anyone went by their own name. Nassar's name was really Nebuchadnezzar. Even Alexander had different names. People called him Iskander, Sikander, Ekeisander, or the

210

'King of Heaven and Earth', if they were feeling poetic.

Onesicrite was feeling poetic. 'O King of Heaven and Earth,' he intoned, 'Will you take this humble servant with you to the marvellous court of King Musicanus so that I may write a full report back to my brother Athenians?'

Alexander raised a tired face to the journalist and frowned. 'Why not? I'll let anyone come who really wishes to.'

'Anyone?' Onesicrite asked.

'Why yes, of course.' Alexander looked over at me and shrugged. 'Why do you ask?'

'It's your lady wife, sire, Queen Roxanne. She wishes to accompany her husband to see the wonders of Indus before we leave this enchanted place.'

I flinched at this *wonderful* piece of news.

'Fine,' he said shortly. 'Tell her to prepare herself. I will bring her to the court.'

Onesicrite bowed very low, then bowed to me and left with a smirk.

I stopped thinking about how much I'd like to see him fall off the boat. It did no good to dream about things like that. I would have to push him.

I sat down next to Alexander and touched his forehead. It was just a reflex; he was always hot. 'Would you mind if I came too?' I asked him.

'I was already counting on you.' He sounded surprised.

'If I come with you, you're going to have to listen to me,' I said sternly. 'You are to be carried in a litter – no riding your horse to the palace. You will drink only what Usse gives you, explaining to King Musicanus that your doctor has prescribed a special diet. You will eat only what can be peeled and eaten, like fresh fruit, or what has been well boiled, like plain rice. You will eat little, drink less, and retire as soon as I look at you like this,' and I widened my eyes.

'Yes.' He sounded suspiciously meek.

'Yes? That's all the protesting I'm going to hear?'

'Who's protesting? I said "yes"! Don't tell me you're not happy with that?'

'Why the sudden excess of good sense? It's not like you.'

'Ha, ha. Very funny. Now that you've managed to ruin my first outing in three months, will you please help me up? I'd like to go to the bathroom, then I want to go up on deck to get some fresh air this morning. Where's Chiron?'

'On deck with Brazza.'

'Brazza should have been a father with twelve children,' said Alexander as I carefully helped him up and walked with him to the chamber pot in the corner of the room.

'He's a eunuch,' I remarked dryly. I helped him sit on the large, earthenware pot. In the back of my mind, I wondered if the pot was in a museum somewhere. Blue and green hippos chased themselves around it.

Alexander frowned. 'I know he's a eunuch. I didn't say he could be a father, I said he *should* have been. I'm not happy about his being a eunuch, but he never complains and I will not insult him with pity.'

'It's a rotten society that castrates its boys,' I said with feeling.

'Didn't you tell me stories of women in your time who were mutilated sexually?' he asked pointedly.

'I think that's horrible too,' I answered.

'Well, at least Brazza can still have pleasure and make love,' said Alexander. 'The women with their genitals mutilated are denied that. It's cruel and vindictive.'

'But Brazza can never have children,' I insisted. I hated arguing with Alexander. He never let me win.

'In some places that is considered a blessing.'

'Are you finished?' I asked. 'I'll take you on deck now.'

'Thank you,' he said, when I finished straightening him up. His cheeks had a faint flush. I knew he hated being helpless. It had nothing to do with bodily functions. They had stopped bothering me around the time I discovered that they bothered no one. It was considered the same thing as eating food or scratching your lice. It was something you had to do. But Alexander hated being assisted. He was embarrassed not to be able to walk, to ride, or to make love. Usse had been quite firm about it.

'No, absolutely not,' he'd said. I slept in a hammock near Alexander's bed.

The day was lovely. As usual, the river was full of fishing boats and traders. Children ran shouting, waving, and laughing along the river banks. Women washed clothing and hung them to dry. Men ploughed their fields and fished. White egrets and singing birds filled the trees. Blue and red kingfishers swooped down to spear little fish.

Chiron had a toy boat. It was tied to a long string and floated alongside our boat. Chiron was securely tied too. Brazza never let him out of his sight. He was so attached to the little boy that sometimes I thought that they breathed in unison. Chiron adored Brazza. He adored everyone, really. He was a funny child. He had an impish look to him, his eyes were tilted up at the corners and they were bright hazel. The sun had turned his curly hair pale gold. His skin was darker than Alexander's or mine. He was as tan as a nut. Right now the little nut was trying to crawl, but he'd wound his leash around the mast and was stuck.

Brazza was motioning to him with his hands, telling him to go back the other way and unwind it, but Chiron was determined to go only one way around. He was not crying yet. But his face had taken on that mutinous cast that said, 'I'm right and you're wrong and I'm going to do it my way!'

When he saw me, he sat down and clapped his hands. He had started to babble clear bright baby sounds that delighted me. 'Paapapamamatee!' he cried.

He was sounding distinctly Greek. I looked around for Axiom. He spoke to the boy as he went about his work. He was Greek and had a strong accent. I smiled; Plexis would be relieved to hear his son speaking like a true Athenian.

Alexander sat in the shade, and Chiron, deciding he'd had enough of being silly, promptly unwound himself and crawled onto Alexander's lap. The little boy grinned, his finger in his mouth, drooling abundantly.

'He's getting a new tooth,' said Alexander, returning Chiron's grin.

'Agawapa!' crowed the baby happily.

I squatted down to see. Sure enough, another white tooth was poking out. 'I'm going to have to wean him soon,' I said with a sigh.

'You keep saying that,' said Alexander, 'And you don't make any attempt to do so.'

'I have my reasons,' I said lightly.

'You don't want another baby?' he asked. He saw right through me.

I sat down, taking Chiron off his lap. 'You're going to hurt your daddy,' I said. For simplicity's sake, Alexander was Daddy and Plexis was Papa. Not being a psychologist, I had no idea what having two loving fathers would do to a

214

child. As well as a besotted mother, a caring eunuch, and Usse and Axiom, who adored him. He would probably be a basket case. *Ha.* I doubted it.

'Well?' Alexander was looking at me, faintly hurt.

'I do, of course I do. But right now you're not in any shape to do anything about that, are you?' I teased gently.

'There's always Plexis,' he said owlishly.

We smiled at each other. 'I already told you. Plexis and I are just good friends. We haven't, well, you know, since …' I turned pink.

'You are a funny girl,' he said laughing at me. 'Since when?'

'I can't remember. It doesn't matter anyway. I don't think about him like that any more. It was just a phase, you know, like sucking your thumb was a phase for you.'

'How interesting.' He wasn't smiling though. 'Am I a phase too?'

'Why did I know you were going to ask that?' I peered at him. 'No, you are not a phase. You are my husband and I love you. I love Plexis too, but it's not the same love. That's all.'

'I *would* like another baby,' said Alexander. 'I miss Mary so much. Sometimes I wake up and I think she's still alive, that it was all a dream. Especially since I was wounded. It's not that I don't love Chiron,' he said hurriedly, seeing the look on my face.

'I know, I wasn't thinking that. It's just that, well, you've never mentioned her name.'

'I'm sorry. It hurt too much before.' He leaned back on the mast and looked up at the sky. 'It still hurts, but it's the kind of hurt I've grown to love. I need to feel the pain of Mary's loss. It's the sweetest one I've ever felt.' Two perfect tears trailed down his cheeks.

I looked down at Chiron. He was sitting still, watching Brazza as he whittled a bird from a piece of wood. The fragrant shavings caught in the breeze and floated away like snowflakes. I put my face in Chiron's curls. His arms crept up around my neck and he nuzzled my breast, always eager to nurse.

For a while we didn't speak. Chiron nursed and Alexander watched, his eyes full of a strange melancholy.

The river swept us on. The brown water swirled and splashed against the hull, the wind flapped in the sail, and the breeze was redolent with the smells of fish and freshly tilled earth. The sky was a porcelain bowl held above our heads. The rim of the bowl was white and the centre a deep, ultramarine blue – as blue as Alexander's mood. He stared at the river flowing by, and nothing I said made him smile.

He picked out a purple tunic and a white linen skirt to go to Musicanus's court. I dressed in Persian robes. Brazza fixed my hair Greek-style, braiding the front into many fine tresses and pinning them to the crown of my head. Then he crimped and curled the hair in the back, which reached my shoulders.

Roxanne's hair reached her hips, and she too had fixed it Greek-style. We stared at each other, each with our identical hairdos. To add insult to injury, we both wore butter-yellow robes. I'm sure she was as mortified as I, but we smiled politely and complimented each other.

She had been raised a princess in a time where princes and princesses were used as pawns in vicious power games. She knew how to navigate all the invisible currents in a court, she knew the strengths and weaknesses of everyone, and she knew how to stay alive in a time where murder was considered 'death by natural causes'.

I had been born into one of the richest families in the United States, sent to a boarding school as soon as I was toilet trained, and had grown up alternately ignored, hated, and envied. I had been raped and beaten by my husband but had managed to escape. I was Roxanne's equal from three thousand years in the future. Except for two important points. I'd never murdered, and I loved Alexander. Roxanne tried to kill anyone who got in her way, and she only loved power. If Alexander lost his crown, she would be the first to leave him.

Nassar told me she was sleeping with Ptolemy Lagos. Nassar was the eyes and ears of the court. I had no idea how he found things out but he did. Knowing how to speak just about every known language helped, I suppose. Ptolemy was ambitious. Since it only involved Roxanne and him, for the time being, we let it be.

An unusual garden surrounded King Musicanus's palace. It resembled a jungle, and he had a wild animal zoo. The park was divided into different sections enclosed within a tall, rose-coloured brick wall.

The Greeks were thrilled to see peacocks. They immediately captured several birds and plucked the poor things while King Musicanus looked on and roared with laughter, and Alexander sat in his litter and fumed because he couldn't chase the birds around the garden.

King Musicanus was a handsome man with jet black eyes and a prominent, beaked nose. He was very impressed with Alexander, despite the weakness he showed from his wound. Alexander was confined to his litter, and Roxanne and I walked alongside him, holding his hands. Roxanne was playing the part of the perfect little wife by copying everything I did. I longed to slap her, but I didn't want to ruin the party.

We walked around the garden on a path of white crushed shells and looked at all the animals. There were tigers, wolves, snakes, elephants, deer, crocodiles, and monkeys. The jewel of his collection was a magnificent pair of snow leopards. They lay on the ground, their emerald eyes fixed on us. They looked dangerous and pitiful, caught in their gilded cages. As big and beautiful as the pens were, they were still nothing but cages. I looked at Alexander and saw he was sombre again.

Dinner was an elaborate affair, as dinners tended to be in those days.

First course: chilled curry-flavoured soup and sixteen different kinds of fruit accompanied by tambourine players and contortionists.

Second course: whole roast lambs with peacock stuffing. Peacock feathers decorated the platter. The feathers gradually disappeared as the platter was passed around. They reappeared stuck in the Greeks' hair. The main dish was accompanied by a lovely lute player and some wild drums.

Third course: something with rice. I wasn't sure what it was, and I didn't really want to ask. Sometimes it is better not to know what you're eating. Let's just say I had the distinct impression it was staring back at me. It was accompanied by a fire-eater and a snake charmer. The Greeks were fascinated. Nobody noticed when I gave my dish to a trained monkey.

Fourth course was fish, and the snake charmer returned for an encore. The Greeks were absolutely thrilled.

Fifth course: more soup, and some wonderful herbed

bread. I filled up on bread. A naked fakir came in and did a show. He sat on spikes, climbed up a floating rope, and lay down on hot coals. The Greeks were speechless with delight. I must admit, we hadn't had such fun in ages. It was better than the circus of Roxanne's court.

Afterwards, there was dessert with biscuits and various honey-sweetened dried fruits. The fakir and the snake charmer were asked to do their show again. The cobras were cranky now, and one of the snake charmers was bitten and died. The Greeks were ecstatic. The show was a huge success, and Alexander immediately asked to have the remaining snake charmers and the fakirs. King Musicanus obligingly gave him three of each.

I insisted they have their own boat.

After dinner there were more dancers and musicians. Alexander leaned back on silken cushions and fell asleep. He was still easily tired. Roxanne had forgotten her copycat game and had gone to see the dancers.

I decided to take political matters in my own hands for once and tugged Nassar's sleeve. He was my official translator and accompanied me everywhere.

'Ask the king if it's true about the Brahmins wanting to fight,' I said.

Nassar frowned. 'This is a dinner party, it's not polite to discuss politics.'

'Just do it,' I hissed.

Nassar blanched. He was also an expert in protocol, and this was certainly a *faux pas*. Nevertheless, he leaned over my lap to speak to the king in a low voice.

The king shot me an irritated glance. He spoke sharply to Nassar, saying, 'Tell your queen that doesn't concern her.'

I sighed and shook my head. 'Tell him that if the

Brahmins attack Alexander from behind, Alexander will lose his temper and make things very ugly. Tell him that I'm an oracle, if you like, and that this isn't a threat, it's a prophecy.'

Nassar translated what I'd said, and the king lost his angry look. His eyes widened. He said, 'Please accept my apologies. I was hasty. Obviously you have great powers. The Brahmins declared that if Alexander made peace with me, they would rise up and rebel. I had to buy them off with gold, so they have agreed not to fight. They will honour their word. I paid them a fortune for Alexander's safe passage through my lands.'

I frowned. In my memory there was the great battle against Porus, and after there was a blank. I simply couldn't remember what happened next. I had studied intensively the time period when I was supposed to interview him, but I hadn't known I would be stuck here. My studies had been academic, but they had been incomplete. So much of Alexander's story had been lost to time. I supposed there was nothing else I could do. To Nassar I said, 'Tell King Musicanus that I thank him for talking to me, and I thank him for the wonderful dinner, but that I'd like to take my husband back to his quarters to sleep.'

King Musicanus clapped his hands and ordered his servants to carry Alexander to our room. We were staying the night in the palace. Alexander was so exhausted he didn't even stir when the servants lifted him up and carried him through the echoing hallways to our bedchamber. I'd made sure that Roxanne had another bedroom, on the far side of the palace.

Chapter Twenty-Five

I woke up with sunshine pouring on my face. The room had a high ceiling and enormous windows. A large balcony overlooking the jungle garden ran the length of the room. The greenery was lush, full of flowers and songbirds. The leopards roared as elephants trumpeted. A monkey leapt onto the balcony, screeched at us, and jumped back into the trees.

I smiled and stretched. Alexander opened his eyes and looked across the pillows at me. His face was still too thin, but colour was coming back and he had gotten his appetite at last. Chiron was on the boat, with Brazza and Axiom. My breasts were full of milk. I had decided to wean Chiron, but it wasn't easy to tell my milk to just go away.

Alexander took care of that. He wrapped his arms around my waist and had breakfast. Somewhere in the middle of it, he forgot his wound and we made love. There was something sensual and decadent about making love in the middle of a huge, soft bed with windows wide open and a hot, fragrant breeze coming in from a jungle. The sun warmed our bodies like golden honey. Alexander moved slowly. His head was next to mine. I put my face to his neck, my mouth touching the hollow at the base of his throat where his pulse beat.

Afterwards he slept again. His breathing was clear, his chest rose and fell softly. I rested my hands on his body and tried not to think of the future.

We left the palace that afternoon, saying our formal goodbyes to King Musicanus. We had come with a chariot full of presents for the king, and we left with two cartloads of gifts including the snake charmers and fakirs – complete with beds of nails and cobras. And another elephant.

Everyone knew by now that Alexander was crazy about elephants. This one was a young cow that Alexander had promptly named 'Nostos' in honour of our going home. Nostos was a sweet, sleepy elephant. She had gold knobs on her short tusks and was always munching on grass. Her driver was named Patto. He was a nice fellow with mournful eyes and a long moustache. He was always sucking the ends of his moustache while Nostos was always champing on a mouthful of grass. Nostos had a fuzzy head, which was unusual in an adult elephant. It was as if she'd kept all her baby hair. Alexander saw how much I liked the young cow and gave her to me. I rode all the way back to the boat in the funny seat the elephants have in guise of saddles. I took Nassar with me; I wanted to talk to Patto.

Four soldiers carried Alexander's litter. They carried him as if they were walking on eggs. Every five minutes they stopped and asked him if everything was all right. Finally, he pretended to be asleep. Roxanne sat with him, waving a fan made of peacock feathers. She'd greeted us quite civilly that morning and didn't make a fuss when Alexander gave me the elephant. I wondered what she was plotting.

'Ask Patto if he wants to come with us back to Persia,' I told Nassar.

Patto replied that it was all the same to him, Persia, India, Greece, wherever.

'But doesn't he have a family?' I asked.

Patto gave me a funny look when I asked this and shrugged.

'He's got six children, all girls, all grown and married. He had to pay dowries for each one and now he's ruined,' explained Nassar. 'But his daughters are well married,' he added, imitating Patto's gloomy voice exactly.

'And his wife?' I asked.

After a long conversation with Patto, Nassar said, 'His wife died three years ago. He was thinking about getting married again and trying for a son, but first he needs to earn some money in case he has more daughters. He's perfectly happy to go with us to Persia, or Greece, or anywhere else, providing that when the elephant dies, he's free to return home with his pay.'

'Of course!' I said. 'Tell him I'll even write a contract for him. He'll be paid a full salary and have room and board. Tell him he can have whatever he wants.'

Nassar looked sceptical but told him anyway. Patto turned and looked at me, his gloomy face almost happy. 'Really?' he said. 'Anything?'

'If I can give it to him, yes,' I said.

Patto asked for a blue silk jacket like the one the chief elephant mahout had. He also wanted a stiff scrub brush so that he could wash Nostos correctly, and he wanted to make sure that he was going to be my mahout and nobody else's.

'Is that it?'

Nassar shrugged. 'That's it. What did you expect?'

'I don't know,' I admitted. 'I would have asked for a huge salary and a gold necklace for my elephant.'

'I'll take those too,' Patto replied promptly.

I now had my own elephant and mahout. I was as

pleased as if I'd just gotten a new Rolls Royce and chauffeur. I made sure that the chief mahout knew that Patto was my employee, and that Nostos had a proper place in the elephant parade. Patto got his jacket, his necklace, his salary, and he stopped looking so mournful. He kept chewing on his moustache, though, and Nostos kept her topknot.

We left the kingdom of Musicanus and started down river once more. We went slowly, no more than twenty kilometres a day, to give the armies on either side of the fleet time to keep up with us. The resulting cruise was a lazy affair that made the days drag by with aggravating slowness.

Out of boredom, I decided to ride my pony, Lenaia. I hadn't ridden her in a while, and I was feeling antsy. Alexander was recuperating well and, for once, was being good about following doctor's orders and not exerting himself. Sitting in the shade talking to our resident wise man, Kalanos, was his most strenuous exercise.

I wanted Plexis to go with me, but he was busy that day with his hipparchia. He had five hundred men under his command, and he'd decided to do some manoeuvres or whatever hipparchies do for exercise, so I took Lysimachus.

The day was warm, and we chatted idly as we rode through the rich countryside. I'd always liked the tall captain, but he was in awe of me. He was convinced I was Demeter's daughter, Persephone. It made his conversation stilted. He was afraid to say something that would anger me. In those days, the gods got mad easily. When they got mad, they turned humans into trees or rocks. Each time we passed a funny shaped rock or bush, there was much speculation about what that former person had done to make the gods so angry.

As we rounded a bend in the path, an Indian armed with a long spear stepped in front of us. Before I could wheel my pony around, another man grabbed her bridle and dragged me to the ground. I hit the ground hard and it stunned me. Then someone threw a large black cloth over me, and I found myself wrapped up and trussed like a cocoon. I heard Lysimachus screaming, then silence. I fainted for a second, then came to.

'Lysimachus!' I yelled hoarsely. I was frightened for him. By the sound of his scream he'd been badly injured.

Then someone hit me on the head, and I saw stars. The cloth saved me from being knocked out, but I think I would have rather been unconscious. I was slung into a cart and we moved off over bumpy ground. I didn't dare cry out. I guessed the blow was to silence me, and I didn't want to give the men who'd kidnapped me any excuse to hit me again. I would pretend to be dead, I decided. It wasn't easy. The cart moved quickly over uneven ground. My body bounced and banged against the wooden sides of the wagon, but I couldn't free my arms or legs to brace myself.

We kept moving. I needed to pee for what seemed like hours. It was agony. Finally I wet myself. I had no choice; it was either pee or explode at that point. My captors didn't seem to notice. We just kept going. It was torture. I must have passed out, because the next thing I knew we had come to a stop. There was a loud conversation in a language I didn't understand, and I was hauled out of the wagon. I had never been a sack of potatoes before, but now I knew how one must feel. I hit the ground and just lay there until someone picked me up again, and with a loud grunt, tossed me into another wagon.

More travelling over lumpy, bumpy ground. More hours of having my body sliding back and forth on a wooden floorboard. I tried to wedge myself into a corner, but that didn't work very well. I was considering dying when we stopped again.

My body was a mass of bruises and welts. I was filthy, bloody, I stank of sweat and urine, and I was afraid that I was about to be very ill. My breasts hurt dreadfully. Chiron had missed at least two feedings since I'd been taken. I felt feverish.

This time, I was carried to a building and shut inside. The large sack was ripped off my body, and someone kicked me before I could move. Nice. I caught a glimpse of night sky before the door was slammed shut. I found myself in a low-ceilinged hut with an earthen floor and a heap of straw. The straw made a bed. I crawled into it, noticed that it was almost clean, and fell asleep. I was exhausted but didn't sleep long. I dozed just enough for the shock to wear off. Then I was awake, and there was a spider the size of a kitten on my arm. I shot out of the straw, screaming and shaking my arm, crashed into a wall and knocked myself out.

Well, it was probably the best thing that could have happened to me. The spider wasn't about to eat me, I was just in its way on its walk from one side of the shed to the other. But I never would have been able to coexist with a spider that size. I would have spent the entire night screaming and dodging. I would have found other night-time denizens of the hut, equally repulsive, and I would have died of a heart attack long before daybreak.

As it was, I was still unconscious when they came to get me. I'd managed to have a good night's sleep.

I was awakened when someone tossed a bucket of

water over my head. I sat up sputtering and peered blearily around. There were four people standing near me. I opened my eyes and glared. This had the hoped for effect – they backed away. I have a fearsome glare.

There were three men and one woman. They didn't look like peasants. The woman had a saffron yellow sari trimmed with gold and scarlet. Her hair was long and carefully brushed to a blue-black sheen. The men wore puffy pants made of raw silk, sleeveless linen vests, and unbleached linen turbans. Their beards were dyed blue and red, and they had tattoos on their thin, brown arms. They shouted at me, but I didn't understand a word they said.

After a few minutes, I tried to get up. I found my legs would carry me, and I walked away. Nobody tried to stop me. I soon found out why. I was in a large pen. There was a high wall, and as I walked along it, I saw I was a prisoner. Well, there would be other ways to escape. The first thing to do was to wash. I returned to the hut and found a basin of water and some fruit. I stared at the bowl of fruit and then cursed. I was being treated like a pet monkey. This would never do. I hadn't gone all the way around the park, but I was beginning to suspect that it was part of king Musicanus's domain. The wall was rose-coloured brick.

I washed myself, washed my tunic and my underwear, and hung everything to dry. I went into the hut, dragged all the straw out and spread it in the sun to air. Then I went back inside and plugged up all the holes I found, intending to keep the spiders out.

At noon, when the sun was at its zenith, I put on my dry clothes and walked around the rest of my prison. It was roughly a hundred metres long and fifty metres deep. The hut was in the centre. A path led to a locked gate. The wall was so high, I couldn't see over it, and I doubted I could climb it. I would have to dig my way out or build a ladder.

I spent two more nights sleeping in the hut, milking myself, cursing in several different languages and imagining all the horrible things I would do to King Musicanus when I saw him. I didn't sleep well. Huge spiders were only part of the crowd that shared my bed. I found centipedes, millipedes, scorpions, and other things I'd never seen before. Every night I stayed awake as long as I could, only dropping off to sleep out of sheer exhaustion. In the morning, there would be new red welts on my arms and legs where the insects had feasted on my blood. After three days, I thought I'd go mad.

I wondered where everyone was. I hoped Chiron was all right. Every time I thought of my baby, I'd cry. I wasn't being very brave. Alexander must be frantic with worry. Poor Lysimachus, I wondered if they'd found his body. I kept remembering his scream.

Chapter Twenty-Six

The army found me. I hadn't been kidnapped by Musicanus; I'd been taken by the Brahmins. They had done it to lure Alexander into battle with them. Actually, to get Alexander to fight, all they had to do was attack. But because of the gold they'd taken from Musicanus, they couldn't attack first, so they'd decided to capture me. The results surpassed their wildest expectations.

Alexander turned his army around and swept back upriver, burning, pillaging, and generally wreaking havoc. He stormed into King Musicanus's palace and demanded to see me at once. Of course the poor fellow had no idea what Alexander was talking about, but Alexander didn't believe him. The Brahmins had done their best to leave lots of clues, and Lysimachus had gotten a good look at my captors.

They had let Lysimachus live so that he could tell Alexander where I was, but in the white heat of Alexander's rage there was no room for reason. I was gone, Lysimachus said I was taken by Musicanus's Brahmins, and Alexander was going to kill everyone until he found me.

I never said he was a diplomat or a politician. He was a tactician, a soldier, and a very lethal one. He killed every single one of Musicanus's Brahmin soldiers; he wiped out his entire army. Then he crucified Musicanus and his advisors in their own citadel.

The army stormed through the park. Alexander was nearly mad with grief because I was nowhere in the palace.

A squadron of the Persian Guards stumbled upon me late in the afternoon. They were led by Oxatres, who was Darius's half brother. Darius had been absolute ruler of Persia before the whirlwind that was Alexander defeated him. Oxatres joined Alexander's army in Ecbatana to try and save his brother when Bessus kidnapped Darius. He had stayed with Alexander, bringing with him his own divisions of soldiers. Now he was one of Alexander's generals.

And he'd found me. I don't know who was happier; Alexander, Oxatres, or me.

I heard the army crashing through the park, and so I was standing near the door when they broke it down.

'It took you long enough,' I said. I was so happy and relieved, I hugged him.

'My lady!' Oxatres hadn't expected to find me. He was staggered.

'Where is Iskander?' I asked.

'In the palace.' Oxatres grinned, but his eyes were concerned. 'He's going to be glad to see you.'

The whole army was worried about Alexander. Usse followed at his heels, trying to get him to slow down, to relax, to rest, but Alexander had gone mad. Oxatres led his horse over to me and boosted me up, then he got on behind me and we galloped off to the palace.

I heard the screaming as we arrived. I felt ill. I hadn't realized what Alexander had done to get me back. A river of blood running down the white marble steps gave me the first glimpse of the horror. King Musicanus was dead, his family was wailing at his feet, his advisors were all dead or dying, and there were dead soldiers lying everywhere.

The Brahmins had wanted a fight – they got a fight. Alexander was standing in the middle of the citadel, his head tipped to the side, his expression grim. When I called his name he jumped as if struck.

'Ashley!' he cried. He ran to me.

'Alex,' I whispered, 'Why? Why did you do this? Couldn't you just look for me? You didn't have to kill everyone!'

He blinked. Nobody ever told him how to fight. He didn't reply, but his face grew stony. He stared at me with an expression I'd never seen before, his eyes blank. It was like staring into mirrors of pain. For the first time, I noticed how laboured his breathing had become.

I felt worse than awful: I was dirty, I had a fever from my swollen breasts, I was covered in bruises and insect bites, and my head hurt abominably. The screams and the blood made everything seem like a nightmare. 'Please, take me back to the ship,' I said, my voice starting to waver.

I must have turned ashen, because Alexander lost his anger. He reached out and touched my arm, and I managed not to flinch. I was horrified by the slaughter, disgusted and saddened, but most of all I just wanted to bathe, hold Chiron to my aching breasts, and sleep. Really sleep; not lie awake with a pounding heart, startling at every rustle in the straw, and whimpering in fear as spiders and scorpions danced across the dirt floor next to me. I laid my head on Alexander's shoulder. It was still bony, but it was strong. He had saved me, I was still whole, and I was with him again. Finally, nothing else mattered.

I closed my eyes to the massacre and left the city. The wails of the women accompanied me. For a long time, I would hear them on the edge of sleep. The screams and the blood would be part of the price I paid for Alexander's love. I didn't want to weigh the consequences. I would learn to live with the nightmares. If he could, I could.

Chapter Twenty-Seven

The voyage was calm after that. There were no more battles. The army marched or rode or sailed in peace, and the river started to rise and fall with the tide. We were approaching the mouth of the Indus.

One day, while we were tacking into the wind, the faint odour of salt marsh came to our nostrils. Seagulls flew over the boats, and the air grew cooler. It made a blessed change after the stifling heat. We slung our hammocks on deck and slept under the stars. The army picked up its pace, and the rowers started singing again. 'Row, row, row your boat,' echoed across the broad expanse of flat, brown water. The banks of the river started to widen, and Alexander made the decision to bring the eastern half of the army over to the western side of the river.

The boat-bridge was set up again, and the army filed across. The elephants swam.

Once the whole army was together on the shore, the priests made sacrifices to the gods. We had a huge banquet. A bonfire was built, and some soldiers went to the river and came back with bushels of oysters. The Greeks loved oysters. They couldn't believe there were so many of them. One of the scribes, in a flurry of enthusiasm, described it as: *'Swarms of oysters, like bees, and if you capture the queen, they all follow.'*

I couldn't figure out exactly what he meant. However, he'd written that after the party – after we'd all drunk prodigious amounts of wine and eaten more oysters than we could count.

We stayed on the boats while the army moved inland. We wanted to see the ocean, so we continued down river. The tides rose and fell, and sometimes they were enormous.

One particularly large tide nearly swamped the whole navy. Nearchus was furious with himself for getting trapped. What happened, was that he had anchored in a calm harbour near the mouth of the river at what he thought was high tide. But during the night, a sudden surge caught everyone unawares. The boats were torn from their moorings and swept inland over the salt flats. The wave ebbed as soon and as suddenly as it had come, leaving many boats stranded on the marsh.

I think there must have been an underwater earthquake or volcanic explosion that would account for the phenomenon, but for the men it was – of course – a sign from the gods that meant, 'Go back! Take the other branch of the river!' There was a meeting with the generals while the men and the elephants worked all day in mud up to their hips trying to move the boats back to the river. Other groups of soldiers waded around picking up all the weapons and baggage that had been lost, now lying scattered far and wide. It was a desolate scene.

The boats were fairly light, being made of wood and reeds, so it was easy to haul them back to the water with ropes and pulleys.

The elephants loved the mud. They would stop and roll in it.

The soldiers, who had camped on dry land, mostly made fun of the unfortunate sailors. It was the eternal conflict between army and navy. The insults got nastier, and then someone started throwing handfuls of mud. Soon there was a full-blown mud fight going on, complete with shouting, swearing, and any rocks that could be dug up from the mud.

To loosen things up, Alexander proposed a series of games in the tidal flats. For the next three days, there were wrestling matches and a huge 'goatball' game that put more men in the infirmary than all the battles in India. The men were in high spirits. Their voyage was touching its end, the sun was shining, and the mud was really slippery.

We found a low hill, built it up, and made a huge mudslide. Even I had fun on that.

When the boats were all back in the water, and the winner of the wrestling games declared king of the hill and pushed down the slide on his face by the losers, we set off to sail into the ocean.

I had made a promise to Alexander, and now I was going to show him something amazing.

The army waited for us in a place called Karachi. We would join them in a week or so. Alexander and I went sailing with Nearchus. The blond admiral was in his element now. For the first time in ten years I really saw him. The sun turned his skin deep mahogany, his eyes were bright blue, and his hair was bleached by the sun to a pale strawberry blond.

Alexander had told me he got seasick, and I hadn't really believed him. Poor fellow, while we were on the river he'd been all right, but as soon as we reached the rise and fall of the waves, the swells, the rush up and down – Alexander hung over the railing, retching miserably.

It was better after a few days, but he was never completely at ease on the ocean.

I was in my element. Perhaps Viking blood still ran through my veins; my future ancestors had been explorers and sailors. My hair turned platinum, my skin tanned, and my eyes were chips of sparkling ice.

Alexander said I had never looked better. I'd never felt better. The sea called me; I was an ocean child.

Plexis had stayed on land. His kingdom was horses. He would have liked to accompany us, but he, Ptolemy Lagos, Perdiccas, and Seleucos were in charge of the army. He watched us leave. He waved as long as we could see him. Even when he was just a speck on the shore, I was sure he was waving still, the wind in his brown hair, his legs apart, firmly planted in the sand. His clear eyes full of sorrow.

Since Alexander had nearly died, Plexis had changed. He had always been the most carefree of Alexander's generals. He had seen the whole adventure as a lark, much more so than Alexander, who saw it as an adventure. Plexis had always been with his hipparchia, riding almost nonchalantly into battle, protected by his gods and his insouciance. I had called him *'le bel homme sans souci'* one day; the handsome, carefree man. Plexis had laughed at the time and shrugged. 'Life is too short to be serious,' he'd said, happily patting his horse on its neck. But since Alexander's near-death, he'd become mystic, sacrificing to the gods every day, asking the priests for portents and amulets, walking about with his face to the sky, looking for signs.

I tried to talk to him, but his sadness only deepened as the differences between us became more apparent. Plexis was a man of his times. He was a pure product of Athens and Greece. He should have been the happiest of the three of us; he was in tune with the century he lived in. But the times, 'They were a-changin', as someone had once said far, far ahead in the future. Everything was quicksilver. The world was changing, and Plexis was sharply conscious that the future was Alexander – and me. I came *from* the future, and even if he didn't know that, he sensed it. He sensed that his way of thinking and his way of life were becoming obsolete. Perhaps it was my gentle teasing about his many gods, or perhaps it was Alexander's evolving attitude towards fate. Alexander was starting to believe that he could make his own destiny.

Plexis was bewildered. Most people were oblivious to the changes. Plexis was too sensitive. He saw the difference in me. It chilled him.

I still loved him and he loved me, but there was something between us now that we both felt. It was three thousand years. The gulf widened when Alexander lay near death. Plexis couldn't understand my refusal to turn towards the gods. And at first, he didn't understand why Alexander seemed to be changing. Then he realized that Alexander had always been like that. Alexander needed no gods, he was his own god.

Plexis watched as we sailed away. He would wait for us on shore with his horses – his precious horses. I would never tell him that they had been replaced by mechanical monsters.

For two weeks we sailed under a perfect sky. We hugged the shore at first, then sailed out into the great Indian Ocean. I was looking for somewhere specific. I had something hidden under a large sailcloth on deck. Something Alexander looked at eighteen times a day but couldn't figure out. I wouldn't tell him what it was. It was a surprise.

We finally arrived at an island. It was a small island but

well protected by a wide coral reef and a deep lagoon. It was perfect. We manoeuvred the boat into the lagoon and went ashore. Alexander was relieved to sleep on dry land.

The next day, I unveiled the diving bell. It was a huge glass bell made by the glassmaker in the last village we'd visited. There had been a glassworks making glass buoys, which gave me the idea. I'd drawn what I wanted, the glassmaker had made it, and I'd been as excited as a kid at Christmas thinking about it.

The idea was simple. The bell was weighted and fastened to a huge rope. The rope went along the mast, ran through several pulleys, and could be raised or lowered with a hand crank.

We lowered the glass bell into the water and then I took a deep breath and dived into the clear sea. The bell had a huge air bubble inside, so I just poked my head under the bell and opened my eyes. There was a bar to hang onto and around me was the coral reef in its splendour. The boat floated along slowly, the bell was trailed along beneath it, and we went all around the lagoon that way. It was perfect.

On board, some sailors hung over the rail lamenting, persuaded I was drowned. I swam back to the surface to cheers of joy. Then it was Alexander's turn.

He was reticent. He didn't trust the sea, but I told him it was because he didn't know it. The bell was raised and then lowered again, changing the air.

'Come on!' I cried, and dived into the water. Alexander followed me. He dived under the bell, and when his head broke into the air he opened his eyes in amazement.

'Everything is so clear!' he cried.

'Shhh, don't talk, you'll fog up the glass. Just look,' I whispered.

Of course he had to talk. He talked so much that we

had to haul the bell up several times to change the air inside it. But he had so many questions.

I stayed with him as we drifted around. An unspoiled coral reef paradise surrounded us. We saw sponges and corals, fish, eels, sharks, octopus, shellfish, and shrimp. The reef was beautiful, and Alexander insisted on using the diving bell at least ten times a day.

Everyone got a turn. Even Kalanos, who couldn't swim, was helped underwater and into the bell by Alexander. He got some water up his nose, but the incredible sight more than made up for it.

Chiron was a water baby, and I swam with him every day as soon as the sun passed its zenith. I even took him into the diving bell. He held his breath naturally underwater, as some babies do. Once in the diving bell, he pressed his hands to the glass and gawped at everything. He loved the bright colours. Some fish came right up to see us.

Nearchus especially appreciated it. He and Alexander took the most turns, I think. They even went down at night and we held a torch above the bow, attracting the fish. The light cast a green glow in the water. It was so clear we could see the bell and the men inside it. There were some big fish at night. Nearchus loved it, but Alexander was slightly green when they swam back to the surface. A huge hammerhead shark had circled them for a while before swimming off into the deep.

That night we celebrated Alexander's birthday.

It was late July, 325 BC, on a hot, sultry night somewhere in the Indian Ocean. Alexander was thirty-one years old.

After dinner, Alexander and I swam to shore. The

water and the air seemed to be the same temperature. We floated over the reef and climbed onto the soft sand. Everyone else was staying aboard for the evening. We had the whole island to ourselves.

'Happy birthday to you,' I sang, 'you live in a zoo, you look like a monkey, and you act like one too.'

'Nice song,' said Alexander doubtfully. 'Is that what people of your time sing to each other on their birthday celebration?'

'The ones who are six years old,' I said. I lay back in the hammock and swung gently back and forth.

'I want to talk to you,' said Alexander, stopping the hammock. Even that motion made him slightly seasick. 'About next year. When I'm going to die.'

'I wish I'd never told you,' I said.

'I want to make plans. You know how I am, everything has to have contingency plans, even my contingency plans.' He laughed but his eyes were sad. 'What will happen to you if I do die? Will you be all right? Will you go somewhere safe with Plexis?'

I shook my head. 'No, I won't. If you die, I will too. I've already decided. I'm going to give Chiron to Plexis and I'm going to commit suttee.'

'What?' he sputtered, 'I forbid it! What are you talking about? I won't hear of it!'

'You won't be around to stop me,' I said gently. 'Besides, I won't last three minutes without your protection.'

'But what about Roxanne? What about Stateira? And Roxanne's child, if she even has another?'

'It will most likely be Ptolemy Lagos's. The child, I mean. Oh, Alex, I don't want to tell you everything, it's hard enough that you know about your own death.' I was shivering despite the heat.

'Hush, don't get upset. You must tell me, please. What happens to my empire, my wives and children? Tell me, please,' he asked again.

'Your empire is carved up into three major parts. Seleucos and Apames get Persia, Bactria, and Sogdia, and they found a great dynasty.

'Ptolemy Lagos gets Egypt. He too starts a powerful dynasty that ends with Cleopatra, the most beautiful queen in the world.

'Greece and Macedonia are claimed by your mother and your brother-in-law.

'Some people believe you are poisoned. Most historians think you died of malaria, some have said alcohol poisoning although that seems a bit far-fetched, seeing how you Greeks water your wine.'

'Not always,' said Alexander. His voice was brittle.

'I'm sorry,' I whispered.

'So am I. I would have liked to rule with you by my side. I would have loved to grow old with my children in the great palaces of Babylon and Alexandria.'

'No, you would not have,' I said, drying my tears. 'It's a terrible life, that of king. Especially now, in this time. When you're a king, you're not human any more. And Alex, you're far too human to be the king everyone wants you to be. Would you rule like Darius? Hidden behind a curtain so that the eyes of the common man never see your face? Would you become as deluded as he became? Thinking that only you could make the sun rise and the fields fertile?'

He snorted. 'No, I've had my fill of fertilizing the fields, thank you.'

'Don't interrupt,' I said softly. 'Listen to me. You

241

could never be happy sitting on a throne. You're a man of action. You need to go places, to explore. I know you too well. You were never made to sit and watch as people fight each other for the right to be near you. The people you love will become targets for the ambitious, jealous subjects around you. How long do you think Plexis, Nearchus, or Perdiccas will last?'

'I never thought of that,' he admitted.

'Well, think now. You're too straightforward to rule. There's not a subtle bone in your body. You'll just bulldoze over everyone, stirring things up, making most people resentful. You already do, but you're at war so it doesn't matter.' I kissed his mouth. The sea had left a faint taste of salt. Or maybe it was tears. My tears.

'My heart knows you're right,' he said, 'But I was raised by a king, I grew up a prince, and I am the ruler. I will always feel as if I had shirked a sacred duty if I run away.'

'You won't be running away,' I said sadly, 'you'll be dead.'

There was little he could say after that. Instead he held me tightly in his arms and kissed me. The hammock started rocking again, but this time the movement was more up and down than back and forth, and besides, it was Alexander making it move.

The night was sultry and we went swimming afterwards. I wanted to show him one more thing. In the warm water, phosphorescence, at the very edges of the waves, gave off a pale green light. I swirled my arms through the water and glowing trails followed my movements.

Alexander smiled. He'd seen glow-worms and the light was nearly the same. We swam together, our bodies outlined in light.

In the shallows, we came together again. We floated, making love slowly, silently, like the creatures of the sea. Just before I lost myself, I took Alexander's face in my hands and looked into his eyes. My breath caught in my throat as my body shuddered against my husband's. He pressed his mouth against mine, the salt of the ocean on his lips. His hands wrapped around my buttocks, pulling me harder and harder onto himself. He gave a gentle moan and then sighed. His hands slid from my hips, rose slowly through the water and found my breasts. Thrusting with his hips he moved into shallower water.

The water was waist deep. I wrapped my legs around Alexander and he lifted me easily, carrying me just to the water's edge. Then he lay me down and drove himself into me again and again, harder and harder, until I cried out as each thrust found its way to my womb. There was urgency about him that he rarely showed. His hands roamed over my body, his lips, his mouth, his cock claiming me for his own. I arched my back, digging my heels into the wet sand. I met him and met him again as he claimed me, our bodies moving on the beach in a rhythm older than time.

Finally he gave a hoarse cry and shuddered, his body jerking in its release. He rolled off me, beads of light glowing in his curly hair and streaking his skin. His face was still, his mouth soft. The phosphorescence still surrounded us. We were in three inches of brightly glowing water. It was like lying in a cloud of stars.

I leaned over him on my elbows and licked the salt off his upper lip then laughed shakily. 'Well, happy birthday,' I said.

'Ashley?' his voice was blurred.

'What?'

'Why have you never told me when your birthday was?'

'No one ever celebrated it,' I admitted.

He got to his knees and then stood up slowly. He looked down at his body, covered with sand and phosphorescence and laughed softly. Then he pulled me to my feet, and we went once again into the water to rinse off. When we crawled back into the hammock, I thought I would fall asleep at once. But Alexander cupped my chin in his hand and asked me again.

'When is your birthday? And how old are you?'

'I'm not born yet,' I reminded him. Then I sighed. 'I'm thirty years old. I was born on the first of April – a cruel joke for my mother who never managed to forgive me. The fact I existed was bad enough, but to be born on that date seemed like an affront.'

Alexander traced the outline of my face with his finger. 'Is the first of April considered a bad omen?'

'It's the day of practical jokes. Not the best day to be born if your parents have no sense of humour.'

'I'm sorry I never celebrated your birthday. I promise that next year I will try. But first you have to tell me, exactly when is April?'

'It's the month of Mounichion.'

'Mounichion? The month of the festival of Artemis, the huntress. Fitting, I think. She is portrayed as being very fair and utterly merciless.'

'Oh, and I am merciless?'

'You are; you make love to me mercilessly.'

'Are you complaining?'

'No.' His voice had a smile in it. 'I'm certainly not

complaining. But I think that if you were born on the day of the practical joke, it's because the gods have a sense of humour.'

Chapter Twenty-Eight

Eos, the dawn, poked rosy fingers at us and woke us up. Even under the shade of the palm trees, the sun, dawn's brother Helios, was bright. Sunlight sparkled on the waves, the white sand, and the glass diving bell hanging from the boat.

Everyone insisted on going for another ride in it. All day long, we took turns gazing at the colourful reef from under the bell. When we weren't diving and swimming, we made sand castles or lazed in hammocks.

Alexander wanted to make love to me underwater in the bell. The glass got all steamed up and we couldn't see the reef any more.

Nearchus took a spear underwater and killed a large grouper, so we had a feast that night. We held a barbecue on the beach. We sang and told jokes during dinner. In the dark, our teeth flashed whitely, and the fire made red shadows on our skin.

We finished eating the fish and lay back, content. Chiron played with a shell Nearchus had given him. The air was warm, the breeze felt like a soft caress. Sparks from the fire soared high in the air as Alexander told stories.

He was a consummate storyteller. I could listen to him reciting a grocery list and not get bored, so when he told stories about the great heroes, he gave me goose bumps.

That evening he told the story of Jason and the Golden

Fleece, one of Nearchus's favourite tales, of course. There was a long sea voyage in it.

Then Kalanos told us a story of the Indian goddess Kali, scaring us all. It was the perfect spooky, around-the-campfire tale. Afterwards, we were all afraid to go to sleep, and Alexander, always very imaginative, woke up in the middle of the night, yelling that he was being strangled. It was just my arm, but some nervous giggles sounded from around the campfire before we fell asleep again.

The next day we lifted anchor and sailed back towards the Indus River. Before we left, Alexander tossed two gold cups into the ocean. They were for Poseidon – one from him, one from Nearchus.

Alexander had lost his seasickness and stood on deck with the wind in his hair, his face split in a wide grin. He looked so handsome that I wished his court painter were here to paint him. I was a terrible artist. I had my own journal and I used to sketch little scenes in it, but when I tried to draw people they came out looking flat and awkward. I leaned my elbows on my knees and sighed. My kingdom for a camera.

His chest had healed. He sported a scar shaped like a perfect triangle between two ribs. His whole body was scarred. His arms and legs were well muscled. His hands were those of a warrior, strong and sure. His tendons showed sharply on the backs of his hands and in his neck. I loved his mouth especially; he had full lips with deep curls at the corners when he smiled.

He knew I was staring at him. He was terribly vain, and loved it when I admired him.

I blew him a kiss and he pretended to catch it. The width of the boat separated us, but only for an instant. His movements were still as quick as when I'd first met him. His gait had changed to accommodate his leg, but it bothered him less now. He gathered me in his arms and held me. I could feel his heart beating. His eyes were brilliant in his tanned face.

'Ashley of the Sacred Sandals, we're going home,' he said.

'And where, exactly, is home?' I asked, teasing him. But he only smiled proudly.

'The world is our home,' he said, and now his voice was ringing. He threw his head back and his words seemed to reach the sky. 'The world is my home now!' he shouted.

'Alexander, King of Heaven and Earth,' I said.

'That's me,' he said modestly, and he kissed me. And anyone who could kiss so well, I thought, might as well be king of heaven and earth.

The Time for Alexander Series

The Road to Alexander
Legends of Persia
Son of the Moon
Storms Over Babylon

Proudly published by Accent Press

www.accentpress.co.uk